The Shadow Over
Deathlehem

The Shadow Over

Deathlehem

Edited by
Michael J. Evans
and
Harrison Graves

A
Grinning Skull Press
Publication

The Shadow Over Deathlehem
Compilation Copyright © 2017 Grinning Skull Press

"The Disturbing Disappearance of Horatio Gristle" copyright ©2017 Leslie J Linder
"Capturing the Christmas Spirit" copyright ©2017 Kurt Newton
"Good Ol' Mrs. Claus" copyright ©2017 Karen Thrower
"Merry Christmas to All, and to All a Bright Night" copyright ©2017 Dan Foley
"Christmas Calendar" copyright ©2017 Christine Lajewski
"Return Policy" copyright ©2017 William D. Carl
"Homeless for the Holidays" copyright ©2017 Gregory L. Norris
"Ho, Ho, Horror Workshop" copyright ©2017 R.A. Goli
"O Little Town of Deathlehem" copyright ©2017 Dan Foley
"The Basket Case" copyright ©2017 G.H. Finn
"Christmas Lasagna" copyright ©2017 Larry Hoy
"Lots of Fun with Mister Snowman" copyright ©2017 Joseph Rubas
"The Illusion" copyright ©2017 Bev Vincent
"The Carolers" copyright ©2017 Mark L. Eshbaugh
"The Gift That Keeps on Giving" copyright ©2017 Sheri White
"Bleeding Out the Christmas Cheer" copyright ©2017 Nick Manzolillo
"Exmas Tree" copyright ©2017 Rose Blackthorn
"Hazard Delay" copyright ©2017 Sheri Sebastian-Gabriel
"Left in a Manger" copyright ©2017 Larry Hoy
"Naughty" copyright ©2017 Steven Van Patten
"Sequel" copyright ©2011 DG Critchley
    An earlier version of this story appeared as "The Sequel" in *Epitaphs: The Journal of the New England Horror Writers*," published by Shroud Publishing. This version has been modified.
"Rudolf, the Gold-Nosed Butcher" copyright ©2017 Stuart R. West
"Creevy's Trees" copyright ©2015 Kerry E.B. Black
    Originally published online by Dark Chapter Press as part of their Christmas Horror Advent Event. Republished with permission from the author.
"Christmas Moon" copyright ©2017 David Bernard
"Goblin Fruit" copyright ©2017 Harold Hull

The Skull logo with stylized lettering was created for Grinning Skull Press by Dan Moran, http://dan-moran-art.com/.
Cover designed by Jeffrey Kosh, http://jeffreykosh.wix.com/jeffreykoshgraphics.
ISBN: 0-9986912-6-7 (paperback)
ISBN-13: 978-0-9986912-6-8 (paperback)
ISBN: 978-0-9986912-8-2 (e-book)

DEDICATION

To all those who enjoy a little darkness
during the holiday season.

TABLE OF CONTENTS

ACKNOWLEDGMENTS

First off, we would like to thank MRGODZILLAJODEDOR from DeviantArt.com for giving us permission to use his Krampus drawing as this volume's interior graphic for this year's volume and Jeffrey Kosh for another great cover.

We also want to thank Dan Foley for rewriting "O Little Town of Bethlehem" and putting a Deathlehem spin on it. The first verse appears on the back cover, and the complete version can be found within this collection.

And, as always, we would like to thank the readers who embrace all things Christmas, light and dark.

HAPPY HELLIDAYS

As the end of the years draws near, I'm always interested to see what controversies will arise as the "War on Christmas" revs up. I'm never disappointed, as there always seems to be something that offends somebody. A couple of years ago it was the Starbucks red cup fiasco. In 2014, the American Atheists stirred the pot with a billboard that stated, "Dear Santa, All I want for Christmas is to skip church! I'm too old for fairy tales." A few years before that, it was, "Keep the Merry! Dump the Myth!" And let's not forget the ongoing campaign to put Christ back in Christmas. For whatever reason, people take offense to being wished a Happy Holiday or Season's Greetings. There's even been a move to eliminate Santa from the holiday, as folks say the jolly old elf detracts from the true meaning of the holiday. The way the religious folks behave, you'd think they had a monopoly on Christmas, that nobody else has a right to celebrate the holiday. Personally, I find this amusing, especially when you consider all the articles that have been published stating there's no way Christ could have been born in December. According to what the experts say, all evidence points to Christ being born during the summer months, but people still insist on ignoring the evidence and celebrating His birth on December 25th.

Now if anybody wants to take offense, it should be those of us who are having Christmas shoved down our throats, those of us who embrace Halloween as their favorite holiday, as there seems to be a conscious effort to squeeze out the scariest of holidays. Christmas trees and jack o'lanterns battle for space on the store shelves as early as August, and unless I'm mistaken (and please correct me if I am), there are three holidays that fall during the final quarter of the year: Halloween, Thanksgiving, THEN Christmas. And I guess that's why Deathlehem still exists. Yes, it is a charity collection (and always will be), and it is done to honor the memory of my mother and sister, but it has become something more personal. For me, it has become a way to push back against those trying to eradicate the spirit of Halloween.

For folks who have made this trip before, you know what to expect. For those just tuning in, the Deathlehem collection contains Christmas-themed horror stories. Just because this is a Christmas collection, keep in mind they are horror stories. There are no happy endings in Deathlehem. Krampus rules, as do the other baddies of the holiday season. Of Santa there is no sign; however, if you do see the jolly old elf around, chances are he isn't who he claims to be. Nowhere is this more evident than in "Naughty" by Steven Van Patten, and after you read "Ho, Ho, Horror Workshop" by R.A. Goli, you'll find yourself questioning the authenticity of everybody's favorite holiday icon. This year, even Mrs. Claus gets a chance to step up to the plate in "Good Ol' Mrs. Claus" by Karen Thrower—and she's not any nicer than Krampus or any Santa you'll meet here.

Will you encounter any other monsters in Deathlehem? Oh yes! "Hazard Delay" by Sheri Sebastian-Gabriel and "Christmas Moon" by David Bernard let us know that there's more to fear than Krampus during the holiday season, and Stuart R.

West shows us in "Rudolf, the Gold-Nosed Butcher" that Christmas doesn't have a monopoly on the holiday baddies. And let us not forget the human monsters, who seem to run amuck in Deathlehem. Just check out Dan Foley's "Merry Christmas to All, and to All a Bright Night," Bev Vincent's "The Illusion," and Gregory L. Norris's "Homeless for the Holidays."

I'll be the first to admit, though, that some of the humans you'll encounter didn't all start out bad, as you'll see in Larry Hoy's "Christmas Lasagna," Sheri White's "The Gift That Keeps on Giving," and William D. Carl's "Return Policy." In these tales, circumstances have pushed people to the brink. Does that make them any less monstrous? Of course not, but maybe you'll have a little sympathy for them.

So without further ado...

Welcome to Deathlehem...
Again.
Remember, trust no one. And whatever you do, don't eat anything, no matter how tantalizingly delicious it might look.

Michael J. Evans
and the staff at
Grinning Skull Press,
Best Wishes for a Happy Helliday
and a frightful New Year!

THE DISTURBING DISAPPEARANCE OF HORATIO GRISTLE

Leslie J Linder

Herein lays the disturbing account of the disappearance of Horatio Gristle. Said gentleman, if one cares to call him a gentleman, served as a porter at the Blessed Cross Workhouse found on the East End of London. Never in the three years since this account began has there been the slightest clue to his fate.

I myself happen to know his fate. Let us see if you can guess it. We can play it as a Christmas merriment, like the old parlor game of "lookabout." In this case, we shall look about for poor Gristle. Shall we begin? Here are the particulars.

On the East End of London in the year when Gristle left us, being the year of our Lord eighteen hundred and forty, disappearances were not uncommon. Thieves and housebreakers ruled the streets of the slums. It was quite unremarkable for many inhabitants of the tenements to be lost each year and never to be sought after by anyone.

But for a man of Horatio Gristle's standing to vanish was cause for an official investigation. This particular gentleman, if indeed you would call him one, was not only head porter at Blessed Cross. More importantly, he was a first cousin to the local magistrate, Algernon Gristle the Third.

You may have noticed, gentle reader, that I have twice suggested you may not wish to call Horatio Gristle a gentleman. I risk slander so boldly because he was universally known to be one of the most draconian and miserly porters at Blessed Cross or any such institution.

If Gristle were to be compared to any other member of the animal kingdom, it would perhaps be a rhinoceros. But such a comparison is unkind to the latter. For where the rhinoceros is merely hard and tough in the exterior, the head porter was all hardness within.

Gristle's inspection of the foodstuffs and clothing that charitable folk would lay in his charge often led to such items being confiscated and thrown out. Alternatively, some suspiciously similar items would soon thereafter be seen in the guardhouse or at the table of the workhouse commissioners.

In all cases, these offerings would be seen as gifts from Gristle and a sign of his proper beneficence toward people at or above his own station. Yet, even his bribes could do little to enhance the opinion of his betters. He was simply too unpleasant in every way.

Even when the kind donations made to Blessed Cross ended on the kitchen midden heaps, they could not be accessed by the rightful recipients. Gristle made it his business to enforce workhouse rules prohibiting any pilfering from the waste piles. And you may believe that during the cold months of winter, the inmates of that dreary place tested his resolve to the limit.

But apparently Gristle's will was as ironclad as the gates that he watched over at Blessed Cross. And he kept these tightly shut, indeed. Since it was the porter's job to admit any new paupers who sought admission from the Master and Matron, few destitute souls ever found themselves at the gates if they had any recourse, whatsoever.

"Better to sleep on the street than to seek mercy from Horatio Gristle," was the wisdom that all the paupers of the East End magnanimously shared forth. For, if the inmates of Blessed Cross were destitute of worldly goods, then so was Gristle impoverished of mercy.

But fate seemed to step in and deal the paupers a change of fortunes in the autumn of the aforementioned year. At just around the time of Stir-up Sunday, which the pious will know occurs on the twenty-fifth Sabbath after the Trinity, Horatio Gristle vanished.

Those of us who recall the events detailing Gristle's disturbing disappearance have a very precise recollection of the date. This is because Stir-up Sunday is the time when the cooks all make up the Christmas puddings, so they might properly season in the five weeks leading up to that most joyous of holy days. And we may remember the disappearance of Horatio Gristle in close connection to the concoction of puddings for reasons that I am about to elucidate.

This is perhaps the proper time in my story to introduce you to Goodie Lovell, who ran the most popular cook's shop on the Baker's Row at Whitechapel. For Goodie Lovell and her employee, George Penny, became central to the investigation of Gristle's dematerialization.

First, it may be helpful for me to describe the good woman in question. Goodie Lovell's Christian name, along with her age, was long ago forgotten by everyone, very possibly herself included. She was a jolly, round woman whose laugh rang like the bells of St. Dunstan's when she greeted her friends on the street. And her friends were many.

Goodie Lovell's cook shop was prosperous not only owing to the proprietor's skill at her craft, though I should say that this was true of the place as well. It often was said that her bread, pease porridge, joints, and chops approached divinity. Even her gravy and mustard sauce were of the very highest quality that could be had in the town.

Not only was her food the best, but also the most economical. Everyone in the tenements said that Goodie's shop could stretch your meat further. If you took her a goose, you would get at least the following—one boil, two grills, a roast, and at least four cold lunches. If you bought right from the cold rooms of the shop, you would get meat and trimmings that had been the most skillfully and most thoroughly cut. No one could clean a carcass like Goodie. She had learned it so young that it was like breathing to her. At Goodie Lovell's, not a scrap of any animal was ever wasted. This was attested to by a simple sign that was painted for the front of the shop on a piece of wood shaped and colored like a copper cooking pot:

Be ye rich men or paupers, we'll fill up yer coppers.

The proof's in the pudding, no matter yer coffers.

But her skill at both butchery and cookery was not the reason that Goodie Lovell was so adored that the common folk and the destitute often called her "Goodie Lovely." Rather, she was beloved because she was one of their own.

Goodie Lovely had been put out to work at a cook's shop when she was barely six years old. This came about when her father (and consequentially the whole family) was sent to the Marshalsea debtor's prison. This had been done over a shortage of only fifty shillings. When a family went to Marshalsea, it was necessary for every able-bodied member to begin raising the money for an expeditious release. Their father had worked at a blacking factory. Their mother had taken in sewing. Goodie Lovell's older brother had joined the army. And Goodie herself had been taken in as a servant in a cook-shop. At that time, she had only been trusted to stir the coppers and to sweep the hearth.

Unfortunately, the circumstances of this little family only grew worse. Within one year of their coming to Marshalsea, both mother and father were swept away by an infectious fever. Goodie's brother never returned from his military service.

In the face of this relentless tragedy, the owner of the cook shop took pity on his little apprentice. Goodie was allowed to live in the attic of the shop and to work for her room and board. In this manner, she was saved from being swallowed up by an orphanage.

Despite her early years of loneliness and despair, Goodie repaid her employer. She continued to sweep the floors and clean the coppers. As she grew, so did her responsibilities. She learned to help with the butchery as soon as she was strong enough to wield a knife. She learned to clean a carcass more perfectly than the worms at Highgate Cemetery. Every duty at the shop became familiar to her. She served her benefactor with such gratitude and industry that the crotchety old fellow, having no children of his own, left the entire operation to her upon his passing.

Goodie Lovell seemed never to have forgotten the momentous importance of her mentor's generosity, for she lived every day of her life showing what could almost be called an apoplectic beneficence. Where Horatio Gristle showed charity to his betters in order to enhance his own position, Goodie Lovely seemed to genuinely care for her neighbors. The more desperate their condition, the more generous she became. She often took soup, loaves, and cakes to her needful neighbors. This included all those who dwelled in the workhouses and debtor's' prisons. And the gifts that were most looked forward to each year were her miraculous Christmas puddings. Every year she brought them far and wide about town. They were said to be the most succulent and rich of such offerings to be found in all of England, regardless of social standing or origin.

Goodie's puddings and stews were not the only examples of her kindness. Her apprentice, George Penny, was a living example of her charitable nature. George had been turned out of an orphanage when he came of age. Rather, when he was large enough to look as if he had. He was thought to have no prospects whatsoever. In general, the people who should have been his benefactors tended to dismiss him as underdeveloped and coarse. They saw in his appearance a born criminal. Their subsequent lack of attention to his development led to manners and speech that showed every sign of confirming their prejudice. But Goodie Lovely saw in George a wayward child in need, even when he was a rather giant specimen of manhood. She took him into the shop and let him live above it in exchange for his labors, as had been done for her when her parents had made the final journey.

Goodie doted on George as if he were her son — or perhaps her long-lost brother. The people who patronized her shop humored her in these opinions. If truth be told, many of them were a bit afraid of George Penny. For one thing, he was well over six-foot tall. He was rather ill-formed in the sense that his appendages and features seemed to have been unnaturally or accidentally tripled in size. George Penny was also so silent in general that many people thought him mute. In reality, he could speak, but he usually found it unnecessary when just a grunt, growl, or chortle would do. In fact, George tended to burst into deep and unsettling laughter at very importune moments, which no one knew what to make heads or tails of. They forbore his presence in their midst for the love of Goodie, but none would want to meet him in a dark alley.

Now we get to the meat of the matter — Gristle's disturbing disappearance. The events that drew suspicion onto Goodie Lovell's cook shop, particularly regarding the person of George Penny, occurred about four days prior.

Many people remembered that Goodie Lovely had gone to Blessed Cross around that time. She there attempted to deliver a pease porridge and several loaves for the poor souls interred within. As was his habit, Gristle had refused to let the items in. When Goodie Lovell came back to her shop, she displayed one of the rare flashes of temper that sometimes occurred when she saw injustice in the world that seemed to be going unchecked.

"Never have I encountered such an ill-humored, mirthless, unkind devil!" she had said.

Rather, it was more of a bellow. More than one patron of the cook shop had jumped half out of their skin at the way she slammed down her empty basket on the countertop. The coppers that were waiting to be filled with porridge and stew all shivered like apple blossoms in a spring gale.

"Did he give it to the greedy guts in the guardhouse?" one of the customers dared to ask. They all knew Gristle's tendencies, after all. This particular patron sought to commiserate with his disgruntled cook.

"Not even that!" Goodie had roared. Her wooden spoon smacked a copper and set off a noise like an East Indian gong. Many of the patrons cringed again. "That evil robber dumped it all on the midden just to teach me a lesson," she said. "You see, I spoke back to him a wee bit when he said it was contraband. I know well that I oughtn't to have done it. Still, what can one do when confronted with such a heartless villain? I reminded him that I had brought the same offerings many times before. Why, only last week the porter let me in with twice as much! But that porter hadn't been Gristle. I vow, he's lucky I'm a peace-loving woman. I'd as soon have his vile guts for garters. Such men really oughtn't to be suffered to breathe."

Many of the customers tutted and nodded. They fully commiserated with their hostess and instantly forgave her intemperate speech. They could well understand the tempest given Gristle's cruelty, combined with Goodie Lovell's untold measure of wasted food and labors.

This was one of those moments that George Penny chose to punctuate with an importune blast of dark, rumbling laughter. He threw his huge head back and roared with glee. Nothing could be seen of his upper regions save a red tongue, a wide chin dark with stubble, and a frightening set of huge, browning teeth.

This gave the customers in the shop some discomfort, as it always did when he laughed so. But Goodie Lovell seemed wholly unconcerned. She waved her wooden spoon at George in an air of command, but not of anger. "Hush, now, George

Penny," she said. "You sound like the devil, hisself." And with that, she shooed him to the back to get more beef from the cold rooms. And no one thought of the matter again, until Horatio Gristle's disturbing disappearance.

By all accounts, this was a baffling event. Gristle left work on Thursday evening and was never seen again by a living soul. There was no trace of his movements and no insight into his social calendar. There was no opinion on his health or his mood. He was corporeal one moment and seemingly incorporeal the next.

As mentioned, no one would have been quite so curious about the porter's change of condition were it not for his first cousin, the Magistrate. But Algernon Gristle the Third was not inclined to suffer the loss of anything, especially a relative.

The police went all over London questioning everyone they could find who had known Gristle as a boy, as a porter, or as a neighbor. If he had possessed any, they also would have asked of his friends. When the inspectors heard about the quarrel that Goodie Lovell had with Gristle only a few days prior to his disappearance, they followed this line of investigation into the depths of the East End. And from further questioning, they learned of Goodie's intemperate words upon the matter.

No one who patronized the cook shop would ever suspect Goodie herself of any wrong-doing. But several had rather chilling opinions about George Penny. And a few of them said as much to the police.

The man who followed up on these reports was Inspector Tobias Little. This inspector was, in fact, quite small both in stature and in standing. When Little heard that Magistrate Gristle was so keen to recover his cousin, the inspector was determined to do the job. He hoped that this would be the path to promotion and esteem. When he swaggered into the cook shop, he was determined to find the truth of the matter as it pertained to the round old woman and her half-mute apprentice.

"Well, well," he said to no one in particular, "let us just see. We shall get to the bottom of this, you can be quite certain."

Goodie Lovell and her customers all stared at Little in confusion. If one or two folks had guessed the reason for his presence or his statement, they did not say so.

"What can I serve up for you, dearie?" Goodie asked. "I've just done half a dozen joints of pork. They are fat and juicy and cleaned of the bones."

"I'm not here for joints of pork; I'm here for Gristle," the inspector replied.

This resulted in a few chuckles from the patronage. As for Goodie, she simply blushed and looked more befuddled. "Surely you don't want the gristle, dearie," she said. "We serve only the finest cuts here. The fat bits are for the puddings, don't you see? For tomorrow is Christmas Pudding Sunday. Then they shall be well seasoned by Christmas Eve."

"Do you mock me, Woman?" Little demanded. The inspector was one of those men who never speak clearly, and then act intemperate when they are misunderstood. In truth, he wasn't well suited for his chosen profession. And at Goodie Lovell's words, he grew russet with rage. "Quite obviously," he said, "I am speaking of Horatio Gristle, the porter at Blessed Cross! I mean that very same man who you threatened to kill only a few days ago."

Goodie cried out and clutched at her chest upon hearing this proclamation. Several of the patrons in the shop gasped, fearful that their beloved cook might collapse from shock or terror.

"See here," said a mill worker at the back of the line, "that is no way to speak to a lady."

"A *lady*?" Little asked in an ugly tone. "Does a *lady* say she wants a respected porter's guts for garters? Does a *lady* say this of a magistrate's cousin, no less? That he ought not to be suffered to breathe?"

"Oh, my heavens!" Goodie said in a faint, breathy voice. "I promise you, my good man, that it were only a moment of intemperance. I had so badly wanted to take porridge and loaves into the workhouse, you see."

"And Gristle got in your way, did he not?" Little retorted. "That problem has been solved, I dare say!"

The patronage gasped again as Inspector Little rushed past the counter and into the kitchen. Goodie gave another cry and fluttered after him. Though since she was a rather large bird, her fluttering resulted in a clattering of coppers.

"Please, Sir, there ain't nothing to see in there," she said. "I keep a clean and simple kitchen."

"We shall see about that!" Little replied.

And he did his best to see while looking over the entirety of the room. To the layman's eye, it did look like a very common kitchen. There were piles of neatly cleaned meat on the counters. It looked to be from several different creatures. Several coppers steamed on the large stove. One in front had a rather hairy item bobbing away in it, boiling heavily. Steam from the coppers gathered at the ceiling like fog. It was as hot in the room as the devil's inferno.

"It's a hog head, dearie," Goodie explained when Little's eyes rested on the pot.

"A head?" he repeated. His eyes narrowed in suspicion, though he did not approach the searing heat of the stove.

"We'll scrape it and take the soft bits out for a sausage," she explained. "I can show it to you if you like."

She moved toward the bobbing item with her wooden spoon brandished aloft. But Inspector Little, while mopping his brow, was already retreating from the room.

"Enough," he said. His voice was tense, but not disbelieving.

Goodie followed him back into the front. She and the customers watched the inspector pace to and fro, his face growing purple from his mental exertions.

"Well, well," he said. "I'm still going to need an accounting. Horatio Gristle didn't disappear into thin air, now did he?"

"I suppose not," Goodie replied, "But I have no idea what he disappeared into. I've been slaving away over the puddings, you see. Everything must be ready."

"Goodie Lovely would never hurt a soul," said a woman who was waiting in line. "When my mother had the fever, it was Goodie what brought her soup and loaves every single day for a month. She never asked for a penny."

"Aye, and she gives those puddings to the poor and miserable every year at Christmas," said another customer. "You'll not find a soul to speak against her!"

"Oh, really?" Inspector Little replied. "And do you all feel the same about George Penny?"

There was silence in the shop. In truth, many patrons were thinking that George was very capable of killing Horatio Gristle if he thought it would please his mistress. But none of them said so out loud, out of respect for Goodie.

At that moment, George walked into the shop. His timing was no better with entrances than it was with laughter. He looked every bit the murderer, with fat joints of roast in his arms and his apron streaked with gore. And when George saw the crowd in the shop looking at him with such attention, he dropped the meat with a violent thud. There he was, left standing before them, awkward as anything and covered with blood.

"George wouldn't hurt anyone," Goodie insisted. "He is misunderstood because he looks so fierce, and doesn't often speak."

"Oh, and I'm to take your word for that, am I?" Inspector Little retorted. "Can he give an accounting for his time, two nights past?"

"I can give an accounting for him," said one of the men in the line. "George were here working all of Thursday evening. I were here dining in, and I played cribbage with the lads till past eleven."

"Is that so?" Inspector Little asked. "Can anyone else recall it?"

At first, there was silence. Then two more men, presumably the aforementioned cribbage lads, gestured as if to say they could. Whether they were in earnest or merely being loyal to Goodie, no one could say. But it did take the wind out of Little's sails.

"Well," he said, "well, well. I suppose. But then, was Mistress Lovell accounted for as well?"

"I was out getting the dried fruits for the puddings," Goodie said nervously. "That were only until eight, or so. That were why George worked out front. I walked clear to a shop at Charing Cross to find the amount that I needed. I am sure they can vouch for me. With my rheumy old legs, it takes me a good three hours to get there and back again."

"Oh, I am sure," Little said, with frustrated aggression. But he looked her up and down, and then nodded when he added, "You do say they can vouch for you, then?"

"I am sure, Sir," she replied. Then she began to cry, exhausted as she was from the strain of the questioning.

"See here," said her most chivalrous customer. "I shall say again, it's no way to treat a woman. She has answered your questions, and we have accounted for George."

"*You* see here, I'm just doing my duty," Inspector Little replied. "A magistrate's cousin has been meddled with! We can't have that, can we?"

"Well, go and find the ones what did the meddling," another customer retorted. "Leave our blessed Goodie Lovely in peace."

"Now, now," Goodie interjected, "don't be hard on the inspector. He is right. Foul play must be answered for if good folk are to be safe."

"Exactly," Little said, seeing Goodie in a lovely new light. "That is *precisely* what I have been saying. I am gratified that someone understands."

"And so I do," Goodie answered. "My good man, do make an old lady happy and take home a joint from this pork. If you come back on Christmas Eve, I shall have a pudding held aside for you."

"Well, I must say I do appreciate it," the inspector said. "Perhaps a joint of pork, then. Thanks very much."

And so Goodie's life went back to normal. The inspector became a regular customer, and he came back for not one, but three Christmas puddings. When the holy day came and Goodie had distributed her treats, everyone claimed they were the best of such offerings on record.

When Goodie took her bounty to Blessed Cross Workhouse, the new head porter allowed her stews and loaves into the dormitories. She was even allowed to bring a large stuffed goose. This was in return for the four wonderful puddings that she sent to the staff and the governors.

Even Magistrate Gristle consumed one and said it was the finest he had tasted. He especially liked the hard sauce, which he said was the most delicious confection he had yet tasted. And with time, his taste for familial restitution was replaced by a taste for Goodie's dainties.

The holiday season came and went, and another and another after that. No one ever found a trace of Horatio Gristle. But can you win our little game of lookabout? Perhaps you would have done if you had looked about in Goodie Lovell's cold rooms the Friday after the disturbing disappearance.

If someone had looked in on the cold rooms in those days leading to Stir-up Sunday, they would have seen a grisly (and a Gristly) sight. For it had not been a pig head boiling in the copper that Inspector Little failed to inspect. And they were not joints of pork that he supped upon that night, or the two nights after.

The carnal remains of Horatio Gristle had been greatly enjoyed by all. His joints had been cleanly cut and deboned. Every scrap of Gristle had, in fact, been preserved, except the bones, which were cleaned by the hogs.

George Penny burned these remnants into ashes, along with all the porter's earthly belongings. For George Penny was always a loyal helper to his mistress. On some years he was the one who collected their holiday offering. But, fortunately for both, Goodie had been just angry enough to kill Gristle on her own.

She had gathered her currants and raisins from an obliging shop at Charing Cross in order to give a reckoning for herself. But she was far younger and could walk far faster than she allowed anyone to suppose, and she had quite enough time on her hands. She had waited for Gristle to leave work. Growing up rough at Marshalsea, Goodie knew well how to knock a man in the back of the head and bring him quickly down. It was not much different from stunning a hog, which she had been taught to do long ago.

Gristle didn't moan or struggle. Goodie felt a bit put out that the offensive man had passed with so little suffering after having heaped so much of it upon the poor. But the brains leaking out over the cobblestone alley assured her that this act of mercy could not be undone.

"The good Lord knows best," Goodie told herself.

Then she had left the body in an obligingly forbidding Whitechapel alley until George Penny could retrieve it. And so, their ruse and their acquisition were complete. Goodie saw the entire endeavor as proof that the Lord favored her work.

Indeed, the puddings that Goodie Lovell had taken to the needful as well as to the magistrates, police, and wardens throughout London over many years had always been made of someone like Horatio Gristle. Every year she made a search for the one most deserving of that fate.

Though she brought many other simples to the poor, Goodie considered the puddings to be the greatest gift of all. There was one less miserly villain polluting the world. To her, this truth was sweeter than treacle.

If you had been in the cold room that Stir-up Sunday, you would have heard Goodie singing as she stirred the gristle from Gristle into the treacle, bread, currants, and other fixings meant to steam into a holiday treat. In accordance with the Common Prayer, she hummed the words:

"Stir up, we beseech thee, O Lord, the wills of thy faithful people; that they, plenteously bringing forth the fruit of good works, may of thee be plenteously rewarded; through Jesus Christ our Lord. Amen."

Perhaps the unseeing eyes of Horatio Gristle, pale and glassy from being boiled like eggs, still managed to look upon her endeavor with gratitude from where they yet bobbed in their pot. For, in death, Gristle did more kindness toward his fellow men than he had done in his entire lifetime.

One humble bird could make a boil, a roast, and many cold suppers. The likes of Horatio Gristle made six boils, a half dozen roasts, innumerable cold suppers, two score of sausages, and three dozen puddings. And, prior to Goodie's hard sauce, Gristle had never been so sweet.

Goody may thusly have provided Gristle with the one convincing argument the porter was able to make to Saint Peter at the pearly gates. He had lived his life selfishly, but had at the end given of himself to the poor. As Goodie thought to herself, he had a much better chance at redemption than if he had been allowed to live out his lifetime according to his own proclivities.

Now you understand the disturbing disappearance of Horatio Gristle. He finally gave something back to the world. In addition, Gristle became the finest hard sauce that Goodie Lovell had ever made. It was the one time he managed to be sweet.

Alas, Horatio Gristle will never have the credit for it. The proof was in the pudding, and the pudding is long since gone.

Capturing the Christmas Spirit

Kurt Newton

First, you set your traps.

That guy who rings the bell outside the shopping mall entrance—you try him first.

You drop a dollar in the bucket, make some comment about the weather and how you can feel the good cheer in the air. Make him smile, just long enough for him to remember your face so the next time he sees it he's not so alarmed.

Later, after the mall has closed, you follow him home to

his one-room efficiency apartment in the north end of town. Of course he lives alone. Of course he has no friends to speak of. He must have something else that gets him through the holidays. Something special inside. Something you need.

So, you knock on his door—and he invites you in, for Christ's sake! Because he knows your face. He knows you donated your hard-earned cash to total strangers. He remembers the remark you made about good cheer. He believes he knows your heart. But when he turns his back, you reach into your pocket as if to give him a gift, but your mission here is only to take.

He barely utters a noise as the blade slips smoothly across his throat. You ease his body to the floor. His eyes are searching. For meaning, no doubt. For a reasonable excuse, as you produce a wide-mouth jar and wait expectantly for his life to drain away.

But he wasn't the one. After the blood and the gasping, there was nothing. But you filled your jar anyway, as a souvenir.

❉ ❉ ❉

Now, you turn your attention to the girl in the pretty powder blue snowflake sweater who sings in the church choir.

Little does she know the baritone who stands behind her lusts not for her body, but for the essence that seems to shine like miniature Christmas lights in her eyes and lifts her voice from the ordinary yuletide hymn to true aural majesty. Surely, she has what you're looking for. Surely, she has a grip on the heel of the elusive Christmas spirit.

Choir practice ends for the evening. The night has turned cold and blustery. Flakes of wet snow shuttle sideways across the parking lot. You've brought an umbrella and offer to walk her to her car. You talk about the music. She compliments you on your voice. And, once again, it is easy to gain the trust of a lonely stranger. She may even like you, but you aren't interested in second-hand grace. With you, it's either all or nothing.

You've made sure to park your car next to hers. And just as you are about to wrap your gloved hands around her soon-to-be screaming mouth, she asks if you would like to go somewhere for a cup of coffee. You smile and say you know just the place.

You bring her to your apartment. And while the cappuccino maker is hissing like Satan's first kiss, she tells you she's never done this before. "I'm kind of new at this myself," you say as you hand her a Santa Claus mug full of hazelnut coffee spiked with enough strychnine to send Rudolph into paralysis. Because you want her awake. You want her eyes open so you can stare down this thing that has eluded you all these years.

In minutes, her body begins to tremble, then flail. This is it, you believe. The exorcism of a spirit is indeed a violent thing.

You open the jar you've retrieved from under the sink. Her eyes bulge, her voice rises to an ethereal caterwaul.

But the seizure ends. Her gaze hardens. Somehow, you missed it. Or it was never there.

Damn.

❄ ❄ ❄

Your search intensifies.

Christmas is only one day away. As the snow falls around you and the sidewalks fill with holiday shoppers, you decide you have been looking in the wrong place. Your sights have been set too high. You look down. And see a child.

The boy is carrying a ceramic piggy bank between his mint green, threadbare mittens. He enters a Salvation Army store. You follow, curious.

The boy selects a long wool scarf off one of the racks. He carries it like it's made of crepe paper. It's for his mother he tells the cashier as he empties the contents of the piggy bank onto the counter. Everyone within earshot pauses to smile. The cashier is nearly moved to tears. The pennies are counted out, and the scarf is bagged. "Merry Christmas," the cashier says, "and don't forget your piggy bank." The boy exits, beaming. You follow.

He's the one, you tell yourself.

There is no car waiting for him, no parents, no brothers or sisters to accompany him home. He must live close by. You don't have much time.

The sidewalks are slippery with slush. The boy heads a-way from the crowds, toward the darker side of town, toward the tenements where babies cry and drunken husbands smack their wives between commercials. You feel naked as you become the only one following the boy. The boy senses this and his street smarts kick in. He bolts, running down an alleyway.

You chase after him. He's quick. His spirit is strong. But your stride is no match for the boy's shortened step.

At the end of the alley, cars flash by on the adjacent street. You are nearly on top of him. The alleyway ends and the boy darts around the corner. You make a lunge for his hood, but the slush takes your footing. Your body hits the sidewalk with a bone-jarring thud.

The boy darts between two parked cars and turns to see if you are still chasing him. He doesn't see the taxi speeding down the street. The impact sends him end over end in a high acrobatic arc, then down onto the pavement, where he lands like a wet garbage bag thrown from a third-story window.

You scramble to your feet. There is still time, you tell your-self. But as you approach the boy, you discover that you are limping. Your thigh burns. The dampness is not all slush. Some of it is warm. You reach down and feel the jagged splinters of glass protruding from the inside of your coat pocket. The jar. Without the jar, there is no capture.

You kneel over the boy anyway. Perhaps your mouth will be an ample orifice, your body a suitable container.

The boy is hardly breathing, but his hands still clutch his mother's scarf. "It's mine," he gurgles, and his voice doesn't sound like a child's at all. It resonates with age, with a knowl-edge beyond time. The boy takes his final breath, and as his lungs relax, his skin begins to glow. A look of contentment dis-places the one of pain and fear that was there just moments before. His pores seem to open wider to allow more of the light to escape.

Your eyes are blinded, your heart is seared. He was the one. Tears sting the corners of your eyes and run hot tracers down your cheeks.

"One minute nothing, next minute he there. Boom!" The taxi driver approaches. "Mister, you see it, right? He like a ghost."

A crowd begins to gather. You hear sirens in the distance.

You walk back through the alley. Back to the shoppers with their armloads of presents. And the children. You notice now that each one you pass has the glow. Just beneath the surface. The skin of the innocent. The face of the Christmas spirit. And you realize it is in each one of them. They are born with it. We are all born with it. But somewhere along the way, it leaves us. We don't know when, and we don't know why. All we know is that one day it is gone.

✳ ✳ ✳

You are now back at your apartment. It's getting close to midnight. The oven door has been open for an hour now, the gas turned on high. You watch the clock as it ticks toward midnight. Five. Four. Three. Two. One.

You strike a match and wait to be reborn.

G᪲ood O᪲l' M᪲rs. C᪲laus

Karen Thrower

manda sat in the only booth that wasn't full of rips and covered in duct tape, her hands wrapped around a hot mug of coffee. She hated the taste, but it always warmed her hands better than cocoa. The hood of her coat was pulled low to hide her new black eye. She hated her boyfriend and wanted to leave, but he had moved them to a town where she didn't know anyone and she had no idea what to do. She had no job, no car, and no money of her own. Her family and friends all told her not to move, not to trust him, but she thought they were jealous of what they had. She hated being proved wrong.

The plastic on the booth squeaked, and she saw someone in red help themselves to the seat across from her.

"Evening."

Amanda looked up. It was a woman, a very pretty woman in one of those slutty Mrs. Claus dresses.

"Oh, that looks painful," she said, pointing to the black eye.

"What do you want?" Amanda looked back down at her untouched coffee.

The woman cleared her throat and stretched her arms over the top of the booth. "Well, it's Christmas. I figured I could help someone less fortunate. You need help?"

Amanda looked across the table. The woman was clearly nuts. She rolled her eyes and stared into her coffee cup again. "Yeah, but nothing you can do."

The woman threw her head back and laughed, her silky dark hair shimmering in the colorful Christmas lights decorating the window next to them. "I knew you'd say that. Everyone says that." The woman reached across the table and touched Amanda's hand. "Try me."

Amanda scoffed and scooted back, taking her hands from the woman. "Everyone says *that* to me. So you try me, weird lady."

The woman snickered and laid her arms on the table and leaned forward. Amanda thought her boobs were going to pop out of that dress the way she was sitting. "What do you want?" the woman asked.

"What do I want?" Amanda sat back and crossed her arms. "I want enough money and a decent car to get home for Christ-

mas. I want enough money to get my own place. I want..."
She stopped. She had never said the words before, just imagined what might happen.

"You want?" The woman leaned closer, almost like she knew what Amanda didn't want to say out loud. "Don't be shy. You want him dead, don't you?"

Amanda gasped and leaned back farther.

"They all want them dead, honey; how dare he put his hands on you, how dare he take you from your support system. He deserves it, doesn't he?"

Amanda shook her head and looked away from the woman. She caught slutty Mrs. Claus' reflection in the window and gasped at the rotting face and red eyes that greeted her. She quickly looked back, but she only saw a live beauty with chocolate brown eyes staring back at her. She looked back and forth a few times, always a rotting crone in the window and vibrant beauty sitting across from her.

Mrs. Claus laughed and sat back, her slender arms still resting on the table. "You aren't going crazy, and he didn't hit you so hard you're seeing things. Not many get this opportunity, Amanda. I'd take it if I were you."

"W-what opportunity," she said as she began to shake. She wasn't sure if it was from the woman or if she was coming down off an adrenaline high.

"Revenge, dear girl."

A waitress walked over, but Mrs. Claus waved her hand and the young girl quickly turned around and left them alone. "Like I said, it's Christmas, and I'm feeling generous."

Amanda shook her head and grabbed her coffee mug to try and steady herself. "I can't—I mean—it's not my place to decide something like that."

"Well, why not?" Mrs. Claus leaned forward. "How often do victims say they want that control, they want that choice?

How many lives would be saved if they did what they thought they couldn't do?"

Amanda scoffed. "Yeah, and be in jail afterward. No thanks."

"No jail, dear girl. You'll be gone by then. Unless you want to watch."

Amanda's eyes widened as a wicked smile spread across Mrs. Claus' face.

"Some do." She shrugged. "I wouldn't deny a victim the chance to see their tormentor punished. I know I would enjoy it."

Amanda sat back and stared at Mrs. Claus' perfectly manicured red nails. It had been so long since she had treated herself to something like that she almost forgot she could.

Mrs. Claus tapped her nails on the table, as if reading her thoughts. "Like them? I love a good diamond top coat, don't you?" she said, admiring her own nails.

"I—I don't know. I've never had one."

Mrs. Claus gasped. "Never? My dear girl, every woman deserves beautiful nails." She snapped her fingers, but Amanda just stared at her. Mrs. Claus sighed irritably. "Your nails, dear girl. Look at your nails."

Confused, Amanda wrinkled her nose and looked down. It took a moment for her brain to comprehend what she saw. Her nails were shaped, not cracked and broken, and they were a beautiful, delicate pink—and so shiny! Amanda sighed at the artistry.

"Wow," she finally said as she held up her hands.

"Much better. Now, what else?"

Amanda looked up at Mrs. Claus and realized whoever— whatever—this woman was, she could get her everything she needed.

She looked down into her black coffee. "I don't want him

doing this to anyone ever again."

Mrs. Claus smiled. "I think I can do something about that."

❄ ❄ ❄

Amanda walked around Ricky; he was unconscious and duct-taped to a chair in the kitchen. She found him that way when she walked into the apartment. Mrs. Claus was sitting on the table, twirling a thick, black baton like the police have.

"So," Mrs. Claus held out the weapon, "do you want to do the honors, or shall I?"

Amanda shook her head. "You do it."

"As you wish," she said, practically singing the words. As she hopped off the table, Amanda heard little bells jingling. They must have been sewn into the dress. She tapped Ricky on the head, and he jerked up. "Hello."

"Who the hell are you!" he yelled. "Get me out of here, you stupid bitch!"

"Hey!" Amanda moved around Mrs. Claus. "Don't talk to her like that!"

Ricky's face turned red with rage. "You bitch! Get me out of here! You and your friend are going to be so sorry!"

Mrs. Claus laughed and struck him across the face with the baton. "He does have a mouth on him, doesn't he?"

"Hey, screw you!" he yelled as blood dripped down his chin. He struggled against the tape, but the tape held him securely to the chair. "Get me out of here!"

"Hmmmm. No," Mrs. Claus said. "You are a wretched being, and you will not hurt anyone ever again."

Ricky looked up at Amanda and his voice softened. "Mandy, come on. Let me out. I'm sorry. You know how I get when I drink!"

She had heard it before and wasn't buying it this time. "I

do," she yelled in his face. "That's why you shouldn't drink! You're a piece of shit, and I'm going to make sure you don't hurt anyone ever again!"

Anger flashed across his face, and he was about to start slinging insults when Mrs. Claus stuffed a sock in his mouth, then covered it with more duct tape.

"You should have thought about how you treated me." Amanda picked up a suitcase and started for the door.

"One minute, dear girl." Mrs. Claus walked over to her, her fingers drumming against themselves. "I do require payment for this."

"Oh. I don't have any money," she said as she began digging in her purse.

"I don't need money, dear girl." Mrs. Claus laid her hand on Amanda's chest, and she felt something being drawn from her. It wasn't painful, but it was the most uncomfortable feeling she had ever experienced. Mrs. Claus took her hand off, and Amanda stumbled a bit. She felt empty and itchy and unfulfilled.

"Ah, perfect. Thank you, dear girl. You go enjoy your life now."

Amanda turned quickly and ran from the apartment as Ricky's screams filled the night.

❄ ❄ ❄

It had been six months since Amanda left her ex-boyfriend. She'd been able to get a job she loved, had a great apartment, and was able to afford a reliable car that she used to visit her family every weekend. Her life was much better. She was getting ready for the weekly family dinner when she heard the front door to her apartment open with a crash. Amanda gasped and snatched up the mace she had on her keychain.

"Get out of here! I'm calling the cops!" she yelled as she locked herself in her bedroom. She dug through her purse, but she couldn't find her phone.

"You mean with this phone right here?" a familiar voice said through the door.

Amanda dropped her purse and felt herself start to shake.

"Ricky?" she whispered. The cheap wooden door burst into splinters, and Amanda ducked away from the debris. When the noise died down, she looked up and saw Ricky standing in the doorway. "No," she said, fumbling for the mace. "You're dead."

He threw the phone against the wall, shattering it. "Not really." He walked into the room, and Amanda didn't hesitate. She sprayed him in the face with her mace, but he didn't react in the usual manner. Instead, he sniffed and licked it off his face. "If you're going to negotiate with a demon, you need to offer more than a piece of your pathetic soul."

"A demon?"

Ricky smiled, and she watched his eyes flash red. "You don't really think Mrs. Claus is that sexy do you?" He walked over and pressed a gun to her head.

"Play with the devil and you're gonna get burned, dear girl."

Amanda's eyes widened as she looked around Ricky and saw Mrs. Claus standing in the doorway in the same slutty red dress. Except she wasn't beautiful anymore; she looked like the reflection Amanda has seen in the window of the diner. Dead and rotting.

Mrs. Claus shrugged dismissively and said with a smile, "His deal was much better. This way I get two souls instead of one."

MERRY CHRISTMAS TO ALL, AND TO ALL A BRIGHT NIGHT

Dan Foley

've been growing Christmas trees for as long as I can remember. It's the family business, after all. We have a hundred and ten acres in upstate New York's Adirondack Park that have been in the family for generations. The park itself contains over six million acres. Over half of that is privately owned land like ours. We grow Douglas Fir, Frasier Fir, Balsam Fir,

White Spruce, Blue Spruce, White Pine, and Scots Pine. Don't get me wrong; I like them all, but my favorite is the White Pine because the needles are long and soft and don't stick you when you're working on them. I've come home many a day with my arms covered in tiny red pricks from some of the spruces.

I started working in the fields when I was twelve. At first, I hated it. My friends would be off playing, having fun, and there I'd be, stuck in acres and acres of trees with nothing but the occasional bird or squirrel for company. I didn't even get paid. My asshole father said I was getting room and board and that I should be happy to pitch in and help. Yeah, right. I worked twenty hours a week and got a lousy ten bucks allowance. That works out to fifty cents an hour. Back then, the cheap bastard would have had to pay anyone else at least five bucks an hour. At least. The day I came home and told him I was taking a job at the local restaurant, the Coffee Cup, he pitched a fit. That's when I got my first "raise." He grudgingly agreed to pay me ten cents an hour over the minimum wage the restaurant offered. He could have got someone for minimum wage, but he would have had to train them. I already knew the business.

Cultivating Christmas trees is actually a lot of work. All the people coming to buy one see is row upon row of well-trimmed trees. It requires year-round attention to get them to look that way. We don't have to do a lot of work clearing the land—that's already been done—but we do have to cultivate and remove the old stumps and roots in order to plant new trees. That can be a bitch. Once that's done, though, things move a little quicker. We rototill the spot, add fertilizer to replenish the soil, and pop in a seedling.

Maintenance is in constant demand. We need to keep the land free of weeds, plants, and other trees that tend to sprout between the rows. There are pests like aphids and gypsy moths to contend with, as well as diseases. They have to be caught early so they don't spread to every tree on the farm.

So, yeah, it's a lot of work.

Like I said, I used to hate it. But somewhere along the line, probably when I started planting the seedlings, I began to love it. Not the work, of course, but the trees. I started to think of them as my children. That's where the trouble started.

It wasn't so bad with the families who would come and cut their own trees. I could see that they were going to a home where they'd be appreciated. But then we started selling live trees with bundled roots. These trees could be replanted once the season was over. *Why can't they all do this?* I wondered, but I knew this was wishful thinking. Not many people want to deal with a tree once Christmas is over.

My life became an emotional rollercoaster that soared with the planting of new trees, leveled out in the summer as they grew, turned to anxiety as Thanksgiving and tree-cutting season approached, and depression, which grew with every tree that was cut down and dragged off the farm. The worst, though, was the anger I felt in the weeks after Christmas when I would see discarded trees lining the road waiting for garbage trucks to pick them up and haul them away. These were my children, used and then discarded like broken toys.

It was the commercial sales that finally pushed me over the edge. My children were harvested like so much chattel. Cut down, dragged out, and stuffed into a bailing machine. They went in, branches full and beautiful, and came out trussed up with twine and looking like concentration camp survivors. It had to stop, but what could I do? It took me years to hit on a solution, and another year to perfect it. And now, finally, this is the year my children are going to get their revenge.

I had to start way back in July to make sure I'd be done by Thanksgiving when the harvest started. I prepared three trees a day, every day. Three trees a day for one hundred and forty-six days. Four hundred and thirty-eight trees with their own little Christmas surprise packed inside.

I got my idea from a safety video I saw on YouTube, of all places. It was a demonstration about how Christmas tree fires can turn deadly within seconds. There are several. Look them up. They're really quite impressive. The burn starts slow, but then it really takes off. Flames engulf the tree, and black smoke rises to the ceiling and fills the room. Within a minute, it's a scene from hell.

My idea is quite simple, really. I filled a small, half-inch plastic tube with gasoline. I inserted two small wires into it from either side and connected it to a tiny battery like you can buy in any hardware store. I got these from the internet. Then I hooked it up to a tiny receiver I could actuate with a cell phone. It took me several prototypes to get them to work properly, but I managed. After that, it was a piece of cake to drill a hole in the trunk of a tree, insert the device, then cover it over with bark. When it was done, only a really close inspection would find it—and how many people inspect every inch of a tree before putting it up?

So now you know the plan. It's Christmas Eve, and my children are dispersed all over New York State. Some are even in Vermont and Connecticut. I'm sipping a fine single-malt scotch and waiting for the clock to strike midnight. When it does, I'm going to make a call, and four hundred and thirty-six Christmas trees are going to light up the night.

CHRISTMAS CALENDAR

Christine Lajewski

"Emma gets Christmas stockings," Charlie told his mother at dinner the last night in November.

"We never had Christmas stockings. Why don't we get Christmas stockings?" said Callie, his sister.

Celeste, ambushed by her six-year-old twins, was hesitant to expand the orgy of commercial Christmas, so she replied, "We never did Christmas stockings in my family. We're Polish. People in Poland don't do Christmas stockings."

"It's a French custom, isn't it?" said Joseph, their father.

The twins shifted accusing stares from parent to parent.

"We open our gifts on Christmas Eve," said Joseph. "How many of your friends get to do that? They have to wait for Christmas morning."

Callie and Charlie were too young to formulate arguments fortified with adolescent logic and legal precedent, but they knew how to pout.

"Finish your dinner," said Celeste. The twins pouted some more, and Callie's lower lip trembled for added emphasis. Celeste sighed, "Don't make me call 1-800-TATTLES." It was a hotline to the North Pole she had created to keep her children in line during the holidays. She picked up her phone. This motion alone usually worked, but this time the threat did not have the desired effect. It gave the pair another line of attack.

"Santa fills the stockings. He doesn't care if we're Polish," they shouted simultaneously.

Celeste began tapping in the numbers. Callie and Charlie retreated from the battlefield.

When Celeste met their school bus two days later, the twins greeted their mother with a new accusation: "Why don't we have an Advent Calendar?"

"Stevie has one. He opened this little door last night, and there was chocolate," said Charlie.

"Emma has one, too, and Liam and Sasha," Callie added.

Celeste promised to see if she could find one at the store, but by December third she still hadn't gotten around to it. Later that evening, she found Joseph checking the sofa cushions for his phone.

"Maybe it's in the study," said Celeste. As she passed Callie's bedroom, she spied the twins hunched over the screen, whispering an urgent message to someone.

"What are you two doing with Daddy's phone?" she asked.

"We had to call someone," said Callie.

"1-800-TATTLES," said Charlie.

"Are you telling Santa on me?" Celeste suppressed a smile.

The twins nodded.

"Is this about the Advent Calendar?"

"And the Christmas stockings," said Callie.

"Well, maybe you can ask Santa to bring you a better mommy. Let's remember to ask next time you want to call someone." She took the phone back to her husband. They shared a quiet laugh over the incident.

The following afternoon, Joe brought in the mail, which included a package for the twins. It had no postage or return address. The parents inspected and opened the padded brown envelope to find two Advent Calendars.

They were both the thickness of a book and made of intricately carved and painted wood, reminiscent of ornaments Celeste remembered from her Babcia's Christmas tree. There were twisted vines and flowers running up the sides, hens and roosters on the roof, and smiling foxes with intelligent gazes seated on the ground. Mischievous imps peeked out from behind the curtains of greenery. An angel with a flaming sword hovered above each child's name over the front door, which was meant to be opened on Christmas Eve. The other twenty-three doors were cleverly camouflaged as windows, flowers, birds, or faces.

Parents and children stood silently before the wonder of these creations. Then Charlie and Callie clamored to open the doors. "How many? How many? How many?" they chorused.

"Its December fourth, so look for numbers one through

41

four," said their father.

The twins located the tiny brass nails that functioned as doorknobs and opened the first gate. Charlie removed a rusted iron nail. Callie found a splinter of wood.

The next three boxes revealed two lumps of putty that looked like chewed gum, nondescript balls of fur, a small piece of dried meat, and a fingernail.

"Oh, my God! Who would send this to a child?" Celeste cried. Joe quickly scooped the trash into his hand and dropped it into a plastic bag. Callie and Charlie looked at the Christmas detritus with puzzled expressions, then at each other, but said nothing. They did not seem to share their parents' revulsion.

"I think we should call the police," said Celeste. "Some freak is watching our kids and sending them sick gifts. Who knows what they'll find next?"

The twins shrieked in protest as their father opened the fifth door, then the sixth, and the seventh. They were empty. The children wept and glared at their father with black fury. "You ruined it!" they cried.

"This isn't an Advent Calendar. This is junk," said Joe.

"Get your coats," said Celeste. "We'll go to the country store and you can pick out your own calendars. Real ones, with chocolate." She hustled her children outside to the car while Joe tied the wooden abominations and their surprises into a trash bag and dumped them.

The twins ate four days' worth of chocolate from their new calendars and seemed mollified when they went to bed that night. "Should we report this to the police?" Celeste asked her husband when she knew the children were asleep.

"I don't want to end up on the news and have this thing blow up on us," said Joe. "It's a sick joke, and I'm afraid other weirdos could copy it and try to go one better." They decided, in the end, to be vigilant, but to keep the incident to themselves.

❋ ❋ ❋

Two days later, Joe went out to move the trash barrels to the street for collection and found one of them upended, the plastic bags spilled out on the driveway. Two of them had been torn open, their contents scattered. He cleaned it up, swearing under his breath and muttering, "Damn coyotes." He finished and was about to go inside when he realized one bag—the one that suggested flat squares and rigid walls—was missing. It insinuated that someone had gone through the trash, specifically looking for the confiscated Advent Calendars.

He told Celeste about this curious development. "Do you think it means anything?" Joe asked, but his wife didn't answer. She was watching the twins watch their parents from the kitchen doorway.

Once Charlie and Callie were on their way to school and Joe off to work, Celeste began turning the house upside down, searching for her phone. She worked from home, and her smartphone was an indispensable tool. She finally heard it ringing and found it tucked between the mattress and box spring of Callie's bed. She finished her conference call with her client, then scrolled through the list of sent calls.

There were three calls placed to 1-800-TATTLES the previous night, well after her children should have gone to sleep. There were also two calls from the same number. In a panic, Celeste redialed. The phone rang and rang. No one answered. She was not kicked over to a voice mailbox.

Celeste did enough work to demonstrate she was not blowing off her day, then took a long break to search the twins' bedrooms. Behind Charlie's bookcase, she found the Advent Calendars. All the doors that Joe had torn open had been expertly repaired. She opened doors for random dates on each calendar, but again found nothing within.

She knew she would never be able to quiet the buzzing in her head unless she continued the hunt. She remembered a pink and purple sealed box made of Legos that sat on Callie's dresser. It seemed no more than a smaller piece intended for a larger structure, but when she picked it up and shook it, it rattled. Celeste broke the box apart and found the plastic bag with the bits of trash Joseph had thrown away. There were six new items: two human molars, two incisors, and two canines.

Celeste was frightened, not only by the interference of some mysterious stranger, but by the secretive behavior of her own children as well. She paced about the house, talking to herself. "I don't want a big scene with them. I don't want a confrontation. What if they get angry? What if everything gets worse?" She halted mid-step as she realized she had never before worried about provoking the twins' displeasure.

"Makes no sense, makes no sense," she repeated as she gathered the calendars and the grotesque playthings and carried them out to the fire pit. The teeth were buried under the compost bin. Everything else was burned. She would say nothing to her twins and hope all of it just went away.

Charlie and Callie came home and played a while before dinner. Celeste had worked hard to put their rooms back together. If the twins discovered anything out of place, they made no mention of it. What could they say? If they brought up the subject, they would have to admit they had retrieved and hidden something their parents did not want them to have. That did not, however, prevent them from fixing their fuming gazes on their parents throughout dinner. Celeste pretended not to notice.

"Is something wrong?" asked Joe. Mother and children

shook their heads and focused on their plates until the twins asked to be excused.

As soon as the Charlie and Callie were out of the room, Celeste leaned in towards her husband and whispered to him the events of her day. "You said there were two incoming calls from that stupid number you made up?" Joe said. Alarmed, he pulled out his phone, but he found no new suspicious calls. He dialed the number, listened for a few seconds, then said, "What the hell. It's a real number. Someone said, 'Complaints' and hung up."

They both decided they would keep their phones close at hand. Celeste went so far as to tuck hers under her pillow when she went to bed that night.

As she slept, she felt the device vibrate through her pillow. "Who's calling?" she muttered into the pillowcase. "I'm trying to sleep."

A muffled voice in a deep, rasping whisper, said, "I'm returning your call. You had a complaint?"

"I don't have any complaints."

"We don't like prank calls. We take our business seriously. Why did you call us?" The voice was just a little darker, a bit more guttural.

Outlines of the bedroom furniture emerged from the blackness and Celeste began to suspect she was not dreaming. "I didn't call you," she said. "Who is this?"

"1-800-TATTLES."

Celeste bolted out of bed, fully awake. She felt under her pillow. The phone was gone. When she stepped out into the hall, she saw the glow of a nightlight under Callie's door and heard the sing-song lilt of children's voices. "We don't know where to keep it," she heard Charlie say.

She threw open the door to find her twins hunched over her phone. "What are you doing?" Celeste demanded.

"Getting instructions," said Callie. She hid the phone behind her back.

Celeste wrestled the phone away from her daughter, whose cries brought her father running. "What is going on?" Joe shouted.

Celeste showed him the phone. A growl issued from the device.

"He was talking to us," said Charlie. "He doesn't like being interrupted."

"Who doesn't?" Joe demanded. He put the phone to his ear and shouted, "Who the hell is this and why are you calling my children?"

"I take complaints," said the voice. "Did you have a complaint?"

Joe pulled the phone away from his head. A cacophony of animals sounds, tinny and distant but just loud enough to be heard, filled the room. It was a long, reverberating chord of squealing pigs, braying donkeys, and bellowing bulls.

Joe and Celeste exchanged looks of horror, but the twins registered no reaction. "You interrupted us," said Charlie.

Callie held out her hand and said, "We need to finish our instructions."

"No, you don't," said Joe, handing the silenced phone back to Celeste. Without a word between them, the parents tore apart the children's rooms again. Enraged, the twins keened with one piercing wail after another as the parents found the Advent Calendars and the bags of horrid holiday favors.

The children had opened one more door, which had yielded two slivers of bone, but the bags contained twice the material Celeste had destroyed that afternoon. Joe brought his foot down on each of the wooden calendars, splintering them to bits. Then the adults collected every last shaving and dumped all of it in the fire pit. Joe doused the pile with gasoline and lit it up. Both mother and father had to restrain their scream-ing children to keep them from trying to snatch pieces from the flames.

"They'll wake the neighbors," Joe said. "Someone will call the police." Almost as soon as he spoke, the children settled into a chorus of dismal whimpers and sniffles. The parents tucked the twins back into their beds. They were soon asleep, but the adults could not relax.

"I'll keep the children home today," said Celeste over cof-fee she had allowed to grow cold. "I want to see everything they do."

Joe nodded. "As soon as the ashes are cool, I'll shovel every-thing in the ash carrier and dump it in the pond behind the house. I don't want them finding those teeth."

The twins slept late. When they woke, the first snow of the season was falling, and they begged to go outside and play in it. She dressed them in their winter gear and set up her lap-top on the dining room table where she could work but keep a good, panoramic view of the deck, backyard, and fire pit. Charlie and Callie made snow angels and played on the swings and slides. When they disappeared into their playhouse, Ce-leste made an excuse to go outside. They seemed engaged in a perfectly innocent argument about their favorite movies. Celeste went back to work and was soon so absorbed she for-got to check on her children.

The wind picked up and slapped big wet snowflakes against the windows. It was time to bring the twins indoors, but when Celeste stood on the deck, it seemed her children had disappeared. She called their names a half-dozen times before the door to the shed swung open. Charlie and Callie peeked around the door frame.

"You need to come in and warm up," Celeste called. "I'll make some hot chocolate for you."

The children happily complied. Their mother said, "We keep a lot of tools in the shed. You know we don't like you to play there without Daddy or me. What were you doing in there?"

"We're sorry, Mommy," said Callie, somewhat too cheerfully. "We were pretending a blizzard came, and we had to hide in a spooky house."

As they drank their cocoa, the twins were animated and excited, as if the chaos of last night had never happened. For the rest of the afternoon, they colored Santa pictures and built a blanket fort in the living room. They engaged in a good deal of make-believe, then their voices dropped to conspiratorial whispers. Celeste moved her chair so she could eavesdrop, but she could only pick out two sentences.

"She'll never find it," said Charlie.

"It's just like Build-a-Bear," said Callie.

Something's in the shed, Celeste thought. When Joe got home, she shared her suspicions. They waited for the twins to go to sleep, then took flashlights out to the structure to investigate.

All the tools hung neatly from the pegboard rack against one wall. The plank shelves resting on milk crates and cinder blocks appeared largely undisturbed. A shoe box with packets of leftover seed appeared to have been gnawed by a mouse that left a sizeable puff of nesting material wedged in the corner of a milk crate.

"Oh, here we go," said Joe as he trained his flashlight on an upended crate of kindling. Most of its contents were sorted into piles: flats of plywood stacked in a tower, sticks and small limbs laid out by length, like the keys on a toy xylophone. Propped against the crate were two small figures fashioned from kindling and wire. Joe held up one as he handed the other to his wife.

They were Y-shaped twigs turned upside-down to represent legs; a cross stick had been wired in place where the arms would go. Jagged squares were awkwardly wrapped with wire and stuck on the necks to represent heads. Dried leaves had been threaded over the arms and legs to resemble a dress on one figure, pants and a shirt on the other.

"A boy and a girl?" Celeste suggested.

"Or you and me," said Joe. "Are they toys, presents for us, or voodoo dolls?"

"Nice, Joe, real nice."

They left the wood where it was and returned the figures to their places next to the crate.

Over the next week, mother and father maintained a careful watch over their children as they prattled happily at the dinner table about the approaching holidays and consumed the chocolates from the store-bought Advent Calendars. But there were dozens of moments, briefly seen from the corner of the eye, when Joe or Celeste caught a dark, threatening glower, or overheard unsettling snatches of whispered conversations:

"How does skin fit over bones?"

"His teeth came out—again."

"We need more instructions."

"They always seemed so happy, so affectionate," Celeste confided to her husband during their night out that weekend. "Now, there are times when I just feel, I don't know, nervous when they're around."

"Ever since they called that number, they haven't been the same," said Joe. He had placed several more calls to 1-800-TATTLES, but no one ever answered. It was as if someone was using caller ID to ignore him. He added, "I still don't get it. You made up the damned number, so who's talking to them? Maybe a hacker pervert?"

They decided that Joe would ask the police the next day

if they could track the number. By the following evening, however, the parents realized a police investigation might not help. As she passed Charlie's closed door with a basket of clean laundry, she heard the twins' voices rising and falling in great excitement. She placed her ear against the door and could hear an animated three-way conversation. She knew her phone was in her pocket, and Joe was talking to his sister. With a bundle of folded clothes in her arms, she eased the door open. She could not see the children anywhere.

"We glued on the skin and hair, but the teeth keep falling off," Callie said. The voice came from the closet.

"Yes, we have tape," said Charlie. "And when we're done, we put them behind the last door?" He seemed to be listening to someone. Then both twins giggled as Charlie said, "They'll be so surprised."

Teeth? Skin? Those grotesque Advent calendars—returned to the children? Celeste threw open the closet door. Her children were seated on the floor. Each was holding one half of a tin can telephone. A growling voice echoed in stereo from the cans: "Are you still alone?"

The laundry dropped to the floor as she snatched the cans away and shouted "Hello? Who's there?" into one of the silent cylinders. Suddenly, she realized how stupid she must look. Her face turned red as she dropped the toy to the floor and made a feeble demand: "What are you two doing?"

"Playing," said Charlie.

"We're playing customer service," said Callie. "We're getting instructions."

"What kind of instructions?" asked Celeste.

"We can't tell you," Charlie replied. "It's a surprise."

His mother forced a smile and retreated. Once again, Celeste and Joe mounted a stealthy search of house and grounds after the twins fell asleep. The wooden mannequins were missing from the shed. There was nothing to indicate those obscene-ities masquerading as Christmas calendars had resurfaced.

The next night, the family took a walk through the light display at the local park and zoo. A light snow wheeled and sparkled through haloes of lamplight along the winding path, exciting cries of wonder from parents and children. As the family neared the end of the tour, Callie was so overcome, she threw her arms around Celeste's waist and stretched on tiptoe to plant a kiss on Joe's cheek. "I love you, Mommy. I love you, Daddy," she cooed.

Charlie hugged his parents, too, insisting, "Don't worry. We don't care about the stockings."

Joe and Celeste hugged their children in return, but also exchanged quizzical glances. They had long forgotten the con-versation they'd had regarding Christmas stockings at the be-ginning of December. Clearly, if the twins were now forgiving them this transgression, they had been brooding about it for the past three weeks. When they discussed it later, Joe seemed satisfied the twins were no longer listing quite so heavily towards the weird. Celeste did not share his opinion, but the final week before Christmas was just too frenetic to allow the luxury of anxiety.

On December 23rd, Callie and Charlie consumed the choc-olate Santas hidden behind the next-to-the-last perforated cardboard door on their printed calendars. "I wonder what's behind the last door?" Charlie speculated.

"It's a big door," said Celeste. "It must be special."

"Not as special as—," Callie blurted before she clapped her hands over her mouth.

"Let's go play," Charlie said quickly, tugging his sister's hand.

Celeste watched them disappear down the hall and de-bated whether she should follow them or wait to investigate.

She decided on the latter and went outside to fill the bird feeders. On the deck stairs, she nearly tripped over a pair of soup cans joined by a tangled length of twine. She had thrown their last telephone into the recycling tote. Her twins had made a new one. Feeling thoroughly foolish, she glanced around, then put one can to her ear as she spoke into the other: "Hello? 1-800-TATTLES?"

There was a crackle of static with undertones of animal grunts and squeals, then a raspy whisper hissed, "Do you have a complaint?"

Celeste's knees shook, and her voice was little more than a squeak, but she said, "A complaint? Yeah, I do. Who returned those hideous Advent Calendars to my children? And exactly what are you instructing them to do?"

"Your children asked for a new mommy and daddy for Christmas," replied the voice. "We are filling their request."

"How?" The voice did not answer. Now Celeste was angry and shouted into the tin can as she paced the deck. "What's wrong with you? What kind of hateful game is this? This is a terrible thing to tell a child. This is not what Santa is about."

"Santa is not affiliated with 1-800-TATTLES."

"Excuse me?"

The voice snarled, "Madam, the complaint line is your invention. Clearly, you did not think through the repercussions. Good afternoon and have a Merry Christmas." The hum of animal voices went silent. No one responded to Celeste's repeated entreaties.

She made coffee and poured in a shot of whiskey. She tried to imagine how the twins would get new parents for Christmas. Maybe someone would plant evidence of horrible, ritualistic abuse. No doubt, that was the intent of the nasty gifts concealed behind those carved wooden doors. Celeste pounded her fists against her head in an attempt to drive away thoughts that were so obviously insane. Two shots of whisky later, she felt calm enough to start dinner. As she rose from the dining room table, she saw her husband standing in the doorway. He held a large black trash bag in his fist. From the angled shapes under the plastic, Celeste knew without asking what was inside.

"This was propped right in front of the garage door," he said. "Whoever put it there didn't even try to hide it."

As Celeste related her phone call, Joe set the wooden calendars on the table. They were perfectly carved and painted, new in every respect. Each door gaped wide except the largest ones, to be opened on Christmas Eve. Without a word, they unfastened the last doors to find the wooden man and woman propped inside. The twigs, however, were no more than skeletal frames for what Joe and Celeste now held in their hands. Each had a perfect little skull and splinters of bone glued to the stick arms and legs. Parchment-like skin was stretched over all, taut enough to allow glimpses of the bone underneath. There were hands and feet, fingers and toes that had previously been missing from the stick men. Every digit had a pearly disc of fingernail. Celeste's blonde hair was glued to the woman's head. Joe's black curly hair topped the man's skull. The teeth, which had been so troublesome to attach, were held in place by clear packing tape, wrapped several times around each skull.

"Callie! Charlie!" shouted Joe, but the twins were already there. His voice faltered as he demanded, "Is this the new mommy and daddy you asked for?"

The twins shrugged. Neither child looked particularly guilty, nor did they seem distressed by having been discovered.

"Okay, we got your new parents right here," he said, striding out to the deck and uncovering the fire pit. He poured gasoline over the abominations and set a match to them. "There are your new parents," he repeated.

The twins were mysteriously silent as the oily flames flickered and pulsed. The blaze brought a flush of heat to Celeste, who suddenly realized she was drunk and exhausted. She wanted to weep and ask her children how a mysterious, inhuman voice had convinced them to carry out such horrifying rituals. She knew that no matter how revolting these dolls were, they were harmless by themselves. They had to be. But they represented resentment, even hatred, planted in the hearts of her beautiful children, and she felt wounded beyond repair.

She brought her hands to her face to wipe away the tears and the sweat. As she lowered her hands, she saw they were smeared with ash and blood and a substance like melted fat. She saw Joe's face was streaked with the same, his mouth silently opening and closing, his eyes wide with helpless terror. His skin turned bright red before her eyes. Celeste felt as hot as he looked, so painfully hot that she was about to pass out. She wanted to scream, but she could no longer work any kind of sound out of her throat. Her mouth filled with hot, salty water. Her children stared with horrified fascination. The dolls in the fire pit collapsed into black heaps of greasy ash, and so did Joe and Celeste.

"What are we supposed to do now?" asked Charlie.

"He said to wait," Callie said. They pulled lawn chairs near the circle of paving bricks to do just that.

Darkness fell, and Christmas lights winked on in yards all over the neighborhood. A gust of wind blew through the yard and ruffled the ashes in the fire pit. In the dim light, one shadowy figure rose from the pit and stepped onto the deck, immediately followed by another.

The creatures were nearly indistinguishable from the twins' mother and father. New Celeste's neck and spine seemed slightly bent, so she leaned somewhat awkwardly to one side. New Joe had one leg that was almost an inch shorter than the other and a perpetually twisted grin. Their eyes had a silvery-gray cast that glittered with a calculating intelligence as they regarded their children's expectant faces.

"You're naked," said Callie, and the siblings giggled. They showed their new parents where their bedroom was. After the adults dressed, Celeste said, "I think we should go out for pizza, and then do some shopping."

The twins cheered and raced to get their coats. The unholy family braved the last-minute crowds at the mall so Callie and Charlie could pick put their own Christmas stockings and the small gifts they wanted to find inside.

On Christmas Eve, the twins ate the last piece of chocolate from their parent-approved Advent Calendars: a candy bas-relief of the nativity. Joe and Celeste suggested they might wish to go to sleep so Santa could make his expected visit. Callie and Charlie complied, sleeping peacefully until midnight. They awoke and crept down the hall to inspect the Christmas tree. There they found their refurbished parents filling and hanging their stockings on the faux fireplace mantle. The six-year-olds exchanged happy, knowing smiles. They had been patient and clever and eager to learn. The payoff now stood before them: New Joe and New Celeste were already turning out better than the children had dared to hope.

And as the children snuck back to their beds, Joe and Celeste turned to each other with their own knowing smiles, their silver-gray eyes glittering with cruel anticipation. So many years of interesting surprises lay ahead for their naughty, scheming children.

RETURN POLICY
William D. Carl

It was the day after Christmas, and the sound of the shop door opening to admit a new customer was greeted with a resigned sigh from the elderly man behind the counter. Sid Trundle had worked every holiday season since he was fourteen years old, and he'd worked in his own antique store—the eponymous 'Trundle's Treasures'—since he was twenty-six. Every year, retail grew more and more difficult, and the customers (he outright refused to consider them as guests) had grown more demanding. He would never admit it, but he was struggling to stay in the black as the assholes who shopped in his place nickeled and dimed him to death. He didn't think he had many Christmas seasons left in him. Retirement was looking more appealing with every indignant, cell phone-checking, online outlet price-quoting bastard that graced his shop.

Looking up as the bell above the door tinkled, signaling the entrance of another deal-seeking jerk, Sid noticed that it was snowing heavily again. There had been a pretty intense blizzard on Christmas day, and he'd expected that to affect the number of unhappy customers seeking returns on the 26th, but he'd already had more than twenty people attempting to return or exchange merchandise. The day after Christmas was always a heavy return day, but this was getting excessive. He wondered if he had enough cash in the till to cover the day.

Of course, several people had tried to return merchandise that was clearly marked as "All Sales Final." Sid didn't have a lot of these in his inventory. Only the extremely cheap markdowns and—special items. He couldn't take those back.

The man walking into the shop shook himself like an animal, snow falling off his heavy black coat into piles that would soon melt into puddles Sid would have to mop up later. As the door closed behind him, he brought a bag out from beneath the coat, and Sid heaved his shoulders in the expectation of the imminent conversation. The man stepped up to the counter, dragging his left leg a bit.

"How can I help you?" Sid asked, the words automatically escaping his mouth, and he raised his head to get a better look at the man.

He was quite tall, over six feet, and he had a girth about him that, when combined with that heavy coat and cropped beard, gave him the appearance of a sad, old bear. The man's eyes were a shocking blue, and they seemed misplaced with his other features. He should have possessed soulful brown eyes, or perhaps hazel, but they were the same blue as the icicles hanging from the back entrance. It was a disconcerting phenomenon.

The man set the bag down on the counter and said, "I need to make a return." His voice was low and raspy, brittle leaves on a frozen sidewalk.

"Let's see what you have here," Sid said, opening the top of the paper bag. "Do you have your receipt?"

The man pawed at his pockets until he pulled out a blue-lined receipt that was undoubtedly scrawled in Sid's signature looping handwriting. He handed it to the old man, and some emotion fluttered across his face, as if another set of features had briefly overtaken the man's sad-bear visage, then disappeared again. Sid perused the receipt, dreading what he had to say.

From the rustling paper bag, the man retrieved a brass lamp, and Sid recognized it immediately. But there was something different about it. Something had been altered.

"Oh dear," Sid said. "This lamp is a non-returnable item. See, it even says so at the top of the receipt. All sales are final. I'm afraid that I can't—"

"I want it out of my house," the man said, his voice still flat and low, almost a growl. The hairs on the back of Sid's neck began to stand up one at a time.

"The return policy is plainly posted here on the counter and on the register, and even on your receipt. I cannot take this item back. I'm very sorry, sir."

"I don't care so much about the money. I want it gone, out of my sight."

Sid touched the base of the lamp, noticing three small dents, probably what had triggered his feeling that something about the merchandise had changed. Glancing back up at the man, he said, "Sir, this lamp has been damaged. So, we couldn't take it back even if it wasn't one of the special non-returnable objects."

"I'm wondering where you got this lamp, Mister Trundle."

"That's really none of your business."

"Because there was something about it, something I noticed even the first time my wife brought it into the house. Oh, it was still wrapped up in a box with ribbons and bow. She loved that shit. She had bought it for me, a Christmas present, something for my desk. I'm a writer, you see."

"No returns. It says so right on the receipt."

"But why are there no returns on this particular lamp? I think I know. It has something to do with the lamp, something to do with its power."

"You aren't making very much sense, sir," Sid mumbled. A cool sweat had emerged on his forehead, tiny beads of perspiration that gave away his discomfort. "It's a lamp. It doesn't have any power, unless you're talking about electricity. Then—"

"Oh, it has a power all right. Ever since Denise placed it under the tree in its colorful box, I could sense there was something fascinating within the wrapping paper and doo-dads. It drew me to it, and I found myself lifting it, shaking it, listening to it. As I placed my face next to the side of the box, I tried to discern a heartbeat. Like it was alive. Like it was waiting for me. And it was."

"You're crazy," Sid gasped.

"I waited and waited until Christmas morning, and I made damn certain I opened that box first. When I looked at it, I was surprised. It was a little brass lamp, heavy, but nothing extraordinary. Certainly not anything that was alive. I thanked my wife—Denise was her name—and I opened the rest of my packages. The lamp was set on our mantle."

Sid interrupted, "And you dropped it and dented it. I get it. But no refunds! No exchanges! Not on this item."

Sid looked down at the damaged base, and he thought he saw a stain, a smudge, near one of the dents. He rubbed at it with his finger, but there was nothing there. Probably a trick of the light.

"All through the day, as the snow accumulated outside our house, I kept circling back to that lamp. It called to me, drew me to it. I touched it, felt the smoothness beneath my fingers. The brass was cold, but there was something else in there, something that throbbed ever so slightly beneath my caress."

Sid looked over at his phone, which was on the corner of a table two yards out of his reach. There were always trouble-makers during the post-Christmas returns period, but this man seemed somehow different. He felt dangerous.

And that thing with his face happened again, as though someone else's features were projected momentarily over his. Sid blinked a few times, and the effect dissipated. He realized the man was still speaking, his cold blue eyes gazing at a point just over Sid's shoulder. The old man turned, but there was nothing behind him except shelves and a wall.

And several of those items. The special ones that he wanted out of his shop so badly that he had ticketed them as non-returnable.

"Then, I would look at my wife, at Denise," the man droned on. "The lamp was in my hand, no longer plugged into the wall, and it felt so very light in my grip. A frisson of some-thing like electricity tingled through me, and I had an over-whelming urge. Have you ever just had an urge, Mister Trun-dle?"

"Er..."

"I mean one that you cannot control. I experienced this urge unlike anything I have ever felt, and I moved across the room. I needed to do it, you understand. Something was making me."

"You're crazy!"

"I raised the lamp just as Denise smiled up at me with her beautiful smile that had always eased the troubles from my mind. Only, this time, I wanted to smash her teeth into her head, to pound her face into meat. I...could see it...all so clearly in my...mind."

Sid debated rushing for the phone. Could he dial 9-1-1 fast enough, before this man caught him and did something terrible to him? Could the police get here in time to prevent the crime, considering how hard the snow was blowing outside the huge plate glass windows?

"I raised the lamp, and I brought it down into her mouth the first time. I felt the teeth shattering beneath the weight and force of the bronze. I could feel them snapping and cracking. Denise gasped, then she opened her wide, bloody mouth again to scream, and I smashed the lamp down into her temple as hard as I could. I don't know why. I love—loved?—my wife, Mister Trundle. I loved her deeply, but I felt I just had to... had to..."

"Oh my God."

The man looked at him, and his face wavered, as though in heat, a mirage of a visage. He didn't stop talking, although his words were growing louder.

"I did it one more time. I hit her again across the temple, and something broke inside of her, cracked like an eggshell under the force of my blow. It was enthralling, invigorating, and horrifying all at once. Something inside me was thrilled with the blood seeping out onto the floor. Something cheered on the carnage in a voice like dead leaves."

Sid started. He opened his mouth, then he decided on a whole new tactic. He said, "Maybe I could give you your money back, sir. On this item. Maybe this time—"

"Where did you get that lamp, Mister Trundle? There was something inside of it, something that called out to me and filled me with irresistible urges. Something evil."

Sid shrugged, trying not to look frightened. "It was just an estate sale," he said, and his voice cracked, dammit! "Just an estate sale like so many others."

"Where was this estate? Was there something—unusual about it?"

"I don't believe so."

The man screamed then; his face went purple with a rage that erupted from some deep part of his psychosis. "Where? Something killed my wife, sir! It wasn't me. It was something that got inside of me, something that sneaked in through the cracks. Wherever you got this lamp, that was a place of evil. Where was it? Where?"

"At the corner of Hoppling and Vine Streets," Sid said, the truth rushing from his lips. In his terror, he told the truth, a truth he had even denied himself. "There had been a multiple killing and suicide. Some man had murdered his wife and three kids with a knife and drew symbols in their blood all over the walls and floors. Then, he—he ate the youngest child before he took a shotgun and blew his own head off. He was just some crazy man, someone who snapped and did a terrible thing."

The man almost whispered, "So, you bought everything he had cheap."

"The house was filled with antiques, but nobody would touch them, like they were the reason that man went crazy. They were just things. I figured I'd offer a couple hundred dollars for them. They would have just ended up at the dump."

"That's where they should have gone," the man said.

"I couldn't believe my luck," Sid continued, looking away from the man, overwhelmed by a wave of guilt. He didn't know why; he hadn't murdered anyone. "But when I got the merchandise back to the store, I began to...sense things about them. Like they were calling out to me. I polished them more than anything else in the shop. I would get shocked by them whenever I touched them, and so I decided I wanted them out of this place. Every time I went near them, I had this wild...you called it an urge. I had a wild urge to harm one of my stupid customers, to bash their faces in, to cut off their fingers, to hit them and hurt them and hit them and hit them."

Sid paused. The man said, "Go on."

"I marked them down, lowered prices, and I put them all in one place. See those shelves over there? That's all that is left, and I still feel as if they are watching me every moment I'm in here. I don't want them here anymore, so I marked them as non-returnable. If you would JUST read the return policy—"

"Fuck your return policy!" the man shouted, and small glass objects vibrated. "My wife is dead. Dead! Do you understand?"

"I'll give you money back, but I... I can't do anything else." The old man fumbled with the cash register. "Take the blessed thing away and toss it in a dumpster. I don't want it here."

"Perhaps," the man suggested, "you should take another look at the receipt. Take a closer look."

Sid held it up, perusing it over the top edge of his spectacles. Beneath the brass lamp, there was another item written in his handwriting. He glanced at the man over the receipt and saw the man's face change into something so terrible, so hideous, he had to avert his eyes back to the receipt.

Beneath the item "brass lamp—all sales final, M Lot, $50.00," there was something else written.

"Silver letter opener—all sales final, M Lot, $79.00."

In the corner of his eye, Sid caught the glint of something shiny and metallic as it was raised directly over his head.

Homeless for the Holidays

Gregory L. Norris

Their place was a rented one-story ranch with stark white walls, builder beige carpets, two bedrooms, one bathroom, and a kitchen sink set at a screwy angle, wedged against the refrigerator and beneath a window impossible to open even when ice running off the roof hadn't frozen it shut. He never took off his shoes upon entering through the back door, and was known to sometimes fall asleep with them on. She never wore shoes unless she went out, a growing rarity as her mental illness and her husband's calculated manipulations conspired to confine her to the house. Alone inside their rental, nobody accused her of being crazy. Her husband didn't, though he knew she was, and he liked her crazy. She was easier to control that way.

Inside their house, which was set back far from the road on a hill and watched over by a dense greenbelt, they played their dangerous little game, pretending that all was well, all was normal, though nothing there ever was.

She only ventured out to attend a local poetry group, where she read the mediocre religious verse she wrote, except when he conspired against her into staying in the house, shoeless and dependent upon him, which was exactly where he wanted her and how he liked things. They had been married for thirty years, a staggering sum total that often got them God-blessed when it was trotted out to new members of the poetry circle, or at church, which they attended religiously every Christmas Eve. Nobody who lived outside the house understood that the long years of their marriage were more curse than blessing; that they had remained together not because they loved one another, but because each half knew the other's darkest secrets, and that to divorce might lead to the exhumation of many ugly buried truths. It would also result in divorcees being forced to live alone with his or her secrets, without the deterrent posed by the other's sins. Without a host, a parasite dies. Their marriage was beyond parasitical.

She said a rosary daily in the room at the back of the house, where her sewing and decoupage and notebooks filled with poetry rose in messy mountains, everything chaotic. She spoke the words but did not really grasp their meaning, the small plastic worry beads passing quickly between her fingers, never there long enough to grow warm. The windows of that room looked up at the trees, the dense gray trunks and green wreaths of which had grown so close together, they formed a living wall. She felt isolated in the room, that house, on days when the meds weren't working. And her husband, who did all the shopping and controlled her comings and goings in their one car, who picked up all her pills at the pharmacy nine miles away—a pharmacological who's-who of psych scrips—couldn't have loved their symbiotic relationship more. Sometimes when lucid, she wondered if she did, too; after all, there had to be some reward for staying with the bastard, who had broken every one of the Ten Commandments. Every last one.

She considered herself a good Catholic, told herself she was progressive, that she believed in pro-choice and marriage equality for all. When she found out that one of the members of the poetry group and his male lover were losing their home to the great, greedy maw of the housing crisis, she offered them charity, a place to stay, until they got their act together. It would be great to have the company, especially that of someone else creative, she told herself when her bipolar personality briefly shifted out of the dark and into the light following a morning of listening to Christmas carols on satellite radio, beamed down through the snowy clouds and into her living room. Just until they were back on their feet. A month, three at the most.

Mostly, she did it to spite her husband, her curse. He had once killed all of the fish in the fish tank—a decade earlier, when she'd threatened to leave. She remembered the little bodies, no longer so colorful, floating in a stew of toxic water.

"I could do the same thing to you," he'd said, and she'd never forgotten. "Slip you something poisonous. Blame it on an overdose. Who would know the difference?"

Yes, she invited the two men to stay in their house, mostly to remind him that, although he had isolated her, she still had the power to wound him.

In her haste, what she didn't factor in was that, with strangers present, the sealed fortress of their world would be opened, and that there would be witnesses to the strange goings-on inside their house, which sat high on a bluff, far away from the street, at the end of a long and winding driveway.

❋ ❋ ❋

The couple came to stay with them, two men who'd found themselves homeless during the holiday season, that time of year when good folk everywhere celebrate the birth of our savior, Baby Jobs; when Saint Gates and his tiny helpers dress in red suits and drive processions of eight luxury vehicles rescued during the automotive buyout through the streets, spreading good cheer and remembering those who are less fortunate.

The homeless, who'd once owned their own home, one attached to a subprime mortgage until that multi-limbed, fanged horror swelled up and adjusted, took the dark room at the back of the place after lugging out all of her many unfinished creative projects and attempting to put order to the chaos. Like so many of her poetry manuscripts, the carpet exposed from the piles of things bore dark stains. Spilled coffee, the homeless poet assumed.

❋ ❋ ❋

"I'm doing this for *you*," he snarled to her, as the couple moved in the few things he'd allowed them to.

"You're a smart man," she said.

And he was smart, as well as crafty. She knew his secrets. He knew hers. Still, the charity came with almost as many strings as the gay couple's old mortgage—*Enclosed, please find your monthly statement, courtesy of your friendly neighborhood lender*—despite the initial promise of being string-free.

He made them get rid of their dog, a sweet mutt they'd rescued during better days. Their car had broken down, was carted off to be repaired, but with no money, it was sitting in a junkyard, likely to be junked. Sobbing, and with no other options, they moved in and tried their best not to be a nuisance, to become invisible, as though not really there.

* * *

One of the two men had lost his job. Both had lost hope. To avoid questions and potential problems with the nosy landlady who rented out the ranch on the bluff, their host forbade them to move in their bed or any furniture. A bed or furniture would be noticed, but an inflatable air mattress could be easily smuggled in, and they were readily available at most supercenters, now open twenty-four-hours a day for the holidays. Out of the goodness of his huge heart, he said, he would buy them one—and made sure to rub this in their faces on their first night in the house.

The mattress felt like sleeping atop layers of garbage bags, and was about as comfortable. Up close, the odor of the stained carpet was foul to breathe in and didn't smell like spilled coffee.

* * *

"I don't want them getting too comfortable here," he said to her, his voice low, clipped, mean. The homeless heard it through the thin wall. "It's not like I even want them in this house."

And he let them know it at every possible opportunity. In the kitchen, where they scuttled to eat what little there was. When they used the bathroom, he pounded on the door. If they did cross paths, he shot them cold looks, mostly said nothing. He didn't have to, the language in his expression clear.

Their strange routine was broken, and the husband and wife fought more and more, louder and louder, no longer bothering to conceal it as one week became two. The charity cases living in the bedroom at the back of the house tried to become even more invisible, while on TV merrymakers were decking halls and running up fresh credit debt and fa-la-la-la-la'ing, the rest of the world oblivious to the truth of what was really taking place in the rented house on the bluff.

Her personality shifted back into the shadows, and she stopped going to their poetry group. Flexing his mean little fingers, he brought home less and less food, though there were more mouths to feed, hoarding most of what he purchased in their bedroom. It snowed. The landlady, wintering in Florida, sent her man out to plow the long driveway. The two guests hid in the back room with the curtains drawn, bullied by their host into avoiding detection.

"You can't be seen. You *can't*. Get in there and lay low, or else."

Being December, the snow partially melted when the sun again came out and then refroze at dusk, creating a slick and treacherous glaze on the drive. To the homeless, it felt like they'd been banished to the North Pole, only farther away than that, to a desolate No Man's Land.

* * *

"Let's just go. Get what little things we have left and go," the poet begged his partner in whispers after their host drove off to work. "We still have each other, and that's something."

The wife, who never left the house, sat on the couch, admiring her bare feet, specifically the nails of her toes, which she had painted freshly in a deep shade of pomegranate. "Where do you think you're going?" she demanded.

The poet said, "Just for a walk. For some fresh air."

She eyed them warily. "Don't forget to scrub the bathroom when you come back."

He smiled sheepishly, nodded. They didn't get far when his partner slipped on the ice.

"Let's turn back," the other man said.

They did.

"It will get better, I promise."

"It can't get any worse," the poet said, chuckling humorlessly. But he was dead wrong.

* * *

Christmas loomed closer, and the homeless discovered that while it's possible to slip through the cracks, attaining nothingness, real invisibility, in a visual sense when you're trapped inside a small house with a pair of monsters, is the true illusion. Homeless can gather in abandoned spaces and under bridges that those with houses would never visit, but the law will always inevitably show up to harass them. Ditto to all who seek a warm bench in a train station or other public space like a store, unless they plan to purchase something at three times the manufacturer's cost. The homeless are never so invisible that those who are in control stop kicking them when they're down.

"Only a month, until we get back on our feet. Three at the most, no longer." That had been the bargain.

"They'll never leave, you know," he whispered to her in the dark, while their houseguests turned miserably on their inflated pallet in the room at the back of the house.

She stared up into the darkness, seeing things not physically there, and hearing other voices. One of those voices, launched from her very own lips, said. "I know."

And so, as yuletide texters texted and video games rang in the cheer—a piece of the Earth, good will to every man in the Top 1% who can afford it—the couple living in the house on the bluff, beneath the brooding wall of trees, reassumed their sinister identities, smiles upon their lips in the blackness of that cold December night.

* * *

They aren't even buying you holiday presents?
Sacrilege!
Heathens, someone tittered on his Titter page.
Devil worshippers. You're stuck with them unless you do something. You have to do something.

She blogged, *They use all our stuff! They never help out around the place! They're there, always there, everywhere I turn!*

Gay and homeless? It's not like they're real people, a friend on FaceSpace urged. *You should just kill them.*

* * *

The husband and wife never missed Christmas Eve services, and didn't this year.

And then, late the same night, they crept into the back bedroom, each brandishing a knife meant to carve meat or debone fish; sharp knives; the ones they always used when the ugliness within them needed to be flexed. The meat was human, sleeping.

"Do it, my love," she urged, giggling.

The gay poet stirred. The inflatable mattress beneath him groaned. "What—?"

Together, husband in shoes and barefoot wife plunged their blades through their houseguests' hearts, through the inflatable mattress, popping it in the process, and unleashed a lovely red torrent across the room, into the pile of the carpet, one that perfectly matched the color of their holiday decorations. Shrieks echoed sharply, but the walls and sealed windows contained them, and they were set far enough back from the road that nobody but those inside the house on the bluff heard the screams.

"I feel better already," she said, promising to clean up the mess on the carpet, as she always did, after she danced barefoot in the blood—so long as he disposed of the bodies in the woods, which, smiling, he promised he'd be more than happy to, as usual.

"Nobody's gonna come looking for them," he said, whistling the statement on a laugh. "They were invisible to begin with."

Nobody did, and on the twenty-sixth day of December, as fresh white powder fell, blanketing the countryside, their life of denial and dangerous secrets in the house on the bluff resumed.

Ho, Ho, Horror Workshop

R.A. Goli

Grace walked the aisle of the store, screwing her nose up at the gaudy decorations. Still, she had to get something; it didn't need to be over the top. The lights flashed brightly, almost obnoxiously to Grace, twinkling in their happy way, as though all was merry and bright.

"You're not enjoying yourself?" the man behind her asked. She spun around, coming face to face with a middle-aged man with white hair and beard. If he'd been wearing a red suit instead of jeans, she might have thought he was Santa Claus, albeit a slim one.

"No, not really."

"You don't like Christmas?" he smiled warmly at her.

"No, it's not that." She wondered how much she wanted to share with a stranger. *What's the harm?* "Bad breakup."

"Oh goodness," he frowned, "and right before Christmas.

"Yeah, what a jerk, hey?" She tried to laugh off her pain, but the breakup had put a dampener on her festivities. She'd expected to spend Christmas with her boyfriend, and now she was alone with no time to make alternative plans.

"What you need is some Christmas cheer," he said.

She smiled and picked up a box of lights, studying the packet, hoping he'd go away. She was all for being friendly, but it was starting to feel awkward. He stepped closer. She swallowed and shifted her feet.

"How tall are you?"

She frowned at him. *What sort of a question was that?* "Um…"

He held his hand at her head height. "Around five-six. A bit tall for an elf, but I could work with that. It's hard to find elves these days." He chuckled. "How would you like to work in my workshop?"

She relaxed a little and smiled. He was just trying to be funny. "I have no experience in toy making," she said, going along with the joke.

He laughed. "That's no problem at all. The elves there will teach you all you need to know."

She chuckled along, though she had a feeling of unease. The serious expression on his face made her wonder if he might be delusional. *Does he think he's Santa?* She decided to politely decline and continue her shopping.

"Well, thank you for the offer, but I think I'll stick to my day job."

"Are you sure? You look like you could use the Christmas cheer, and you can have all the egg nog you can drink."

"I'm sure. Excuse me." She returned the lights to the shelf and continued down the aisle, moving away from him. She turned into the next aisle and started searching through the tinsel. Her stomach sank when she saw him loitering at the end of the same aisle. She pretended she hadn't seen him and slowly walked in the opposite direction. When she reached the end, she turned and was shocked to see he was heading towards her. He smiled and nodded, and she walked quickly to the exit, forgoing her shopping.

She reached her car just before the rain started pelting down. *Screw the decorations.* She'd go back to Christmas Land tomorrow. Or better yet, go somewhere else. Sure, the decorations would be more expensive, but it's a price she was willing to pay to avoid the creep. For all she knew, he hung out at the store every day hitting on women. *Was that what he was doing? Surely not,* she reasoned. He didn't seem flirtatious, and he was far too old for her. She concluded the guy was just weird and put him out of her mind as she continued home, the wiper blades melodic swishing soothing her nerves as the sun set behind her.

She felt the impact before she heard the sound of crunching metal. Her car fishtailed on the wet road, but she managed to control it and straighten it out, but then the jerk hit her again, and her car careened off the road and into a tree. Her body was flung sideways; her head hit the window, and her world went black.

✳ ✳ ✳

Grace's head throbbed as she awoke to complete darkness. She was blindfolded and lying on her side with her arms tied behind her back. She shifted her legs and found her ankles were bound, too. Her chest tightened, and she felt the burning taste of bile at the back of her throat. She could feel the rhythmic motion of the car; she was in the trunk. *Is there any point in screaming?* She wriggled her head, trying to pull off the blindfold, but it was wrapped around half of her face and tied too tightly. It wouldn't budge. She remembered seeing a movie where someone trapped in a trunk had kicked out one of the tail lights so the car would be stopped, or something like that; she couldn't remember. She couldn't think with her pulse pounding in her ears. With nowhere to go, she tried to relax, but it was difficult with the noise of her own breath echoing back at her, sounding loud and desperate. She started kicking out blindly, trying for the tail light. She continued until her legs ached and her breath became rasping pants. She was unsuccessful. Her face was beaded with sweat, and her underarms felt clammy. She'd been trying to keep it together, but the hopelessness of her situation dawned on her. No one was expecting her. No one would look for her. The air was thick with her fear. Her bottom lip trembled, and she sobbed in the darkness.

Bang.

She heard the slamming of a car door. She must have drifted off. *How long have we been driving?* The car had stopped, and she heard footsteps approaching. *Oh God, oh God, Oh God.* The trunk opened, and she felt a rush of cold air. She shivered, not from the cold alone. Big hands untied her ankles before pulling her from the trunk and standing her on her feet. With one hand gripping her upper arm, he slammed the trunk shut.

"Walk," the voice came from behind her. The hands urged her forward, guiding her. Another door opening, then the surface changed. She was inside. More doors, and the sounds of locks being opened. Finally, he pulled off the blindfold. She squinted against the light. Once her eyes had adjusted, she gasped.

It was Christmas. She was staring out across the warehouse floor of a workshop. Through the office window, she could see dwarves, all dressed in red and green like Santa's elves, working at a long bench. The bells on their pointed hats jingling as they moved. Some were painting toys, others were gluing wooden pieces together, and several more were wrapping the finished products as gifts. Just like in classic old tales. Wooden train sets, dolls, dinosaurs, and soldiers.

The floor was blanketed in fake snow, and in each corner stood the most impressive Christmas trees Grace had seen outside of a department store. Each was decorated differently. Shimmering tinsel, colorful baubles, and twinkling lights assaulted her eyes. Sparkling icicles hung from the ceiling . It really did look like Santa's workshop.

"Do you like it?"

She turned, not surprised to see it was the man from Christmas Land. A knot formed in her throat and tears pricked the back of her eyes. "What are you doing? Please let me go," she pleaded, her voice cracking. Her temples pulsed, and her breath came in small gasps.

"I can't do that. I need more elves, and you need Christmas cheer." He urged her forward. Reluctantly, she shuffled forward. He was obviously crazy; she'd have to wait for the right time to escape. Her stomach squirmed with terror, and her heart raced like a runner's as she contemplated what he might do to her. *Rape me? Kill me?* She needed to calm herself. She took a few steadying breaths as she walked, her mind ticking over with thoughts on how she could escape.

"There are so many children. I like to donate the toys to charities and orphanages. The elves work hard all year so I can deliver the gifts at Christmas."

So, he thinks he's really Santa. Grace was already devising her plan. Christmas Eve was only two days away. If that's when he was planning on delivering gifts, that's when she would escape. Until then, she would play into his game, be nice and earn his trust.

"That's amazing. The kids must really love it."

"Oh, they do. It's so rewarding."

"Well, I'd like to help."

"You would?" He stopped and looked at her, beaming.

She smiled and nodded. *Sucker.*

"Sure. I love kids. And Christmas," she added as sincerely as she could.

"I knew it. Once I got you down here to see the workshop, I knew you'd get your Christmas cheer back. Everybody does."

She smiled as he untied her hands, then opened the door they stood in front of.

"You'll join me for dinner." He led her to the table, and she sat. There was a pair of handcuffs attached to the chair, and he snapped the other end around her wrist. "I don't want you running away now," he said with a chuckle.

She smiled. "I wouldn't run away."

He grinned and sat beside her. The table was already set for two, with several cloches sitting in the middle. He lifted the first cloche, and she was surprised to see a whole turkey. He carved them both a slice, then removed the lids of the other cloches and served up potatoes, roast vegetables, cranberry sauce, and gravy.

"Who cooked all this?" she asked as he cut up her food into bite-sized pieces. She had a plastic fork, but no other cutlery. Before her sat a plastic cup, like one you would give to a clumsy child, and her plate was made of melamine, so smashing it against the crazy man's head would be pointless.

"The elves, of course. I told them I was hoping to bring someone back."

The words made her stomach drop, but she tried to keep her expression neutral. Her temples began to throb, and she took a few slow and steady breaths.

"But we'll never eat all this." She stabbed a piece of turkey with her plastic fork, dipped it into the cranberry sauce, taking her time, wondering if the food was safe to eat. She watched as he stuffed a large forkful into his mouth and nodded for her to do the same.

"The elves will eat after their shift. It won't go to waste."

She tentatively put the food into her mouth and chewed. It was delicious. Her stomach growled, and she suddenly realized she was starving. Her abductor talked as though he was St. Nick, discussing the workshop and the elves, and she smiled and nodded along. Towards the end of the meal, he threw his hands up in an exaggerated gasp.

"Ah, I almost forgot the eggnog." There were two small glass jugs filled with creamy liquid at the end of the table. He grabbed both of them and smiled at her.

"Alcoholic, or non-alcoholic?"

"Non, please."

He poured her a cup, then poured himself one from the other jug. "Don't judge, but I like the alcoholic one," he said with a laugh, then guzzled down his eggnog in a few large gulps. He put down his cup and watched her as she took a small sip.

"Don't be shy," he said, and tipped her cup so she was forced to drink a large gulp. She immediately panicked and tried to shove the cup away with her free hand, but he was too quick. He grabbed her hair and yanked her head back. Prying open her clenched lips with the cup, he forced the thick fluid into her mouth. She gurgled and spat, the eggnog spilling over her chin and down her neck. Once she'd swallowed, he released her, put the cup aside, and handed her a serviette.

She sputtered and wiped her mouth, then blew her nose. He watched as she caught her breath, then leaned in closer. It was the first time he wasn't smiling. A tingling fear spread through her, covering her skin in goosebumps. She felt like she'd swallowed a ball of lead as she tried to focus on his face.

"They always pick the non-alcoholic one," he said.

How could I be so stupid? Her mind raced as she started to sway in her chair. Already she felt dizzy. Her vision blurred, and she let out an incoherent sob. She felt drool run down from the corner of her mouth, and for the second time that day, her world was plunged into darkness.

❋ ❋ ❋

She woke slowly, feeling woozy. She could hear a steady beeping, quiet, but close by. She opened her eyes and looked around. She was in a hospital room. No, not a hospital. She was in bed, her left arm attached to a drip line pumping clear fluid into her body. There was a note attached to the machine.

Don't pull out drip line. It has morphine in it.

Without it, you'll be in too much pain.

Too much pain? The morphine was making it hard for her to concentrate. The muscle near her left eye started to twitch. She felt weird, but nothing hurt. *Did it?* She focused on her body, bit by bit, like she would do in a meditation class. *My legs? Why would my legs hurt?* She struggled to sit up, and through her morphine-induced haze, saw something strange.

Understanding and panic hit her like a wave crashing against rock. She threw the blankets aside as a scream clawed its way out of her throat.

Dark inkblots of blood stained the bandages that covered her legs. *Too short!* Her screams reverberated around the small room, making her head throb. She wailed like a mother mourning the death of a child. She swore, screamed, and begged until her throat was hoarse and she'd exhausted herself. Then all she could manage was breathless sobbing. Her foggy mind tried to comprehend why this psychopath would cut off her legs just below the knees. *So, I can't run?*

Then she saw the elf uniform hanging on the back of the door, the bell on the hat hanging sad and silent, and she understood. They weren't dwarves she'd seen making toys the day before. They were amputees, like she was now. And when her legs healed, she would be joining them in the workshop.

✳ LITTLE TOWN OF DEATHLEHEM
Dan Foley

O little town of Deathlehem,
  Within you death doth lie!
Beneath thy deep and rutted streets
  Tormented souls do cry.
Yet in your dark streets shineth
  A cold and ghostly light.
The fears and tears of all the years
  Are met in thee tonight.

The night is filled with horror.
No light shines from above.
The undead creep, and mortals weep,
In a town that knows no love!
Night walkers mourn together,
Waiting for the yearly birth,
Of Santa's evil brother,
Who this night walks the earth.

How silently, how silently,
The tender flesh is riven.
A feast is made of human hearts,
The spikes are deeply driven.
All men will fear his coming,
For in this world of sin,
Greed and hate will call him,
As he gathers sinners in.

Children roam from door to door,
No succor do they find,
It doesn't matter, rich or poor,
Your streets are too unkind.
No charity, no kindness waits,
To ease tormented minds.

Unholy child of Deathlehem
Descend to them this day.
Judge their sins and enter in
as each one you do slay.
We'll hear the fallen angels laugh
As you ramble on your way.
O come to us, abide with us

Our Dark Lord we do pray
O come to us, abide with us
On this, unholy day.

THE BASKET CASE

G.H. Finn

8:13 p.m., December 5th

Belschnickeldorf, a few miles from Salzburg.

It was normally a typical quiet Austrian village. This evening was different. Horror stalked the land. Everyone was looking forward to it. It was part of the traditional pre-Christmas celebrations. *Krampusnacht*. The night before the Feast of Saint Nicholas. The time when the old yuletide devil, Krampus, appeared to punish the wicked. First, Krampus would scare all the children into behaving themselves, and the next night Saint Nicholas would bribe them into being good until Christmas.

Saint Nicholas and Krampus. The carrot and the stick.

But tonight would be different. Tonight, there would be blood on the snow. There would be death by midnight.

It wasn't a threat. It wasn't a prophecy. It was a promise.

❄ ❄ ❄

The parents of the missing child were terrified. He watched them. Outside, in the darkness of an Alpine winter's night, they waited, desperate for news.

The parents were an American couple. They were shivering. Not from the cold. The father was as white as the newly fallen snow, shaking, but as silent as the night. The soundlessly sobbing mother had driven her long nails into the palms of her pale hands. She stared blankly, seeing nothing but her fear. The couple was distraught. Inconsolable. Scared out of their wits.

He turned away from them and walked back to the brightly lit hotel, taking a deep breath and running his tongue over his teeth. He considered the situation, composed himself, making sure he looked every inch the image of a seasoned police investigator. He flashed an old, crumpled identification card to the uniformed officer at the entrance. The man came swiftly to attention, saluted, and began to say, "Herr Inspektor," but was ignored.

He walked past the young policeman, pondering. Annoyed. Angry. He'd been looking forward to tonight. It should have been fun. He'd been expecting to be out, enjoying himself, drinking fruit wine... This wasn't at all how he'd planned on spending the first hours of Krampusnacht. But maybe it was fate.

Just as he was passing through the town, he'd heard the call. He couldn't ignore it. He had to answer. It was his duty. He'd sworn an oath to protect the innocent and punish the guilty. He thought again of the frantic parents, then glanced once more at the recording from the CCTV camera behind the reception desk. His eyes narrowed and his heavy jaw set. He had indeed sworn an oath to protect and punish. That was his role in life. But *this*... This was *personal*.

He watched the video footage again. Studied it carefully. The camera was mounted over the reception desk, facing the hotel's main entrance and lobby. It recorded everything. Picture and sound. According to the time stamp on the video, it had been 6:32 p.m. when the figure had first entered the hotel.

He was tall, but the massive, pointed horns made him look taller still, with a gargantuan body entirely covered in shaggy gray fur. It looked dirty and matted. His eyes were dark, overly large, and bulging. Fangs jutted forward, with a long snaking tongue sticking out from his grinning mouth. Each of his bony fingers ended in vicious hook-like talons.

He capered forward, cavorting and dancing mockingly. Half-comic, half-terrifying.

In one hand he carried a thick bundle of birch twigs. Across his shoulder was slung a large, sturdy basket emblazoned with the word "Kinda."

Children.

The receptionist looked up from her desk and recoiled in shock as she saw the newcomer.

Then she smiled in relief.

"Gruß vom Krampus!" she said with a grin.

The figure leered back at her, asking, "Room 512?"

"The Royal Suite?" She nodded, "Take the elevator to the 5th floor, then turn left as you get out." The receptionist paused, staring at the demonic-looking giant grinning down at her.

"Shall I call ahead to let them know you are coming?" she asked.

The figure shook its bestial head, replying "No, this is a surprise visit. I'll scare the living daylights out of the child. Little children must learn to behave themselves properly. Otherwise, they can be sure I'll come and carry them off to the underworld!"

The receptionist laughed and nodded, waving to the gigantic figure of Krampus as he disappeared into the elevator. The camera lost sight of the suspect as the doors closed.

"Herr Inspektor?" asked a voice, interrupting his viewing of the videotape. He paused the playback and glared. "What?" he asked, curtly.

"I'm sorry to bother you. I'm Herr Schultz, the hotel manager. It's just that when we reported the abduction, we were told a uniformed officer would be here almost immediately, but that it would take hours for a plain clothes detective to arrive. Because of the snowdrifts blocking the road, we were told. You got here far sooner than I'd expected."

"I was already in the area," replied the Inspector.

"Ah, of course," said the hotel manager, "but even so, would you mind if I saw your ID? For all I know, you could be a reporter."

A very official looking ID was immediately thrust under the manager's nose, and he peered at it carefully. It had apparently first been issued in 1962. The Inspektor was evidently older than he looked. Schultz compared the photo of the steel-eyed, dark-haired, sour-faced individual on the ID card to the glowering man standing before him, while reading aloud, "Inspektor, em... Markus P. Drosselmeyer?"

He got a brisk nod of confirmation.

"Ah, well, that all seems to be in order. I'll leave you to your investigation." He began to depart, but was stopped in his tracks as the Inspector snapped, "Halt, Schultz. What do you know about these Americans?"

The manager turned reluctantly back. He prided himself that he ran a respectable, discrete establishment. Normally, he would have feigned ignorance if asked anything about his guests, even by the police, but this was not a normal situation. There was a madman dressed as Krampus taking children away in a basket! Guests were missing! Abducted from *his* hotel! Besides which, there was something about the glint in the Inspector's eyes that made Schultz think that not cooperating would be a *very* bad idea indeed.

"I know little about them, Herr Inspektor. The child is just like any other. A young girl. Maria, I believe. Quite polite. I recall she likes marzipan and gingerbread and lollipops. We have them at reception for our guests. Like most children, she seemed easily excited, but fairly quiet. The parents are typical tourists. They filled out the register when they checked in. The father is some kind of lawyer. The mother is, I believe, an accountant. Their family name is Schwartzstein. They come from some American town that I have never heard of. About the only thing I know for certain is that they are rich. *Very* rich. We are an exclusive hotel. They booked our two best suites—one for the parents, and one for the young daughter. The rooms connect, naturally."

Schultz was about to leave, but the Inspector growled at him impatiently. "What else?"

The manager shrugged. "I gather they have Austrian ancestry and chose to come here on holiday to visit what they think of as 'the old country.' I believe they brought their daughter here for the Saint Nicholas Day celebrations tomorrow. But really, that's all I know."

The Inspektor snorted. "Saint Nicholas?" He grumbled a few more words disgustedly, but Schultz was too busy quietly slipping away to notice.

The Inspector turned back to the video. He already knew what had happened next, but he wanted to see it again.

The huge, deformed, and monstrous shape of Krampus emerged from the open elevator and leaped into the lobby. Its massive mouth gaped as it danced and frolicked its way toward the exit, although it seemed less sprightly that before, weighed down by the heavy burden of its tightly bound basket.

The receptionist looked up and laughed cheerfully, waving merrily at the beast-like demon. The costume was eerily impressive. It must have been very expensive, a real work of art. It was uncannily realistic and all too believable.

"All done?" she asked, smiling.

"Yes," replied Krampus. "I have captured a naughty child, and now I'm dragging the unlucky little girl down to the underworld. Into the deepest, darkest pit."

Krampus gestured with a razor-sharp claw toward the basket on his back, which contained something moaning pitifully and wriggling wildly.

The receptionist and Krampus both laughed their farewells, wishing each other a good Krampusnacht.

And with that, the Krampus left the hotel, heading out into the snow-covered night—

—carrying Maria away with him. The terrified little Schwartzstein girl disappeared into the darkness, still struggling in the basket.

No one had attempted to stop the demon. It had never even occurred to the receptionist to try. This was Krampusnacht! Everyone expected to see men dressed up as Krampus, donning the wildest, most elaborate, and horrendous costumes. Krampus was *supposed* to appear unexpectedly. Frightening children was his *job*. The whole point of Krampus was to scare the young ones into being good so they would avoid being judged naughty and escape being carried away into the night.

Children were told that they must obey their parents, just as long ago they were told they must honor their ancestors. Both the living and the dead. Now the young were told not to be naughty. Not to break the rules. Just as in the past the children of the Alpine clans were taught never to break the tribal taboos. *Be good little ones, or Krampus will come for you.* Naturally, these days, amusing the tourists was good for business, too. A Krampus with a sack full of naughty children was *precisely* what everyone expected to see. The receptionist had assumed the heavy basket, moving about and making sobbing and wailing noises as it was carried, was just a gimmick. Probably with some simple animatronics and an MP3 player inside.

When she found out the basket really *did* contain a kidnapped child—the sweet, little Schwartzstein girl being stolen away into the dark night—the poor woman had hysterics and was led away to an empty room.

The Inspector left the lobby to speak briefly with her. It quickly became obvious there was nothing she could add that would be of any use. She kept crying and pleading, "You will save the girl? Won't you? She's a nice little child. Maria is a good girl. You will save her, won't you?"

The Inspector looked grim, but nodded. It didn't seem to reassure the receptionist much. Someone had given her a shot of schnapps for her nerves. And then another one. And another. She was well on the way to becoming insensible. His nostrils flared as he sniffed the peach liquor scenting the air, wishing he could merrily get drunk himself.

She spoke again. "I never imagined... I just thought... It was meant to be fun. A joke. But he took her... Just like the real Krampus..." For a moment, she locked eyes with the Inspector. "I know it sounds silly," she said, "but...the way he took the girl... It couldn't... I mean... That wasn't *really* Krampus, was it?"

The Inspector looked at her with scorn, his voice full of disdain, "Of course not. Don't be ridiculous."

She hung her head, embarrassed, as he strode away, muttering over his shoulder. "The real Krampus? Stupid. Everyone knows Krampus only takes bad children."

He left the building, angrily letting the main door crash shut behind him. He turned his back on the bright illuminations of the hotel and glared into the darkness, narrowing his eyes. He sniffed the cold night air, then paused, deep in thought. He was hunting now. Tracking his prey. He already had a clear idea of where this little girl, Maria, had been taken. It was the only place for miles around that would serve as a suitable hidden lair. What were the words he had heard on the video? *"I've captured a naughty child, and now I'm dragging the unlucky little girl down to the deepest, darkest pit."*

He started walking. Swiftly. Feet crunching in the snow. Striding towards the nearest mountain, heading for the old, abandoned mines...

❋ ❋ ❋

Flakes of snow were falling heavily. He made good time despite the slippery ice and the drifts across the road. He might be old, but he was as swift as ever and as sure-footed as a mountain goat.

The old mines were swathed in darkness, barely touched by the pale moonlight. The night was still. As silent as the grave. There was nothing to indicate anyone had been here recently. If there were footprints, they'd been buried beneath the freshly fallen snow. But even without the presence of footprints, he knew this was the right place. He was certain. Every instinct told him he was right. The little girl was close. So close he could almost smell her. Noiselessly, he slipped from one patch of darkness to the next as he approached the mine entrance, keeping himself hidden with an ease and expertise born of from many long years of practice. He became a shadow moving among the shadows. He crept into the old mine and worked his way downward, deeper into the darkness, listening the entire time. Then he saw the pale flickering light. Someone had lit old oil lanterns down inside the mine, totally concealed from the outside world. Nothing was visible from the surface. Of course. This would be a perfect place to hide. Anything could happen here. Even the most terrible, most secret, most baleful of deeds. Out of sight. Invisible to the world above. No eyes to witness anything. No ears to hear screams, frantic sobbing, or desperate pleas for mercy. It was a hidden place for a dark death and dreadful, bloody deeds. He stopped, his ears pricked. He could just make out muffled sobbing. The dampened sound of tears and moans coming from behind a gag. Naturally, the child would have been blindfolded and bound hand and foot. Probably rags had been stuffed in her mouth to keep her quiet. The method was familiar to him. Very familiar.

Then he saw it.

It was huge. Towering far taller than a man.

Horned. Fanged. Clawed. Bestial. Demonic.

Just as it had appeared in the video.

Except now it sagged. Lifeless. Empty.

He had to admit, it was a pretty good costume.

He was wondering where its owner was hiding when he felt the cold metal barrel of a gun pressed against his neck.

A voice whispered in his ear, "Don't move."

He froze.

A hand reached out and expertly patted him down, searching for a weapon and finding none. The hand slipped into a pocket and removed his ID.

The gun disappeared from its place behind his ear, but he could feel it was still pointing at him. The ID was held up to an oil lamp. The voice read aloud, "Inspector Markus P. Drosselmeyer. So you're police..."

There was a pause, then, without apparent concern, the voice asked, "'S'up Mark?" The gun barrel glinted in the lamp-light as the voice continued, "How did you find me? I'm impressed Inspector. I haven't even sent the ransom note yet. Who knows you are here? And don't try and tell me that the mine is surrounded; I know the roads are blocked, and you can't have more than one or two men with you."

The Inspector turned slowly to face the gunman. "No one else knows I'm here. I came here alone."

The gunman raised an eyebrow. "Really? What is this? A double-bluff? Are you telling me you're alone so I'll think you are lying and believe you've got reinforcements?"

The Inspector shrugged. "Think what you will. But I tell you I came here alone. I told no one I came here."

"Why?" came the response, the gun now pointing directly between the Inspector's eyes.

"Because I wanted to see you, privately. Face-to-face."

The gunman paused. "Drosselmeyer?" he said, "Why do I know that name?"

The Inspector smiled. "Oh, it's the name of the godfather in Hoffman's Christmas story of *The Nutcracker*. Drosselmeyer is an inventor and toymaker, and also a rogue and a magician. It always amused me that 'drossel' can mean 'to throttle' or 'choke.' But enough about that. Tell me, why did you take the child?"

The gun remained trained on the Inspector's head, and the reply seemed casual. "Money, of course. I don't kidnap children for the fun of it. I was hired to do this job. I've been planning it for weeks. Watching the hotel. Waiting for the Schwartzstein family to arrive. I had all the details I needed about them. The Schwartzsteins are rich, and they don't know Austria well. They'll pay a fortune to get their little darling back. Especially if I cut off a finger or two to prove I have her."

The Inspector shook his head. "I can't let you do that, Hans. Really, I can't. Maria is a good girl. An innocent child. She doesn't deserve to be treated that way. But you..."

The kidnapper laughed. "What are you going to do to stop me?" Then he suddenly paused and asked, "Hey, how do you know my name?"

The question was ignored, but the Inspector continued, "I have my duty. I have two roles. Two tasks in life. To protect the innocent. And to punish the guilty."

The Inspector broke off, smiling as though admitting a small deceit as he said, "Well, I say '*protect* the innocent,' I suppose '*spare*' them may be more accurate, but as for punishing the guilty... Oh, I do that. I enjoy that part. A lot.

"Which category do you think you belong to, Hans? Are you innocent? Of course not. You are guilty. Very guilty. I know a *bad boy* when I see him. You were naughty when you were a child. Very naughty. When you grew up, you took an extremely crooked path. You are not a good boy, Hans. I know. I know *all* the bad ones. In fact, I would say you have been a *very* bad boy indeed."

Hans, the kidnapper, began to look worried. "Who are you, Drosselmeyer? Who are you, really?"

The Inspector shook his head. "Forget 'Drosselmeyer.' It's not important. *That* is not the part of the name you should be worrying about. You should have known better. I don't like people who take my name in vain. I have a reputation to consider. If you had only kidnapped a *naughty* child, I *might* have overlooked it, but I really can't have you dishonoring my name.

Everyone knows I come for the bad children. All of them. Eventually. Most of the bad children think they have been spared. They grow up. Then they think they are safe. It never occurs to them that sometimes... *I'm just biding my time."*

Hans was sweating, pale. Fear gripped him even as his finger began to tighten on the trigger. But he was far too slow. The oil lamps flickered as the Inspector disappeared. A vast, dark, primeval shape took his place. The lamps cast shadows on the cavern walls. Twisted horns. Jutting jaws. Dripping fangs. Crooked claws to clutch and catch.

Hans managed to fire a single shot before the lamps went out.

He turned, pointing his gun in every direction. He fired blindly into the darkness. And again. He heard a jolly, devilish laugh that was full of the merry joy of malice and slaughter. Hans emptied his gun into the deep, underworld blackness of the mine. And then, as the echoes of the gunshots died away, silence fell.

Hans felt hot breath on his neck as a voice whispered in his ear, "You should have been a good child when you had the chance. It's too late now."

Hans screamed.

The whisperer hissed, "You shall learn why they call me *Krampus.*"

Maria Schwartzstein was found the next morning, safe and well. She had been given a bright, multi-colored lollipop. The young girl couldn't remember what had happened to her. The authorities decided it was all just a Krampusnacht prank that had gone a little too far. Distressing, but no real harm had been done.

Hans was never seen again.

Most of his body is still down there, in the mine, waiting to be found—if anyone were willing to search enough places to find the few parts large enough to recognize...

Yes, *most* of his body is hidden within the mine. Most.

But not his head.

That had been carried away in an old, well-worn, blood-stained basket to be placed at the top of a magnificent, ancient evergreen, deep, deep in the primordial forest. Far away from the sight of any human.

Around the tree, in the snow, cloven hoof prints and splashes of blood marked the ancient ritual. Hans' head stared down, eyeless and unseeing. The latest addition to countless skulls decorating the evergreen branches. Hanging like baubles on the boughs. Shining. Glistening. Bone white and blood red. Silent as the night.

And there, Krampus danced his timeless dance, through the bright white winter snow and the dark red ice formed from frozen blood. Capering forever under cover of eternal darkness, on a Krampusnacht that would never end.

CHRISTMAS LASAGNA
Larry Hoy

arco stared at the tree; even though it was Christmas Eve, it was nearly empty of decorations. One thing stood front and center among the branches: a red envelope marked with the Delta Airlines logo. Inside, there were two one-way plane tickets to Italy. At the front door, a pair of suitcases waited. He and his son were returning to Italy on the red-eye Christmas morning.

The apartment was now mostly empty and very quiet.

Paolo, his son, was still sleeping. Marco didn't dare wake him. The boy cried himself to sleep most nights, and today was going to be a long day. There was still a lot to do.

With a sigh, he turned away from the Christmas tree and walked into the kitchen. He promised he'd make a lasagna for the homeless shelter, and with this being Christmas Eve, it had to be a big one.

In the kitchen, he started pulling out the remaining pots and pans; the majority of his kitchen was gone, sent to Salvation Army the day before. Once everything was in place, he rested a moment, his hands pressing on the kitchen island, just gathering his thoughts. This was his last day in this apartment, his last day in America. He took a deep breath and started to gather the rest of the things he needed. He moved without thinking. It still hurt too much to think about how his life had been turned upside down. Now and forever he would think of America as the place where he lost his wife.

It had started on Thanksgiving Day with a stupid argument.

✳ ✳ ✳

"What do you mean you're going to stay and help clean up? *Bella*, they're homeless, not disabled. They can clean their own kitchen, *porca vacca*." Marco struggled to keep his voice low, but with his thick Italian accent, there was little chance of being understood even if he'd been overheard.

"Marco! They are going to hear you," Nadia hissed. She opened the kitchen door, then she ushered her husband outside the shelter.

"*Non parlano italiano.*"

"No, they may not speak Italian, but Paolo does, and if I hear him using that language, I'll know it came from you.

Madonna!"

"*E tu*? Listen, I'm tired, Paolo is tired, you have been here all day, and it's obvious that you're tired. Let's go home."

"It's not going to take that much longer." She picked at the hem of her apron and started wringing her hands. She always fidgeted when she lied.

"Did you see how many people they served?" He pulled out a pack of cigarettes and lit one. Through a cloud of smoke, he continued. "Dozens came through the service line. They won't be finished cleaning till *notte*. I've got better things to do than clean up after a bunch of bums, *cazzi*."

"Stop. Times are difficult; besides, have you forgotten our first year in America? We had dinner here, too."

"*Una volta*, and I had a job. We just hadn't been paid yet. I bet most of them haven't worked all year."

"I'm sure many of them have jobs."

"I see them all the time hanging out at the exit ramps off the highway, just begging for change."

"We only do this *una volta* a year."

"No, I only do this once a year. How many times are you up here? I bet you are here more often than you are at home. Have you forgotten that we have *a bambino*?"

"I only help out on the weekends." Her mouth had drawn tight. They'd had this argument more than once before.

"I don't understand why these people are more important to you than we are."

"Our family is the most important thing to me, but they need me here."

"Yea, and we need you at home." He dropped the cigarette and crushed it out on the ground. "It's late. I'm taking Paolo home. Come home when you are done, or don't. I'm not waiting up." He turned to the door. That is when they both saw their son standing on the other side of the thin screen door. "Go take your apron off. You and I are going *la nostra casa.*"

"Is Mamma coming, too?" Paolo had just turned six; his dark hair and eyes spoke to his Italian heritage.

"She will be home, *dopo*, later tonight. She is going to stay and help clean up. You'll see her in the morning. Go give her a kiss and then we'll go."

Paolo banged through the screen door and gave his Mamma a hug. She bent low and gave him a kiss on the cheek. "Be good for Papa. Maybe tomorrow we'll go shopping for *un albero di Natale.*"

"Can we get a really big one this year?"

"As long as the tree fits in the front room."

Marco returned from the kitchen; he was carrying his son's jacket. "All right, *bambino*. Let's get in the car. We are going home."

Nadia waved as they drove out of the parking lot, then returned to the kitchen.

❅ ❅ ❅

"Goodnight, Nadia. Thank you so much for staying 'til we got everything cleaned up. I know the serving line is a huge job, especially on Thanksgiving. We could never have done this without you. Please pass our love to little Paolo, too. He and your husband were both a great help. It is a shame they had to leave early."

Nadia Rossi stood beside the open door to her car. "We were happy to help. Oh, I brought some of Marco's old clothes. They are in the trunk. Would you mind?"

"Not at all." Michael opened the trunk of her Maxima and pulled out a garbage bag stuffed with clothes, then shut the trunk. "Nadia, thank you again. Happy Thanksgiving." Then he turned and walked back into the shelter's kitchen.

Nadia got into her car and pulled out of the Hope House parking lot. As she drove the empty streets of Bangor, she thought back to all the people she had helped. She had only lived in America for a few years, but the Thanksgiving holiday was a time that her family embraced. For the last five years, they had spent each Thanksgiving serving dinner at Hope House, a homeless shelter. This year her family made two dozen pumpkin pies and twenty pounds of turkey dressing.

As she neared the corner, the stop light switched to red, and Nadia slowed her car. As the car came to a stop, a dark figure ran up from the side and ripped open the driver's door.

Nadia looked up, a startled scream escaping past her lips.

"Move over, bitch." The man was wearing a dark hoodie pulled low over his head, hiding his face in shadow. In his hand was a snub-nosed revolver.

Nadia froze in fear. Her jaw had dropped open, and she took a deep breath, preparing for another scream.

The man smashed her in the face with his gun. Her world exploded in a white-hot burst of pain. Blood erupted from her nose, instantly coating the lower half of her face. Her eyes filled with tears, and she brought up her hands to stem the flow of blood.

"Slide over, bitch. I ain't gonna ask you again." The man reached across her and hit the button to release the seat belt. Then he smashed the butt of the gun against her forehead and pushed her across to the passenger seat.

Nadia instinctively curled up, turning away from the man climbing into her car. Tears and blood covered her face as she broke down, deep sobs racking her body.

From far away, she heard a car door slam shut. Then, with a squeal of tires, she felt herself pushed back into the seat. Then she felt something hard crashing down on her again and again. He hit her in the head and on her arms, back, and ribs. He continued to beat her as he drove one-handed.

Eventually, the car came to a stop inside an old, empty warehouse. The man climbed out of the car and opened the passenger door. With a handful of what used to be dark silky hair, now matted with blood, he dragged Nadia from the car.

Nadia weakly tried to swat at his hand as he pulled her along the warehouse floor, but it was no use; the beating she'd suffered during the ride had made it difficult to think. One of her arms refused to work. A thick trail of blood ran from the car door to a dark back corner of the room. With a grunt, the thug tossed her onto a pile of mildewed blankets.

"Lady, this is it for you. You are dead, but before you go, I'm going to share something with you." He unzipped his pants and let them fall to the ground. He stood before her, laughing as she tried to crawl away. "Don't go. You and I are going to spend some quality time together," he cooed.

* * *

The lights in the front room were low. Paolo had gone to sleep long ago. Marco was waiting for his wife to come home. He was relieved that they had put another Thanksgiving behind them, but he was still kicking himself over how they had parted.

Marco checked his watch again. It was almost two. Nadia should have been home by now.

He grabbed his phone from the charger and pushed the speed dial number assigned to his wife's phone. The call immediately clicked over to her voice mail. He tried again and got the same result. He thought for a brief moment that maybe her phone battery had died, but there was no way she'd let that happen. Not when she had to drive through some rough parts of the city.

He opened the contact for the shelter and thumbed the number. He hated that he needed to have that number, but when Nadia was at the shelter, she didn't always answer her phone. After six rings, it switched over to voice mail. He re-dialed with the same result. After four more attempts, some-body finally answered.

"Hello?" a voice thick with sleep mumbled. It was Michael, the supervisor of Hope House.

"Michael, this is Marco, Nadia's husband. I was wonder-ing if she was still there."

"Marco, she left here hours ago. She should have been home by now unless she gave one of the other volunteers a ride home." After a moment where he seemed to be considering something, he said, "That must be it. Maybe they got to talk-ing and forgot about the time?"

"Yea, maybe you are right. I'm sure it is nothing, but I'm going to drive out that way. Maybe her car broke down. Could you check the parking lot and give me a call?"

"Sure, Marco, I'll turn on the outside light. Please call me when you find her."

"Of course. I'll talk to you in a bit."

It only took him a few minutes to strap Paolo into his car seat. The boy was still dressed in his pajamas; he never even woke as his father carried him to the car. Marco drove the route from his house to the shelter, and by the time he pulled into the parking lot, his nerves were frayed and his thoughts were running wild.

He drove back home, then repeated the entire process one more time before finally returning home to stay. He was there only long enough to shower and drink a large mug of coffee.

At seven o'clock in the morning, he pulled into the police

station to file a report on his missing wife.

* * *

It was three days later when there was a knock on the door. Marco opened it to find a young man in a dark Bangor police uniform standing on his doorstep. "I'm sorry to disturb you, sir. I'm Officer Joseph Allen. Are you Marco Rossi?"

"Yes." Marco felt a sinking sensation in his stomach.

"Mister Rossi, you reported your wife missing a few days ago, is that correct?"

"Yes. The day after Thanksgiving. Did you find her?"

"We believe we found what might be some of her personal items. Would you be available to come down to the station with me to identify them."

"I'll have to get a sitter for my son."

"Let's bring him. We have an area where he can hang out. I don't really know how long this will take; there might be additional questions."

At the police station, Marco confronted the awful truth regarding his wife when the police officer handed him a photograph. It showed a young woman lying on a steel table. Her eyes were mercifully closed, and her hair had been drawn back to reveal her bruised face. One eye was swollen shut. Her nose had been savagely broken and was twisted to the side. Over one temple was an oval bruise that was almost black. The bruising continued down her neck, all the way down the edge of the picture.

As he stared at the picture, it started to move in and out of focus as tears filled his eyes and rolled down his face.

"Is this your wife?" The deep voice now came in a low whisper.

All he could do was nod. He kept hearing his final words

to his wife echoing over and over in his mind. *Come home when you are done, or don't.*

"We found her in an abandoned warehouse downtown. I understand she was serving dinner at a shelter last Thursday and never came home?"

Marco barely heard the question, but he nodded all the same.

"You think she went missing about midnight, is that right?"

Another nod. He couldn't look away from the picture. It was obvious she had suffered.

"We believe she was car-jacked and killed. The car is still missing. That area of the city has a few chop shops, so there are officers out there right now looking for the guy who did this. Do you have anyone you can call to come get you? If not, I could have an officer take you home."

Marco nodded. "I can call someone."

❊ ❊ ❊

"Is this Marco Rossi?" a young girl asked when Marco answered the phone. He didn't recognize the voice.

"I'm Marco."

"Sir, my name is Kathy, and I'm calling on behalf of Hope House Homeless Shelter. I understand that your family has helped us out in the past on the holidays. I want to thank you for all your help and ask if you'd be interested in helping us this Christmas."

Marco's mouth fell open. A rush of emotions flowed through him. His wife has just been killed working for these people, and now they wanted his help as though nothing had happened. A wave of heat hit him; anger burned red hot. None of that reached his voice as he said, "Kathy, please put me down as an extra set of hands. I'd be happy to help." He could taste the bile starting to rise as he imagined helping the people he blamed for the death of his wife.

"That is fantastic. Could I also put you down as providing a dish? We are open to anything."

His anger continued to rise, but his voice remained pleasant. "Of course. I make a mean lasagna. How would that be?"

"That would be wonderful!" The girl was almost squealing on the phone. "We are planning to start serving dinner at six, so could you come by around five? That will give everyone a chance for last-minute preparations."

"Five o'clock? We'll be there. We wouldn't miss it for the world."

"Thank you so much. I just want you to know how much your support means to the shelter." The chipper young thing hung up the phone.

Marco made a few calls that evening. He called some of his Italian friends who had helped him out over the years. It can be difficult leaving your home country to start all over again, but fortunately, Marco had friends. It was going to take some time, but he was pretty sure he would be able to find everything he would need.

* * *

Marco pulled out a giant saucepot, into which he poured a quarter inch of extra virgin olive oil. Next, he dropped in three large diced onions. With a wooden spoon, he slowly started to stir the onions. With a face as expressionless as chiseled stone, he looked through the onions, through the stove, through the floor. Marco looked down to the very depths of hell as he started on his Christmas lasagna.

It was less than a month ago that some worthless piece of trash stole his beautiful wife from him. "My Bella, my beautiful," he said as he stirred the onions until they started to sizzle in the pan. They quickly turned soft and translucent as he sautéed them.

On the plate beside the stove sat piles of ground beef and ground sausage. One by one, he dropped them into the pot and stabbed at them with his spoon, breaking them up and stirring the meat as it cooked. "My *bella donne*, my beautiful, beautiful woman. Why did you leave us?"

As the meat browned, he added salt and pepper, twisting the pepper grinder savagely as the pot's contents sizzled. The aroma of the meat mixture filled the kitchen. Behind him, he heard the tiny feet of his son as he inched into the kitchen.

"Papa, what are you making?" Paolo pulled a stool to the island in the middle of the kitchen. A giant aluminum pan was on the table, along with four large bowls of cheese, two bowls of dried herbs, a bowl of small, black berries, tomatoes, and six large boxes of lasagna noodles.

"I'm making lasagna. It's Christmas Eve, and I thought we could bring dinner to the shelter. Like we did with Mamma on Thanksgiving. Don't you think that would be nice?" Marco reached for a large can of tomato paste and slowly spooned it into the stew pot and mixed it with the ground meat.

"She would like that." He reached out and plucked a few berries from the bowl and was about to pop them into his mouth when his father grabbed his wrist.

"Paolo, those aren't for you. This is for those people at the shelter." Marco forced his son's hand open, took the berries from him, and returned them to the bowl. Then he took a washcloth and wiped the small hand clean. "Now, go and wash your hands. I'll get this simmering, and then we can play with your video games for a while. How does that sound?"

"Okay, Papa. Can we play the race car game?"

"Of course. You go wash up, and I'll be right there."

Tiny feet sped out of the kitchen. Marco picked up another large can of tomato paste and slowly added it to the sauce-pot. Next, a half can of water. "Why *Bella*? Why, my beautiful wife? Why did they take you from us?"

Marco took the bowl of herbs and tore them into small pieces, then dropped them into the pot. Finally, he added the bowl of black berries. He pulled the spoon through the mixture again, breathing in the sweet aroma of the meat sauce. He turned the burner down to low and placed a lid on the pot. The lid sat just off center to allow the steam to escape.

"Buon Natale, and to all a good night."

* * *

"Time out, little man. It is time to boil the noodles." Marco sat his game controller on the floor and stood up. "You want to help?"

"Yes, Papa!" Paolo had been winning most of the races. Usually, his father won, but Marco was distracted. "Can we play some more later?"

"You bet. I want a chance to win."

In the kitchen, he filled another pot with water and set it on the stove to boil. Marco threw a small handful of salt into the pot. That was something he learned from his Mamma. Boiling the pasta in salt water added just a bit more flavor to the pasta. When the water started to boil, he opened a box of noodles and passed it to his son, who emptied it into the boiling water. Five minutes later, they removed the pasta and started on the next box. While Paolo boiled the pasta, Marco sliced some tomatoes nice and thin.

Once the pasta was cooked, they started building the lasagna. Paolo drizzled olive oil into the giant aluminum pan and brushed it around, coating the sides. Then Marco ladled some sauce and smeared it over the bottom of the pan. Next, they put down a layer of noodles. Together, they spooned in a thick layer of ricotta cheese and smeared it over the noodles. More sauce was ladled onto the cheese. Next, they added a layer of tomato slices and covered them with mozzarella cheese.

Paolo shook a little more olive oil, sprinkled a layer of parmesan, and finally, more sauce. They repeated this build over and over again: sauce, noodles, ricotta, sauce, tomatoes, mozzarella, oil, sauce, and parmesan. When the pan was finally filled to the top, Marco slid it into the oven.

"All right, little man. Go wash up, and then we'll have a rematch. What do you say?"

❄ ❄ ❄

When the lasagna came out of the oven, the smell of it filled the kitchen. Marco placed the tray on the island to cool. The cheese bubbled and oozed. More meat sauce was ladled across the top. The aroma even made his mouth water.

"Papa, that looks yummy." A finger was making its way to the pan.

"No!" His father stopped the boy's finger with a word. "This isn't for us. This one is for us to share. Now go get dressed." Paolo was still wearing his football pajamas. Green, white, and red stripes loudly declared allegiance to Italian soccer. "Put on your Christmas sweater. We are going to the shelter today."

❄ ❄ ❄

Michael met them at the door. "Marco, I'm so sorry. The girl who called you was new. She didn't know about what happened. I didn't realize they called you until I got the attendance roster a few minutes ago. I'm really sorry. Please, take the night off; we have plenty of help."

"It's alright. I'm already here, and I brought some lasagna. Paolo and I would like to serve tonight to honor Nadia. This is something she would want us to do."

Michael stepped to the side and held the door for them. "It smells fantastic. Come on in."

"Can I pour the ice tea?" Paolo asked as he walked into the kitchen. "I promise I'll be careful. I won't spill it."

Michael grabbed a small hand towel and draped it over his forearm like a waiter in a fancy restaurant. "I'm sure you'll do a great job."

Marco went to work slicing the lasagna and putting a generous portion on each plate. The cheese slowly oozed down the sides. The layers of pasta, cheese, and meat caught the eye of both servers and residents alike. With each piece, an extra ladle of meat sauce was poured over the top.

Michael came up behind Marco and placed a hand on his shoulder. "Wow! That looks fantastic. You really went above and beyond."

"This is a very special recipe, and this is what you all deserve." He poured another ladle of the sauce over the pasta.

As the night moved along, he closely watched the people in the room to make sure they had each gotten a piece of his lasagna. The recipe was one he usually used, but this time he had added one special ingredient.

In Italy, *bella donna* meant beautiful woman, but belladonna was also the local name for nightshade, a poisonous herb that grew wild in parts of Italy. Its leaves could be dried and had a flavor similar to basil or oregano. The plant also produced little, black berries that possessed a sweet flavor.

Marco had filled the lasagna with it. Now it was all over except for the wait.

"Papa?" His son tugged on his trouser leg.

"What's wrong, little guy?"

"I don't feel good."

Marco looked down and his breath caught in his chest. He got down on one knee to get a better look at his son. Across one cheek was a bright red smear of tomato sauce. "Did you eat dinner here? I told you this was for the guests." Tears started to slip from his eyes. "I told you we would have something when we got home."

"Mister Michael gave me a plate. He said I should have some of your special lasagna, too."

"Marco, I saved you a plate," a voice came from behind him. "It wouldn't be right for you to miss out on this fantastic treat."

Marco stood and turned. Michael was holding out a dinner plate to him. On the plate was the lasagna. Sauce and cheese slid down the sides. He took the plate and stared at it.

"Is your son feeling alright?"

"It is just a little upset stomach. The food might be a little rich for him. He'll be all right in a bit. We all will." He took a hefty forkful, raised it as he would were he toasting with a glass of champagne, and said, "Buon Natale."

L<small>OTS</small> <small>OF</small> F<small>UN</small> <small>WITH</small> M<small>ISTER</small> S<small>NOWMAN</small>
Joseph Rubas

oddamn kids!"

George Kraus stood on his front porch in his robe and slippers, the Sunday paper tucked under his arm and forgotten.

The previous night, close to eight inches of snow had fallen on Brandywine, covering the jagged and crusted remains of an earlier snowfall. Sometime in the morning, someone stole onto his front lawn and built a seven-foot-tall snowman, complete with a stovepipe hat and pieces of black coal for eyes. The snowman, smiling like a damn fool, faced the house, one stick arm bent as if in a wave.

Kraus looked balefully around. The other houses on the street were quiet and shuddered against the cold. Only a few people were out shoveling their driveways. No cars moved in the street.

"Goddamn kids," Kraus muttered again, shaking his head, and went inside.

In the den, Kraus sat down in his La-Z-Boy and opened the paper. On TV, the Channel 5 weatherman was standing in front of a map of the region and predicting more snow over the coming days. "Looks like we'll have a white Christmas after all," he said with a smile.

"Like we need it," Kraus said, snapping the paper. He hated snow. It was cold and wet and turned his lawn into a soupy mess.

He hated Christmas, too. All the crowds and chaos, fake cheer and "gimme, gimme, gimme" bullshit. Kids were too damn spoiled these. Why, when he was young, you were lucky to get a toy and some candy for Christmas. Now kids weren't happy unless their parents went into bankruptcy over it. Sniveling little shits deserved coal crammed up their asses, not fifty presents and a stocking full of diabetes. So loud and rude and ungrateful. Kraus hated kids. He was damned glad that Martha had been barren.

George shuddered at the thought of Martha. She'd taken a handful of pills in January and convulsed to death on the bedroom floor. *To get away from you,* the note pinned to her housedress had said. She'd been alive when he found her. He could have saved her. Instead, he had sat on the bed with his arms crossed and watched her die. Served her right.

Martha had been on his mind a lot lately. Christmas was

always her favorite holiday. He almost went all out and decorated. *Look at me, Martha,* he would say, looking down as if into Hell, *it's Christmas. Do you have Christmas down there?*

Shaking his head again, he scanned the headlines. President Trump was in the soup over an offhand comment; the president of the Philippines was boasting about strangling "a drug dealer with each hand last night"; and one of those Hollywood sluts was mad about women's rights. George uttered a hateful laugh. In his day, women didn't get uppity like they do now. They shut up and did what they were told. None of this feminism bullshit. That's one thing he had liked about Martha: She knew her place, and when she forgot it...

When he was done ingesting the morning news, Kraus went into the kitchen for another cup of coffee. Looking out the window over the sink, he saw that stupid snowman waving at the house like a pedophile. He'd have to get dressed later, he thought, and go knock down the son of a bitch.

Surveying the dumb thing, George noticed something that he hadn't before: The snow around it was pure and unbroken. No footprints. No bare patches stripped of snow for the snowman's head or balls. It was like the little demons carted in their own stock.

Back in the living room, the news had given way to one of those stupid daytime courtroom "reality" shows. A black woman in a black robe sat on the bench and listened to a big fat black woman tell her story: "Well, I done axed him where he were, and he said..."

Stupid niggers. They could barely speak English anymore. At least Martin King could formulate a goddamn sentence.

When the show was over, George resolved to get up and take care of the snowman, but he was suddenly tired, so he closed his eyes and didn't open them again until the noon news was almost over. Feeling groggy and sore, he went into the kitchen to brew another pot of coffee. The snowman was still there, only something looked…different about him. George couldn't quite place it, but something had definitely changed. George watched him (it) as the coffee brewed, filling the kitchen with its rich, warm aroma. He didn't like its eyes. They seemed to follow you no matter where you went, like a creepy painting in an old movie. In his bedroom, he drew aside the curtain and confirmed this to himself: The snowman seemed to be watching him, waiting for him to undress so that it could masturbate itself. George briefly thought of fetching his old .22 from the closet, leaning out the window, and blowing off its ugly head, but decided against it. The last thing he needed was a couple of lamebrain cops taking him to jail. Maybe after dark, he thought, when no one was out and couldn't tattle.

Back in the kitchen, he poured himself a cup of coffee and drank it as he walked from one side of the kitchen to the other, the old linoleum popping under his feet. That snowman was really bothering him now. What was different about it?

By the time he was done with his second cup, he still didn't know, but he knew that he wasn't going to worry about it anymore. He dressed, pulled on his coat and his winter boots, and went outside. The world was silent, save for the stupid, ear-piercing laughter of kids playing several streets over. A little red sedan passed by, nearly losing its traction on the ice several times before steadying itself. George watched, hoping the miserable bastard went off the road and into a ditch. Serve him right for being out on a day like this.

When the car was gone, George sighed and trudged through the ankle-high snow to the little detached garage where he kept his tools. Inside, he reached for a shovel, but stopped and grabbed an ax instead. He chuckled.

"In the meadow, we can build a snowman—" he sang as he approached the towering figure. It was taller than it had looked from the kitchen. "—and pretend that he's a circus clown—"

Oh, he was going to enjoy this.

"—We'll have lots of fun with mister snowman, until the other kiddies knock him down."

George was standing directly in front of the S.O.B., so close he could reach out and punch him in his icy testicles, if he had any.

Damn kids. Damn women. Damn Christmas and damn niggers. George hefted the ax over his shoulder and let fly, burying the ax in the snowman's soft center. *Take that.* Again. *And that.*

George was pulling back for a fourth blow when a car horn honked. He turned, and it happened: The snowman's twiggy arm lashed out, scraping George's neck and knocking him down, sending the ax flying from his hands. Gasping, George rolled onto his back, but the snowman was perfectly still, waving at the house, all smiles and gay, happy greetings.

Trembling, George pressed his gloved fingers to the skin of his neck: They came away bloody.

Inside, George stood in front of the bathroom mirror and examined his wounds: Two brief, but deep scratches. He wetted a cotton ball with a draught of alcohol, pressed it to the gashes, and then taped a Band-Aid over it.

As he worked, George replayed the incident over and over again in his head. A gust of wind. That had to be it. A gust of wind hit the branch and forced it down. The thing was, he didn't remember a gust of wind. He remembered the horn, turning away, and *POW!*, he was lying on the ground and bleeding all over the place, practically half-dead.

In the living room, George drew aside the curtain and

studied the snowman. It looked different again. It looked... closer.

Snorting at his own foolishness, George let the curtain fall back into place and went to his chair, where he sat heavily. He turned on the TV and went casting for a good program. He finally settled on a black-and-white war movie playing on Turner Classic Movies. American boys moved stealthily through a godforsaken jungle while Japs leaped out of the bushes at them like the buck-toothed cowards they were. At one point, a gook attacked a G.I. from the back, dropping his knife and running away when the American fought back. Then, the G.I. scooped up the knife, called, "Hey, Jap, you forgot something!" and threw it after him: It struck the slant-eye in the back and knocked him down. George laughed so hard tears streamed down his face.

When the movie was over, George got up and went to the bathroom. In the bedroom, he pulled back the curtain. The snowman was where he'd left it, watching the house with those dead, malevolent eyes. George shivered. He should really go out there and take it down for good, even if he had to run it over with the snow blower.

Instead, he went back into the living room and watched another war movie, this one about Normandy. John Wayne was in it. George liked John Wayne.

By the time it was over, twilight had settled over the world. He went to the living room window and peeked out.

The snowman, he saw with a jolt, looked closer. A full foot, maybe.

No, couldn't be. Unless some damn fool kids were play-ing a trick on him, hiding behind it and pushing it toward the house.

Still...

He made himself a frozen chicken dinner and ate it in

his chair. He was finishing up when a knock came at the door, and his heart leaped into his throat.

It came again, and a ripple of fear ran through his stomach. *Get ahold of yourself, damn it!*

Sighing, he got up and went to the door, opened it.

Five children in ugly red sweaters crowded onto his porch, a woman with a stupid hairdo standing behind them, smiling smugly. As soon he made the mistake of stepping out, the kids began to sing, reading their lines from sheet music.

"We wish you a Merry Christmas, we wish you a Merry Christmas—"

"Take your Merry Christmas and shove it up your ass," George said. "Santa Claus isn't real. And neither is Jesus."

With that, he slammed the door and went back to his chair. Damn fools. Didn't they know he got enough of that terrible music on the radio and in the grocery store? Did they really have to bring it to his home?

After the six o'clock news, George made another pot of coffee and looked out the kitchen window.

The snowman was standing on the walkway, a good five feet diagonal from where it had been that morning.

That does it.

George went into the bedroom, grabbed the old rifle from the closet, and took down a box of rounds from the shelf. He sat on the edge of the bed and loaded it. Damn kids playing tricks on him. He'd blow that snowman to hell and hopefully hit whoever was behind it.

Gun in hand, he went the window, lifted the sash, and dropped to one knee. "Have some of this, you…"

He stopped.

The snowman was gone.

There were no tracks, no piles of snow to suggest that it had fallen or been knocked over. It was simply gone.

Impossible.

Holding the gun tightly, George crept down the hall and into the living room, his heart pounding and his breath caught in his throat. He checked the kitchen, the pantry, even Martha's sewing room, which had been standing empty and unused since January.

Moving slowly, cautiously, he went over to the front door and pressed his ear to it. He didn't hear anything. He sighed, *Alright, you bastard,* and turned the knob.

The door swung open, and the snowman was there, standing larger than life, its shiny eyes the color of midnight and its psycho smile frozen in place.

"Hello, George," it said, speaking in his late wife's voice.

"Martha?" George asked dumbly, his heart seizing.

"I came back for you, George," it said, its smile unmoving. *"You made me miserable for all those years, George. You hit me, you cussed me, you made me want to die. Now it's your turn."*

The world swam out of focus. George's heart was pounding fast, too fast. Pain like the thrusting of a thousand knives flooded his chest. He cried out and dropped the rifle.

Martha's laughter tittered forth.

The world began to gray then. George clutched his chest and slumped against the wall. His knees gave out, and he fell to the floor, blackness stealing over him.

The last thing George Kraus saw before he sank into death was an empty doorway.

Martha was gone.

THE ILLUSION

Bev Vincent

The man in the Santa Claus suit waves his arm in hopes of flagging down a ride on the third morning of the New York transit strike. Despite freezing temperatures, heavy snowfall, and a severe wind chill, sweat streams across his face.

He tried to tell the woman with the heavy accent who called the night before that today wouldn't be good, what with the strike and the snowstorm, but the caller couldn't be persuaded to change the schedule. The man was up almost all night getting everything ready, organizing the contents of his sack just so. He's sure it will pass muster.

Instead of settling for the stereotypical fake cotton beard and rouged cheeks, he wears a flesh-like mask that clings to his face and covers his entire head. The beard and long white hair were threaded through the rubber a strand at a time by someone in a factory on the other side of the world. The cheeks are plump and rosy, the mouth small and pursed into a coy, disarming smile.

At the neck, his mask connects to a body suit of the type supplied to actresses who need to look pregnant on-screen. Beards get tugged. Hair gets pulled. Stomachs get poked. He wants nothing to spoil the illusion. Only his eyes are exposed, and even these are covered by blue-tinted contacts.

Over the padding, he wears a Coca-Cola red jacket and pants trimmed with white, and a black belt. His boots and gloves are black, too. The conical red hat with white trim and pompom complete his disguise. He's the picture perfect Father Christmas. Norman Rockwell could have used him as a model, that's how properly he's done up.

He hopes it won't be long until someone stops. Who wouldn't give Santa a ride in December if they could?

A car slows. There might have been enough room to squeeze in an extra passenger, even an oversized one, but there's clearly no space for his enormous sack. As he waves his thanks to the driver, steam emerges through the openings at his nostrils and the small puncture between his rubber lips. He suspects he's running late, but he isn't wearing a watch. That would have been out of character. Santa never needs to know what time it is. He's magic, after all.

The snow-lined streets are filled with pedestrians and people on bikes, scooters, and inline skates. Anything to get them wherever they need to be, no matter how cumbersome or clunky. Men and women wear parkas over business apparel as they hold aloft cardboard signs hastily inked with their destinations. Turtle Bay. Lower East Side. SoHo. Battery Park.

Drivers who've never stopped for a hitchhiker in their lives are picking up strangers to satisfy the enforced limit of four-per-car for vehicles heading into Manhattan south of 96th. The red BMW rolling through that stop sign might contain a lawyer, an office temp, a doorman, and a plumber. In addition to the deliveryman, the brown courier van speeding past might hold a CEO, an architect, and an exotic dancer — or a con man, a terrorist, and a hooker, for all he knows. People who wouldn't have given each other the time of day under normal circumstances. None of the vehicles have room for a fully loaded Santa Claus, though. Several drivers hold their hands up in a universal gesture that clearly conveys the sentiment: "Sorry, but what can I do?"

The man rubs his gloved hands together for warmth and jostles the sack on the ground beside him with his knee to re-assure himself of its presence. He reviews its contents over and over again. He's on a tight schedule, and the woman on the phone knows the kind of people who could make his life miserable if he doesn't do what she says.

Though he's hesitant to stick out his thumb, he steps toward the street more assertively. What would a child passing by think if their parents left Santa in the lurch on the side of the road?

Finally, a black Escalade with two people up front and a third in the back seat pulls over to the curb. The man peers through the cloud of warmth escaping the open window. "We're going to Washington Square," the driver says.

Close enough. The man opens the rear door and places his sack on the seat, making sure the drawstrings are pulled tight. He loops his left arm around it like a teenager on a date. He senses he's interrupted a conversation in progress, so he tries to break the ice with an old standby. "Stays like this, we'll have a white Christmas after all."

The others, two men and a woman, smile and nod in response. They introduce themselves. Heidi, in the front seat, wearing a white down jacket with a fur-trimmed hood, says she's a lawyer with one of the big firms on Madison Avenue. Herschel, bespectacled, with a computer on his lap, is a technology consultant. George, the driver, in a dark overcoat, teaches at NYU.

"What do you do?" Heidi asks, then covers her mouth with a white mitten as she bursts out laughing. The others join in. The man's laughter is deep and jolly, well-practiced and natural sounding. People trust him because of that laugh, if for no other reason.

Herschel says, "I heard about this guy who put an ad on the internet night before last. Free rides. No one answered. He put up another one yesterday morning, this time asking for money. He had fifteen replies in five minutes." He shakes his head. "It's crazy."

"I like what happens to people when there's a crisis in this city," Heidi says. "They're nicer to each other than usual. More trusting."

The man nods in agreement.

"Wouldn't it be great if a strike happened more often?" George asks. "There's no traffic."

The man in the Santa suit checks the digital clock on the dashboard. He's glad to see they're making good time. Feeling hot inside his costume, he's tempted to roll down the window, but he doesn't want to freeze out the other passengers. "Not everyone's nice in a crisis," he says, remembering an ugly scene that happened earlier, people yelling at cops and at each other over something. His left arm rests protectively atop his sack.

George shrugs. The streets are slippery and hard to manage with ice. He seems to be concentrating on his driving, peering through the windshield as the wipers push aside the heavy flakes streaming toward them.

"No, not everyone," Herschel agrees.

The man listens to the other three as they banter about the strike, its side effects, the weather, and anything else that comes to mind. He's relieved that none of them have commented on his outfit or the fact that he's kept his mask on the whole time. He asks if they've just met or if they knew each other before today.

From his position in the back seat, the man sees Heidi glance first at George, then over her shoulder at Herschel.

"We've known each other a long time," she says.

"Long time," Herschel echoes.

"Waiting for circumstances like these to go out and gather people willing to join us," Heidi continues.

George clicks a remote control on his visor. Through the frosty windshield, the man sees a garage door opening ahead.

"Eager to join us," Herschel says. "People who'll get in the van without question. Without putting up a struggle."

The Escalade veers sharply into the opening and the darkness beyond. The man has only an instant to consider how easily he was tricked. How perfect the illusion they had created.

The Carolers

Mark L. Eshbaugh

    "I mean, look at me. You don't see me flipping out about being wished a *Merry Christmas*. It doesn't hurt my sensibilities, offend me, or shake my faith. But I don't see anything wrong with just simply wishing everyone a *Happy Holiday*. I mean..."

"Mhmm. Yes, dear," I muttered to my wife as she continued her diatribe. I tried to subtly drown her out as I turned up the radio. The Fools sang away about Norbert, the nearsighted reindeer, but she just kept on talking through the under-appreciated Christmas classic. To my dismay the two songs that followed, "Grandma Got Run Over by a Reindeer" and "Run, Rudolph, Run," achieved similar results. So it was with no small sense of relief when we pulled into the drive-way. At home, I could escape, but in the car there were few options. I had stopped listening to her about the time I pulled out of the parking space at the grocery store some fifteen minutes ago. I'm not even sure if she took a breath the entire drive. My mind was on all the things that still needed to be done today and getting through tomorrow.

"...and, Michael, you really need to take care of those icicles on the front of the house. You don't want it to create ice dams like last year. We just got the house fixed up from the water damage. The insurance barely covered the repairs, and it took three coats of paint to cover the watermarks on the wall," Rachel continued as I parked the car.

In the brief silence where she took a breath, I said something profound like "Yup" to whatever it was she was going on about now and set about taking the groceries inside. It's not that I didn't care about what she was saying, it's just that I really had zero interest in anything said to me at all today by anyone. Today was Christmas Eve. One of the worst days of the year. Followed only by Christmas Day and the week leading up to New Year's Day.

I've always hated Christmas, personally. It's not because I never got anything I wanted, or anything like that—though I didn't. And it isn't because nearly everyone becomes so phony and tries to kiss your ass—like that few weeks of niceties between Thanksgiving and Christmas will outweigh treating you like garbage the rest of the year. For me, if I had to try to pinpoint my hatred of the holiday season, it started around age eight when my grandmother stopped coming to Christmas because it was too far to travel. It was set a little more when I was ten and my scout leader died from complications from Alzheimer's disease. And it was really set in concrete when I was twenty-five. That was the year when my best friend throughout high school was murdered the day after Christmas.

Every year the depression sets in, and I have just done my best to get through the season. Those few people who have noticed I've told I have Seasonal Affective Disorder. Which usually has them responding with something stupid about needing a tan and I'd feel better. But every year I go through the motions and do my best to smile.

I thought I would have some reprieve from the Christmas gloom when I married Rachel on account of her being Jewish. But as my luck turns out, we've just celebrated both Christmas and Chanukah from that point on, and I've made the best of it for my son's sake. So every year we have a tree in the living room, and in the dining room, a heavy brass menorah about a foot tall sits unassumingly on the server along the wall, just below a similarly sized crucifix adorned with white string lights. The crucifix was a decoration courtesy of my overly devout eighty-three-year-old mother, who also happens to live with us since dad's passing four years ago.

Most years the holiday season drags out with Chanukah falling a few weeks before Christmas, each day coursing with the slow and steady reminders of how much December sucks. But every few years, like this one, you get an explosive holiday burnout I like to call Christmukah, when each holiday adds its own brand of misery to the chaos of the season by overlapping.

"I'm going upstairs to check on my mother," I said as I finished putting away the groceries. "I'm secretly hoping she's decided not to go to midnight mass, so I won't have to stay up to drive her."

"Okay. I'll go out and get the mail, then start on dinner," Rachel replied.

I made my way upstairs, turned left at the landing, and gently knocked on my mother's door. I could barely hear her grant me audience over the blaring television. I walked over to the set and turned the volume down from rock-concert levels. "Geez, mom, turn up your hearing aids," I said sarcastically while rubbing my ears, turning towards where she sat on the bed.

She responded simply by sticking out her tongue at me and rolling her eyes. "What time is it?" she asked.

"It's just about four. Rachel's starting in on our dinner. Have you eaten?"

"I had a grilled cheese a little bit ago. Do you have every-thing set for tomorrow?"

"Yes, everything is fine," I lied. "Matthew should be home around eight-thirty. If you still want to go to mass tonight, we'll take you. We would have to leave about eleven to get there and get seats along the aisle."

"That sounds fine. Tell Matt I'd like him to sit next to me at mass," she said. "I was just planning to take a nap for a few hours."

"Good idea, Mom. It will be a late night for everyone," I said as I turned to leave. "I wish I could nap until next week," I added grumpily.

"I know you hate this time of year, Mister Grinch, but I—we all—appreciate everything you do for us," she said. "Would you mind waking me up at least an hour before we have to leave. By ten o'clock?"

"Sure, Mom. Get some rest," I replied, turning back and leaning down to kiss her forehead.

"You're a good kid. Thank you."

I smiled at her and turned toward the door, saying over

my shoulder, "What can I say, my heart grew three sizes today."

As I closed the door upon exiting the room, I heard my mother muttering, "Hmphh, yeah right," under her breath.

"Everything okay with your mother? You get out of taking her to mass?" Rachel asked as I walked in the kitchen.

"She's fine. And no," I replied. "She wants Matt to sit with her during mass. Anything worthwhile in the mail?"

"Nothing for you," she said as she chopped vegetables for our dinner. "Just a few bills and a holiday card to me from my dentist's office."

"'Rats. Nobody sent me a Christmas card today. I almost wish there weren't a holiday season. I know nobody likes me. Why do we have to have a holiday season to emphasize it?'"

"You're just lucky, Charlie Brown," Rachel replied with a knowing wink. "Didn't think I'd catch that quote did you?"

"Not really, but I knew you were smart when I married you. I have to wake mother about ten. You sure I can't talk you into going to mass with us?"

"One of the few perks of being Jewish," she said, winking at me as she began setting out our dinner at the table. We ate as we talked. "Hopefully, Matthew will be good. He's not easy to deal with when he doesn't get enough sleep."

"He'll be Fine. He went last year."

"Yeah, but whatever you do, don't feed him after midnight," Rachel said. "You know what a rage monster he becomes if he eats too late."

"All too well, dear," I said. Matthew had just turned eleven in September. And as much as we would like to deny it, the truth is that, even at that age, the hormones have already started surging. Resultantly, Matt was already a rage monster at any given time. One minute he'd be whining and crying over some damn video game that "cheated" or "glitched," the next minute he'd be angry over some perceived slight by any one of us, or one of his friends.

These past few weeks Matt has been most angry with us over the "big lie" surrounding Santa Claus. Honestly, we were surprised it took this long for that little gem to come to light. And today he's already pissed that his grandmother talked me into taking him with her to midnight mass. These are just a few of these reasons why both Rachel and I were grateful for a few hours without him.

Matthew was with our neighbor, Glen, and his son, who was also eleven; they were shopping for gifts. For some reason, Glen always thought shopping on Christmas Eve was a good idea, which I will never understand. I hate shopping any time of year, but I can't think of a worse time to do it than the night before Christmas. There is already so much that has to get done that I could hardly imagine taking out time to shop for gifts.

Rachel and I finished our meals and preparations for the morning. I looked at the clock. *8:00 p.m. Not too bad,* I thought. *A little time to relax.* Rachel decided it was time to light the menorah rather than wait for Matthew to get home. He didn't really care about either of the religious portions of the holidays. Like any eleven-year-old, each holiday was only about what new toy he was about to receive. Rachel, however, took her religion very seriously—at least on the big holidays. She set up everything for her evening prayer as I watched. When Rachel had everything set out, she lit the Shamash candle.

"*Ba-ruch A-tah Ado-nai E-lo-he-nu Me-lech ha-olam a-sher ki-de-sha-nu be-mitz-vo-tav ve-tzi-va-nu le-had-lik ner Cha-nu-kah,*" began Rachel as the doorbell rang, interrupting her prayer. "Hmph, did Matt forget his key? Who is ringing the bell at this hour on Christmas Eve?" she asked, blowing out the flame.

I opened the door and looked out. At the bottom of the porch steps was a group of five carolers who immediately launched into a horrid rendition of "Silent Night." Long-tailed cats and rocking chairs came readily to mind as I stood there listening. Rachel came up beside me as I took in our little choir. They were peculiarly small, each of the five carolers standing about three feet high, and they had a sickly pale, almost greenish, complexion. They were abnormally thin and lanky, with long aquiline noses and pointed chins. I noticed that two were women, the other three men. They were dressed primarily in emerald green except for their hats. Each wore a red cap, which at first glance I took to be a Santa hat, but on closer inspection, I realized they lacked the white trim usually associated with Santa, and they were a bit darker red in color.

I looked around the neighborhood as they continued their singing. *If you could call it that.* Every house on the street had a group of carolers at their doors. At least three or more at every house, all dressed the same and equally short in stature. *That's odd,* I thought. But perhaps I was just being overly suspicious. Rachel didn't seem to notice anything out of the ordinary.

As the carolers' caterwaul came to an end, they each bowed low, then the caroler in the middle stepped forward. "Merry Christmas, kind sir and madam," he croaked. "I am Kelan, my wife, Mairwen, my brother, Torquil, his wife, Eveleen, and my brother, Tierney." He pointed at each one as he said their names. "Do you have any requests that we might sing?"

"Thank you for the song, but no. We have no requests. We should get back inside. It's a busy night," I said while closing the door slightly.

"But, sir, it is customary to invite carolers in for a cookie or cocoa. Would you not be a gracious host," Kelan said.

"I... Well..." I began, looking at Rachel. Though I was skeptical and inclined to send them on their way, Rachel gave me her "Have a heart" look. I slumped my shoulders and shrugged.

"Yes, won't you come in?" said my wife after seeing my resignation. "I'll make some cocoa. This is Michael, and I'm Rachel."

"Thank you for your kindness," replied Kelan. "My brothers and I are delighted to accept. My wife and sister-in-law must move on to the next house to assist our kin folk with their singing."

"Very well," I said, holding the door open as they shuffled past. "Come on in. Just to the left there."

"Please have a seat. I'll set the kettle for the cocoa," Rachel added as she headed down the short hallway to the kitchen.

Our three guests sat beside one another on our couch while I took one of the reclining chairs. The three brothers looked even more pallid in the brighter interior lighting. It was almost comical how their feet barely touched the floor on account of their short stature. Their heads were even with the top of the back cushions. *If anyone were to look in the window, they'd have no way to see them. They'd just think I was sitting here talking to myself,* I thought.

"What a lovely home. Is it just the two of you?" asked Kelan as he looked around and appeared to appraise the room.

"No. Our son is out with the neighbor and should be home soon," I replied.

"And Michael's mother is upstairs napping," said Rachel, returning.

The next several minutes consisted of painfully awkward small talk that included topics like the abnormally mild weather, which lead to global warming, which then dangerously flirted into politics. For such strange guests, they were surprisingly well informed, educated, and polite. Each of the brothers courteously let one another talk without speaking out of turn. In fact, just as I was noticing that the each one spoke in ordered succession—first Kelan, then Torquil, then Tierney, always in that order—Torquil stood abruptly and spoke out of turn, interrupting his brother. "I'm sorry," he said. "Not to be a bother, but would you have a lavatory that I might use? Please?"

The abrupt break in the almost hypnotic pattern jarred me a little, "Yeah, sure. It's right at the top of the stairs," I said tentatively. "You can't miss it. The light switch is just inside the door."

"Thank you. I'll be right back," replied Torquil with a slight grin.

The conversation began again, the brothers each speaking in turn, rehashing previous subjects for a few minutes. I looked over at Rachel with a questioning look, but she either didn't notice or thought nothing out of the ordinary. "It's nice of your family to go out caroling. Not very many people do that anymore. Do any of you have any children?" she asked, steering the conversation in a new direction.

"Oh yes! We each have children. Many children in our family. Tierney's wife is home tending to them all, so that we may indulge this evening," replied Kelan with a broad smile just as the kettle whistled in the kitchen.

Rachel excused herself to finish the cocoa. Kelan, Tierney, and I sat in silence, looking at one another quizzically as Rachel vanished into the kitchen. She returned a few minutes later, struggling to keep the five cups of cocoa on a serving tray without spilling any contents. I stood and met her halfway across the room, taking the tray from her hands and set it on the coffee table in front of our guests.

"Thank you," said Kelan. "It looks delicious. But, perhaps, I should let it cool." He turned toward Tierney as he said it and nodded slightly.

"No need to rush it down. We wouldn't want to burn our mouths," Tierney said in response to his nod.

Feeling a growing sense of unease, I said, "Your brother seems to be taking a long time in the bathroom. Should someone check on him?"

"Oh, no! I'm sure he is just fine," Kelan replied enthusiastically as a loud *thump* reverberated through the ceiling above us.

I looked up, startled by the noise. "Excuse me a moment. I'm going to check on my mother. It sounds like she might have fallen out bed," I said. I jumped up and hurried up the stairs.

As I made the landing at the top of the stairs, I saw that the bathroom door was open, but there were no sign of Torquil. I hurried down the hall to mother's room. I noticed as I approached that her door was slightly ajar. I skidded to a halt at the threshold and tentatively pushed the door open to see my mother on the floor surrounded by blood. The arm closest to me had been nearly severed at the elbow, and Torquil was leaning over her body as he tore a large chunk of flesh from her neck with his teeth. Upon hearing me enter, he looked up and smiled at me with a bloodstained grin, crimson rivulets running from the corners of his mouth. He spit the flesh from his mouth in my direction. A fine mist of blood and spittle erupted from his mouth with his every breath.

Fear and adrenaline surged through me as I rushed the little demon, knocking him backward into the bed. He kicked at my midsection, trying to keep me back, but his smaller stature left him at a disadvantage. My right hand found his throat, and I squeezed tightly. He thrashed wildly beneath me. A lucky strike to my groin forced me to loosen my grip enough for him to turn and sink his razor-like teeth into my forearm. I rolled to the side as the pain shot through my arm and used the momentum to throw the creature across the room.

We both scrambled to our feet and launched at one another again. He was fast. I had the size and strength advantage. He thrashed for all he was worth, but I managed to get him in a headlock. He scratched and clawed at my sides. I looked down at him and then toward my mother's lifeless body. My anger and anguish rose within me. Mustering all of my strength, I lifted up the small monster with an abrupt jerking motion and wrenched his neck as swiftly and violently as I could. When his neck snapped satisfyingly, I dropped his lifeless body to the floor.

With that little demon dispatched, I was able to refocus, and that's when I heard Rachel screaming from below. The sounds of a struggle and running footsteps echoed up the stairs and along the hallway. I needed to get to her as fast as I could, but needed to make one small pit stop on the way. I ran the length of the hallway to the master bedroom, darted inside and dove across the bed, then yanked open the nightstand drawer. I pulled the Heckler & Koch HK45 pistol from the nightstand drawer. I grabbed the full magazine beside it, slammed it home, then chambered a round. Gun in hand, I was down the stairs in a flash.

I reached the bottom landing and took in the situation. I had no way of knowing what had occurred while I was upstairs, but Rachel and the other two had left the living room. I heard Rachel yelling from the dining room at the back of the house. I moved as quickly as my feet would go.

Turning the corner into the dining room, I saw Kelan grabbing the menorah from the service table. I watched in horror as he swung it toward Rachel's back. It looked as though she was heading toward the backslider, attempting to get out of the house. Sensing the movement behind her, Rachel turned just enough for the blow to glance off her shoulder. But it was still enough to disorient her. She looked dazed as she fell forward into the corner of the service table and the wall. Her hands smacked violently against the wall, causing mother's crucifix to slide down in front her. Whether it was luck or instinct, I couldn't say, but she grabbed the crucifix tightly and swung it as hard as she could. She made contact, burying half of it into Kelan's skull with a sickening thud. "Well, what do you know? Jesus does save," she muttered as she staggered forward. The crucifix was pulled from her grasp as Kelan's body fell to the floor.

For a fraction of a second, relief flowed through me. *My wife is safe,* I thought as she turned toward me. I just stood watching in shock as her face contorted into an expression of pain. She dropped to her knees before me, her legs buckling awkwardly beneath her. She fell forward, smacking her face on the floor with a heavy thud. It was then I realized that Tierney had come up behind her and buried a large kitchen knife in her spine. He cackled as he looked at me, brandishing a cleaver in his other hand.

"You'll shoot your eye out kid," Tierney croaked when he saw the gun in my hand. He lunged forward, the cleaver leading the way. I raised the pistol and squeezed the trigger. Tierney's head vanished into a crimson fog. His body continued its forward movement, flying into to me and knocking me to the floor. I rolled his corpse off me as the warm red blood began to spurt from his neck. I quickly crawled to Rachel only to confirm she was gone. Heartsick for the loss of my wife, I thought, *Matthew! I have to get to Matthew!*

I held the pistol tightly in my hand as I ran to the front door and yanked it open. As I stepped into the cool night air, I heard a yell from above me. There was someone on the roof. Swinging the pistol upward as I turned, I looked toward the source of the sound. I saw nothing but a monstrous icicle falling, heading for my left eye. Ducking to the side just in time, its sharp point pierced my shoulder as the weight of the creature hit me. As I fell to the ground, my head cracked sharply on the pavement. Then the world went black.

* * *

I awoke to the sounds of beeping that synced with the rhythm of my heartbeat. I tried opening my eyes, but my head felt strangely damp and was heavily bandaged, covering a portion of my eyes. The room was so dark that I couldn't make out anything in what I could see of the room.

"Finally awake, I see. Good. Good. It's been almost a week since you were brought in," said a high-pitched voice to the right me. "You're lucky to be alive. Your wounds could easily have been fatal. What's the last thing you remember? Can you tell us your name?"

I tried to speak but couldn't form the words. A low moan was all I could manage.

"No worries. Don't rush it. Just get some rest," said the voice. "I'll check back on you later."

I drifted in and out of consciousness, still unable to make out my surroundings, even when I was more alert. Whether it was from my injuries, or being sedated, I found I couldn't move my legs at all. My arms were heavy, and an IV had been inserted in the crook of my right arm. The doctor (or doctors) checked in on me at regular intervals, though I could never see them in the darkness. Time was indeterminate. When awake, I worked my voice, trying to speak. On the doctor's next visit to my room, I managed a whisper, which gave way to recounting the events up until this moment. "What day is it?" I asked finally.

"Why it's New Year's Eve," said the doctor. "Time to look

forward to new beginnings, and what a great year it will be!"

At the doctor's exclamation, the lights came on, blinding me. I instinctively struggled but still could not move as my eyes adjusted to the new lighting. The room swam before me, slowly coming into focus until I saw the doctor standing before me. Sharp-toothed grin; pointed chin; pallid, green complexion; and a red cap upon its head. It bounded from the room, laughing, as I looked down at where the IV entered the vein in my arm and noticed an unusual greenish tint to my skin.

The Gift That Keeps on Giving
Sheri White

I t was Christmas Eve, and she was sure she'd just heard a jingle of bells from the living room. A sudden swirl of cold air entered the room, and she puzzled over it for a minute. Sliding her feet into warm slippers, she padded ever-so-quietly out to the living room. There, under the tree, was a beautifully wrapped gift box with a flowing red ribbon. "Merry Christmas to YOU!" the card read. Curious, she approached the box to open it.

The smell assaulted her as soon as she took the lid off the box. Her eyes watered, making it impossible to see. She wiped away the moisture. Her vision restored, she peeked into the box. Her husband's head lay nestled in tissue paper. Amanda nodded, satisfied. It had been done. Expensive, but worth it. The cheating bastard had gotten what he deserved.

Amanda had discovered her husband's affair just weeks before. She had been in her Lexus, listening to Johnny Mathis singing her favorite Christmas tune. While at a red light, she had been going over her list when she casually glanced at the car to her right. It was her husband's BMW, but he wasn't alone. Tracy, her sister—HER SISTER—was in the passenger seat, holding up her hand and admiring a huge emerald ring. Peter was smiling and nodding his approval. The light turned green, and Amanda sped off, rage and sorrow squeezing her heart.

It hadn't been hard to find someone who would take a hefty sum to perform the grim task. Her sister would be taken care of shortly; there would probably be another box delivered in the next few days.

Amanda decided to take the head to a dumpster in another town the next day. Tonight, though, she would unwrap the gifts her husband had left under the tree for her. She couldn't wait to see what crap he had gotten her after blowing his wad on her slutty sister.

She tore the paper off, finding pretty much what she had expected. CDs, DVDs, pajamas that wouldn't fit. *Figures*, she thought. Then she reached into her stocking hanging over the fireplace. She pulled out a small, hard object. It was a jewelry box, the kind a ring might come in. And inside... An emerald ring. "That fucking bastard! He actually got me the same ring he got my whoring sister!" She tossed it into the fire.

The phone rang.

THE SHADOW OVER DEATHLEHEM

She stalked over to it and picked it up. "Hello!" she said harshly.

"Amanda! Did you get it yet?" Her sister's bubbly voice set Amanda's teeth on edge.

"Get what?" *Tramp. Tramp, tramp, tramp. I hate you.*

"The ring! Peter had me go with him to help pick it out. He was so excited and couldn't wait to give it to you."

Amanda's legs went weak. Her stomach roiled. "No. Dear God, no," she moaned.

Suddenly her sister screamed through the phone, "Amanda! Oh my God, someone's breaking in! Call the police!"

The screams quickly changed into shrieks of pain. The connection went dead. Amanda fell to her knees, knowing another package was on the way.

B*LEEDING* ❄O*UT THE* C*HEER*

Nick Manzolillo

ll of reality bends with a single thought, and yet I'm still here. When I close my eyes and try to wish for a better place, it gets worse, and the line of grumbling customers grows longer. Fuck Christmas. "Dominic the Donkey" blares over the radio for the fourth time today, one of my fingers bleeds from the razor-sharp edge of the display case of dollar shots, and the never-ending line of customers with arms full of booze sends forth one stupid bozo after another. The rush,

the mania that's the day before Christmas, is brought on because none of these people had the foresight to do their shopping earlier.

I'm halfway through an eight-hour shift, and it never ends,
that fucking line. They shuffle forwards like zombies from *The
Walking Dead*, a ceaseless horde of idiots that spew question
after idiotic question. "Can you wrap this?" Yes, allow me to
wrap your six bottles of wine while the thirty customers behind you wait and grow stupider by the second. "Hey, can
somebody get me a thirty pack from the cooler?" Yes, the
cooler that's twenty feet behind you, in plain sight, yes, we'll
send somebody back there because you're too fat and lazy.
"Is this red wine?" Well, yes, it's red. The flat-out worst I hear
is when each and every customer says, "Boy, it's busy, huh?"
or "Hey, that Christmas music going non-stop must be annoying, huh?"

I'm missing dinner with my family. Now I'm not a sucker for a warm and fuzzy holiday get together, but I've only
got one and a half pairs of grandparents left, and I want to
make those moments count. In twenty-six years, I've never
missed a single Christmas Eve dinner, where my Italian parents
don't hold back from their heritage, and they cook the good
stuff, from fish to calamari to perfectly spiced pasta.

I'm here until ten. What kind of liquor store stays open
till ten on Christmas Eve? Nine-sixty an hour because I couldn't
find a bar that would hire an inexperienced bartender—they
only wanted me to be a grease-stained busboy.

"Happy Holidays," the customers remember to say after
they comment on my tie, argue the price of their wine, or
mumble something I have to ask them to repeat until it becomes English. The shelves behind the counter, which are
adorned with pints, half pints, and nips, give my vaguely OCD-
ridden mind a vague satisfactory sense as they begin to empty.

In a way, I find myself wishing for the entire store to eventually empty, like checking off a list until everything's sold so everyone can leave. But there are stacks below the counter, refills for the nips and pints, and, just like the customers, it's a never-ending, incomplete cycle that feels more like a dizzying spiral of consumption and supply that I could just puke over.

The man with streaks of dirt on his face slams both his arms down on the counter, making the poofy end of his Santa hat jiggle. The hat's too white and clean for his grimy head. His face is covered with so much brown, fresh dirt that it looks like tufts of hair. He didn't bring anything to the counter, which means he's going to ask an exceptionally stupid question or ask the prices of the pints behind the counter before going with the cheapest bottle of well-vodka. He's looking me in the eyes and... Is that dirt on his eyelids? Clinging to his pupils? Instead of wet marbles, his eyes seem clumpy; they're brown, hazel, but they're lumpy, like something's growing off them. The man grins, and I ask him what he wants.

"Well—" It pops out of his mouth like tires on a gravel driveway. He licks some powdery grains of dirt off his lips as he swallows and points a finger at me. "—you don't want to be here, huh?" He nods. He's getting streaks of dirt all over the counter. A dirty customer is nothing new.

"It's about what you want, buddy. Whaddya want?" I gesture to the pints and accidentally make eye contact with the pug of a man and his bird-faced wife standing behind the dirty one. Like all customers not at the front of their line or peering into their cellphones, they seem irritated, like they're divinely owed fast and professional service.

"Well, I want my ride so I can get to where I need to be for a Yuletide celebration like no other."

"You need a phone then?" I don't hide the confusion and

irritation that drools from my scrunched-up face as I raise an open hand to him—the universal sign for "what the fuck."

"No, they'll be here soon." The man smiles as dirt falls from his stretching lips.

Let's make this simple for the guy. "What do you want to buy?" I turn to meet my co-worker's glance. Ashley's been here six years and won't listen to any of my complaints. I think she's become so frustrated with these people that her anger has frozen into a passive misery that leads to her having one tone of voice and a pair of un-batting, unfazed eyes toward the mad demands of the customers.

"Buy? Don't you need money to buy stuff?" The man raises himself up, and here it is, what I've been dreading and half-fantasizing about. It's a common trope, somebody robbing a liquor store, and this place, for whatever strange reason, doesn't have any cameras. I've got no reason to resist, though; if this guy's about to stick a gun in my face, then he gets every-thing. Hell, I'll even help him carry the cash to his getaway car. I will then quit and sue this place for psychological damage because the owners' lack of installing surveillance equipment was an invitation for the store to be robbed, and I, the in-nocent employee, have been mentally scarred in the process. Not that having a gun stuck in my face wouldn't also be the coolest thing to ever happen to me.

"Would you give me money if I needed to buy some-thing?" The dirty man's leaning over the counter now, looking my co-worker/partner in misery up and down. The manager's at the bank getting us more change because customers think it's acceptable to pay for ten dollar transactions with hun-dred dollar bills.

The pug behind the dirty man finally speaks his mind. "What the hell is this, buddy?" The dirty man immediately whirls around to face him, and the bird-faced wife gasps and the lines of customers are now honing in to the scene, drawn by the magnetism of breaking the norm.

"Would you give me money if I asked for it?" The dirty man, who is only a little over five-five, is leaning toward the pug's face, whose arms are full of dual thirty racks of Narragansett. Angry muttering begins to form a rhythm among customers forming the lines winding through the aisles. Everybody's hands are full, which makes them helpless, now that I think of it. The dirty man steps out of line and addresses the room while "Rudolph the Red-nosed Reindeer" begins to play over the radio. "This is a strange place for such a special time of the year. You all are very strange."

"Buddy, you should take your drugs somewhere else," a thick-armed customer scoffs from over in Ashley's line. She has just rung up a young couple who are now carrying their box of wine and a twelve pack of bottles to the door, and that's when things become a little clearer.

"I have a bomb!" the dirty stranger shouts, raising his arms. "And if any of you move, you're all going to die!" He shakes dust off himself. Despite the radio's exclamations of a flying deer with very bright and shiny nose, the room freezes.

"Oh God," an older woman mutters. There is a consecutive shudder coursing throughout the room, contagious as a yawn.

"Don't move. Stay right where ya'll are. Touch me, and we go up. Touch me, and we erupt!"

"What do you want? You can take everything, and just go," Ashley's begging, shouting across the room, and the murmur of the thirty or so customers fills the room. Ashley's cell phone is on a little table behind the nip rack. Her fingers are sliding over her phone, across a nine and a one and a one, and then a green little call button.

"I want you all to cheer up! It's Yuletide, and there's a full moon for the holiday! The holy day!"

How I wish I wasn't working tonight. I could've found that missing, magical part of my childhood while I got drunk with my family and played pool with my uncle and grandpa.

You're all so sad and desperate you can't even be yourselves! You can't even be sober with your family!" The dirty man approaches the register and stares at me. "You can't even give something to somebody else. I came from the ground tonight! I came from the earth!" The stranger faces the room, growing more excited as the crowd gives him all their attention.

"I mean what I said. I'm waiting, and now I think y'all might as well wait with me."

It's starting to snow; soft, eerie snowflakes flutter and stick to the windows. It's snowing despite it having been sixty-eight degrees a week ago. That's probably New England being New England. Of all the times for it to start... Ah shit, it's dawning on me that because it's suddenly snowing, we might have closed early. If not for this...

"He's too thin to have a bomb," somebody's shouting from Ashley's line. A black man is clamping a hand across the dirty man's jacket, and it's true; I can almost see his skin beneath the black or brown shirt he has on beneath the jacket that looks like it's been clawed and chewed up. What did he mean when he said he came from the ground?

"The doors won't open!" The young couple Ashley already checked out are trying to pull the automatic door by the side of the register. They're too stupid or nervous to realize the door should be pushed, but either way, something weird is going on. Suddenly, the black man is screaming, and the chaos of the moment causes the whole world to become unfocused in a blink, and you miss what happens next. The man is on his knees, the dirty stranger holding him by the wrist... No, the stranger's fingers are not holding, but burrowing into the man's arm. He pulls back like he's revving a chainsaw and pries back a long fragment of bone from the screaming man's arm in a quick geyser of blood that eerily mirrors the red of the Santa Claus hat. This is the moment everyone really loses their shit.

People are running, screaming, stomping over one another towards the door as bottles of wine drop like fireworks, exploding violet and bubbling white across the floor. Thirty racks geyser and erupt; the pug-faced man falls through a display case in a creaking shower of crunched gift baskets and shattered wine glasses. Customers are banging on the doors while others are running to the back room. A shelf of craft beers is overturned in aisle six. The man with thick arms is grabbing the stranger, and there's more blood as I catch a flash of something squirming from the stranger's fingertips, like his fingers are hungry little mouths, little worms brought up from the dirt. *Jingle Bells* is shrieking over the radio, blood is spurting all over the counter, and the entrance behind the registers is blocked by the crowd of people pulling and pushing on both ends of the automatic doors.

The snow is sticking, freezing against the windows, and the stranger is humming to the song as he's working on a third man, driving his hungry fingers into an exposed neck.

"Alright, alright!" The dirty man is tilting his head and shouting at the ceiling. "Come on, everybody, let's gain some composure here! Come on now! Let's get our spirits roaring!" His teeth are falling out, and there are black, squirming things in his mouth as he strolls towards the register; my back is to the rows of pints, and they drop and shatter to the floor around my untied shoes.

"Are you a good boy?" The stranger is leaning over the counter just like before, dripping crimson all over the dirt-strewn metal. "Do you know what Yuletide is about, more than anything else?"

"Being kind... Being... Being good, thankful..."

The stranger grins, revealing a mouth full of what looks to be wriggling leeches, then he spits a tooth at the glass and alcohol pooled around my feet. "That's for Easter, and that's for Thanksgiving. Yuletide's about sacrifice. It's about feeding the things that build up an appetite over the course of one year. It's about giving something up."

The wind is howling, hurling snow against the windows, twirling white powder and frost. The howling, it's starting to seem almost like a series of strange flutes, piping cylindrically in a vortex of sound. "How about you step over that counter and walk me to my ride, and I won't kill any more of these fine people. Be the ultimate employee here. How about you show the customers how much you care about them?"

I'm thinking of the three men, crumpled up and bleeding all over the floor. I'm thinking of the stupid sheep that have flocked to the doors. I'm thinking of that fantastic meal that's waiting for me at home. I hate this job and everything. I wouldn't kill anybody. I wouldn't... I... I climb over the counter.

I'm shivering, noticing how the temperature has dropped as the stranger waves me closer to him, and then he begins leading me to the back of the store, and I'm keeping my eyes on the dirt clinging across his jacket. What the fuck... What the fuck... I'm stepping over bodies; my work boots are stained red. I follow the stranger to the back of the store where a huddled number of the smarter customers are crouching, hiding, trying to open the exit door. They step aside so the stranger and I can leave, and they don't follow us into the mad whirlwind of snow that soon swallows up the liquor store as I follow the stranger across a frozen parking lot. I always thought reality tended to blur around the holidays...

Something's moving up ahead. Something's alive, wriggling through the frost. "The snow's like a special lens," the stranger is marveling, shouting over the flutes that the wind plays savagely across our ears. "Will you come with me? Or will I have to go back inside and start emptying people until I find someone who will?"

I consider running, but the ground is so slippery with the sudden spread of ice that my feet are sliding along as I follow the stranger. That moving, living something up ahead, it's making sounds like a whale and a jackal combined. The worms are still in the ground all through the holidays. They don't just disappear, they hide.

"Look at you, look at you, look at you, one foot in front of the other." The stranger is walking backward, curling his carnivorous fingers as he urges me to follow him. "You're a human, after all. I could've sworn you were something else, as strong as the hate rolling off you is. You do care about people, huh? You forgot you were a nice person, huh? Oh you, oh the people like you, I could smell you from a mile away. You're exactly what we're looking for. You're exactly what we need! Here you are, following me into the pale. Here you are, and you still hate them! Here you are, following me, because you know you'll feel guilty if you don't. It's all still about you. You hate them more than I do. You hate them so specially... Come on, come on, spend the holidays with your own kind." The stranger is whirling by my side, gesturing toward the massive wiggling outline, nearly imperceptible through the snowfall. It has spines and hair that looks like Christmas trees, like a massive holiday worm, something ungraspable that has come with the snowfall and hides in plain sight. It has frozen wings and a wide maw full of stalagmites, and there is more of it I can't see, and the liquor store is so normal, so secure and sane, full of typical, comfortably dumb people. What have I done? What have I given up? I turn to run, slip, and fall, shattering my jaw on the frozen pavement. Then hands of dirt, grime, and cleansing snowflakes are grabbing my ankles and dragging me away from my place of work, my register, as my fingernails dig into the ice, and then crack, break, and grind away.

E✻XMAS T✻REE

Rose Blackthorn

"What is it?"

Sal looked at Den, half surprised and half suspicious. "Serious?"

He nodded, cocking his head to one side, trying to figure it out.

"It's a Exmas Tree."

Den chewed on his bottom lip, thinking. He'd just been a baby when things changed, so he didn't have the same kind of memories Sal had. "Exmas Tree?"

Sal nodded, tucking stringy hair behind her ear. "Yeah. It'll look better when the decorations are on it." The tree wasn't very big, maybe five feet tall from base to twiggy top. It didn't look like the Exmas Trees she remembered from childhood, either. This tree had been dead probably a dozen years, if not more. All of its needles were long gone, and a lot of its bark had sloughed off. She'd been careful bringing it home because its remaining limbs were brittle and liable to break. But she was sure it was the right *kind* of tree, just by its shape. And even if it weren't exactly right, Den wouldn't know any better.

"Decorations?" he repeated, tipping his head to the other side as he concentrated. "Like shiny tinfoil bits and paper flakes?"

Sal nodded, smiling. He was remembering. "All kinda pretty stuff, Den."

"And lights?" His dark eyes gleamed.

"Whole bunches of lights," Sal agreed, then went over to put an arm around his bony shoulders. "We're gonna make it the purtiest Exmas Tree ever. Gotta do it all just right, like Mama and Daddy taught us."

For a moment, Den's expression fell. Mama and Daddy were long gone and still missed. But then he smiled, gazing back at the sorry-looking tree leaning in the corner. "Gonna make Mama and Daddy proud."

* * *

Amazingly, they still had a few things left over from childhood stuffed in an old trunk in the back of what had been the cellar. Den helped Sal wrestle it out and unload it. Spread out on the floor, they admired the old decorations. There was a plastic star with most of the gold paint still intact for a topper; one ratty length of tinsel so brittle that it shed silver flecks wherever it was touched; some mismatched plastic figurines in the shapes of elves and reindeer and red-and-white striped candy canes; and last, a box of glass bulbs in faded tones of green and red. A few of the bulbs were cracked, and some had popped into sharp, curved pieces. The cracked ones could still be hung on the tree if they were careful, but Sal sighed at the shattered ones. She'd save the pieces of glass because you never knew when they'd come in handy. She thought wistfully of glue.

At the bottom of the trunk, wrapped in heavy brown paper with half a dozen small wooden balls, was a thick red velvet coat and pants with a matching floppy hat. Den's eyes got very big when Sal unfolded the paper covering. The faint scent of cedar from the wooden balls brought back hazy memories of her mother's cedar chest.

"What is that?" Den asked, breathless and amazed as a child.

"Don't you remember Santy Claus?"

Den nodded, but she wasn't sure he did.

"Well, this is a Santy suit."

His mouth made a perfect O, and he never looked away from the suit.

"We still need to decorate the Tree, though," she reminded him, folding the paper back over to hide the suit, and Den blinked. A doll suddenly come back to life. "Maybe we can make some more decorations to put on, besides what we already got. You think there's anything outside that'll work?" Part of the reason she'd decided to do a Tree this year was because it had been so long, and she'd been thinking about the holidays from when Mama and Daddy were still there. Mostly, though, it was a way to cheer up her little brother.

There wasn't a lot to be happy about these days. They should remember their family traditions and find ways to count the blessings they did have.

Den nodded, dark eyes glittering. "I'll go look," he said, and gave her a broad smile.

* * *

It took the rest of that day, and most of the next, to set up the Exmas Tree and decorate it. Den had scrounged around for most of a mile around their dilapidated house and brought back boxes filled with rusted cans, braided lengths of multi-colored plastic-coated wire, faceted yellow and red and clear covers for headlights and taillights and blinker lights, and the strands of lights that had once lined the parking lot outside the junkyard where they lived. With rusted tools, including tin-snips and pliers and hammers, they made stars and moons and triangles out of pieces of the cans. The plastic-coated wires were separated and used to hang the metal shapes, or they cut them shorter and twisted them into psychedelic flowers or multi-pointed stars. The faceted light covers were also hung, interspersed between the old decorations from their childhood. The long string of lights they gently wrapped around the denuded branches, being careful not to break any. Sal made sure none of the bulbs were broken, then dropped the plug end on the floor.

"Lights?" Den asked eagerly.

"Almost, Den. Almost." She stood back and admired their handiwork. Except for the unlit lightbulbs, it was the most festive thing she'd seen in years. "Can't light it up 'til we're ready to celebrate, and we can't celebrate 'til we're ready to sit down for our holiday dinner."

He frowned when she said can't, but then smiled when

she got to holiday dinner. "Can I help?" he asked, watching her now instead of the Tree.

"Couldn't do it without you," she said, leading him outside. The sun had dropped behind the hill, and soon it would be coming on dark. She grabbed her gloves and filled a faded red wagon with what they would need. "Let's go get us our dinner."

* * *

Sal rested in the shade of an overhanging rock. The sun was just coming up, and shadows stretched long across the broad, flat bowl of land before her. On the far side was a dome. It shimmered like a mirage, looking almost like it was floating in a lake. Lakes, she thought. Those were fine things, gone like everything else. Behind her, snug against the back of the overhang, Den slept the sleep of an exhausted little boy. Even though he was a man grown, only six years younger than she was, he still seemed like a child. He'd been hurt when he was little, and that's why she took care of him; that, and the promise she'd made to Mama and Daddy. Sal thought about them while she waited. She was tired, too, but someone had to stay awake and watch.

When she was little, there had been snow. There had been pine trees, live ones that smelled like winter even in warm weather. There had been TV and music and the scent of things cooking in the kitchen while Mama hummed. There had been an Exmas Tree that filled a corner of the living room, covered with twinkling lights and delicate decorations. There had been plenty to eat and to drink, and soft beds to sleep in, and arms that held her safe when she was scared.

All of that was gone now. After the sun got hotter, when the bombs finally stopped falling and the water dried up because it never rained, then Mama and Daddy got sick. They taught her everything they could and fixed up the old house in the junkyard where she and Den still lived. Daddy sank a well so they would have water, and Mama taught her how to cook and do first-aid. They both taught her to use the crossbow and the rifle, but she'd long run out of bullets. Even though it had been a long time ago, she remembered all their lessons. Now, she was putting one of Daddy's to use.

The little metal and plastic box had belonged to Daddy. He had taught her how to keep it clean, how to check the wiring, and how to change the batteries. He had even shown her how to change the transmission, but said that this one was the best to use. She had never asked him what *Essoess* meant, or why it was best. She had used the box before, and it had worked like Daddy promised. She only hoped the battery was still strong enough.

When the machine came across the wide, flat valley on its fat black tires, it headed straight toward her little box. Den was still sleeping, and Sal stayed quiet and still beneath the overhang. This was the hardest part, the anticipation. She held the crossbow ready, but hoped she wouldn't need it. She crossed her fingers and waited.

Sal checked on the machine parked behind the house under the rusted lean-to in deep shade. There would be time to scavenge it later. Now, it was time for their holiday celebration.

Den, always handy with wiring and machinery, used a battery cell from the machine to give power to the strand of lights on the Tree. Some of the bulbs remained dark, but quite a few of them glowed, making glass globes and tin can stars sparkle. A fire burned in the woodstove, raising the temperature in the already warm house, but the smell of dinner cooking excused the heat.

The two occupants of the machine that came from the dome had been surprised by the pit-trap Sal and Den had dug. Trussed up in their bulky protective suits, they hadn't noticed anything but the blinking light on the transmitter. One had died in the fall, thankfully. The second screamed and cried when Sal and Den appeared above. Sal aimed the crossbow at it. She remembered Daddy's lessons about hunting. "Don't let it suffer. Kill it quick."

She had only hoped for one, but two was better. Their holiday dinner would be memorable, and they'd eat well for a long time after.

"What it is?" Den asked, sniffing the redolent air. Ignoring the heat, he wore the Santy suit with the hat pulled down low, covering the worst of the scarring and deformity left over from the war. "Smells so good!"

Sal smiled, deeply content to see him so happy and excited. "Mama called it Exmas ham."

Hazard Delay
Sheri Sebastian-Gabriel

Chandra rubbed a sweaty palm on her Cheetos-encrusted jeans and licked her cracked lips. She'd almost jackknifed the whole damned rig after some cocky little shit in a Dodge Ram cut in too close. Her load shifted when she jammed the brake harder than she should have, and she'd watched the trailer swing out into the center lane. She could still feel the tires skidding along the layer of snow.

The whole ordeal left her desperate to steady her jittery

hands and ease onto the next exit ramp. The green highway sign about a mile back said there was a greasy spoon down Route 539. A hot meal seemed like a good excuse to get out of the snow and get her heart rate back to normal.

Gusts shifted the trailer. *Great way to spend Christmas,* she thought. She should've pulled into Atlanta two days ago, just in time to sit down to ham and dressing with Auntie Gloria and Nana. Saliva gathered at the corners of her mouth at the thought of Glo's sweet potato pie, so rich and buttery, it'd make you slap your mama. Instead, she was trapped in the fucking Pine Barrens of New Jersey. Whiteout conditions in New Hampshire held her up, and now getting home seemed like a carrot dangled at the end of a fishing line that she just couldn't catch up to.

As she approached the exit, the red brake lights of a salt truck glowed against the white flutter of snow. The knot in her shoulders eased as the roadway turned liquid-black in the salt melt. Then she maneuvered onto the exit ramp, disappointed to leave the safety of the salt truck so quickly.

Away from the headlights, deep in the dark recesses of New Jersey's backwoods, snow glowed blue in the shadows. Chandra's mind wandered to legends truckers told each other huddled shoulder to shoulder at truck stop counters, desperate to stave off boredom long enough to stay awake and deliver their load and move on to the next stop. Stories played an important role in her life, and she gathered them like souvenirs. They'd kept her awake on long trips. Hell, legends, myths, and stories kept her sane during every deployment she'd ever served.

She recalled the intensity in the brown eyes of Italian city boy named Dom as he talked about feeling the wings of a blackened figure whoosh and flutter just above his rig as he raced with a heavy load around sharp bends just to escape to the highway.

"Whatever you do," he'd said, leaning in close, "do *not* stop in the Pine Barrens. There is some weird shit in that place. I'm talking monsters. Oh, and Fort Dix is down there. I'm telling you, there's gotta be some strange military experiments going on. Some of the people... Well, they're just weird."

A lot of good that warning served now.

The walls of snow on either side of 539 closed in around her. A hand went to her throat as the frigid, white claustrophobia piled up. Angry red traffic lights glared off the slick roadways. The brakes moaned as she shuddered to a stop. Red glared off her streaked windshield. Evergreens sagged heavy with snow, forming a canopy across the roadway in places. She shivered as the light turned green. Empty roads stretched on, illuminated now in the faux green cheer that reminded her all too much of the twinkling strings rounding the girth of the Douglas fir in Auntie Gloria's parlor.

A sign spattered with white informed her that Prendergast's 539 Café and MotoLodge was only a quarter mile away, lauding its world-famous chocolate pudding cake. Damned if she'd ever heard of it, world-famous though it may be.

Prendergast's appeared like an L-shaped beacon, thick snow fluttering down, lit by the ugly yellow glow of sodium vapor streetlights. She maneuvered the truck into one of the long spaces reserved for rigs and pulled her iPhone out of the rucksack in the sleeper. The screen light blinded her momentarily like a flashlight in the cold, stony darkness of the cab. Four missed calls and three texts. Chandra knew the number all too well. She opened one of the texts.

Bae U still coming? Can we talk when U get here?

She pressed her finger against the power button and toggled it off. Better to leave it alone. Even if she'd made it to Atlanta days ago, the word *talk* was a euphemism for *booty call.* That's the last thing she wanted to be right now.

She pulled her wallet from the sack, swung open the door, and locked down the cab. Her boots skidded against the snow as she hopped down.

Snow silence was special, almost sacred. It muffled the vulgar sounds of humanity. In the subfreezing parking lot of Prendergast's, her pulse slowed and she sucked in a long, low breath that cleansed the anxiety that gripped her on the open road.

Prendergast's wood panel walls were lined with silver and gold garland, buck heads, antler trophies, archery bows, and rifles. *Charming,* Chandra thought. *Great place if you like Bambi's murderer.* A couple of the deer wore Santa hats in a festive ode to the season.

A snaggle-toothed, bug-eyed woman with stringy blonde hair approached the hostess station. "May I help you?"

Chandra's throat went dry. "I'd just like to sit at the counter."

The hostess sneered, cocked her head sideways, and shoved a grease-smeared menu at her. Chandra took it, revolted by the slippery plastic and the spite barely contained in the blonde lady's bulging blue eyes.

She rounded the corner. Her breath caught in her throat. Plastic tables lined the wall of windows facing Route 539. Almost every person seated at the six or so tables looked identical to the hostess. Sparse, fibrous blond hair stretched across massive, melon-like heads. Their eyes all bulged out slightly, like Louis Armstrong blustering out notes on his horn. Unlike Louis, their skin was milk-white. No one had so much as a brown freckle. Their front teeth rested slightly on their bottom lips, giving them a perpetually confused appearance.

Jeans and flannel lined the counter. The uniform. Chandra swallowed the lump in her throat and walked to an empty stool near the end of the counter. Being among other truck-ers made her feel only slightly more comfortable.

A line of red baseball caps bobbed up and down over tittering heads. Bellies jutted over belts. A man with a salt-and-pepper beard down to the center of his chest growled, "Well, you know where I think Obummer should be right now."

His voice boomed throughout the restaurant. Heads nod-ded, and laughter followed.

Chandra sat, and the cacophony hushed. Her face burned as they stared. It wasn't the only time she'd felt scared being a black woman in a room of white people—hell, that was life, especially as a trucker. But something about the lookalikes watching her and the truckers craning their necks to check her out made her stomach churn and the fine hairs on her arms prickle. Suddenly, food was the last thing she wanted.

Another blond lookalike, this one a moon-faced, acne-pocked guy with an orange-smeared apron, appeared at the counter in front of her. "Get you a cup of coffee?" he grum-bled.

Chandra nodded. Her gaze settled on a Confederate flag hanging on the wall, along with more buck heads, in a larger seating area in the back of the restaurant.

She was being silly. Should she feel uncomfortable every time someone made a comment that was counter to her own political views? Of course not. She'd finish her cup of coffee, see if she was safe to keep going and haul the hell out of Hill-billy Heaven. That was the plan.

The crater-faced man brought her coffee, and it sloshed onto the Formica countertop. She mopped up the overflow with a wad of napkins from a silver dispenser.

The truckers picked up their conversation, turning away from her, but she could still feel the blond people watching.

Chandra inhaled the slightly burnt coffee. The acrid aroma

nearly made her toss a couple of dollars down and leave it un-touched, but the snow piling up outside made her realize she probably wouldn't be safe. The trailer load was too light, and the thought of jackknifing made her hands clench involun-tarily.

She picked up the chipped, white ceramic mug with her fingertips and blew across the dark liquid, dissipating the steam. Then she slurped the lava-hot liquid, and it scorched the walls of her throat on the way down. It was just about the worst coffee she'd ever tasted, and she'd had her share of sludgy, stale, weak, and otherwise shitty truck stop coffee in her lifetime, not to mention the roofing tar the U.S. Army served. It was a caffeine delivery system, and it would do in that capacity.

A small window to her left displayed the fat snowflakes that drifted unyieldingly, adding to the drifts. Getting out of here tonight seemed unlikely, but Prendergast's seemed like it was a slightly less-creepy Bates Motel with free HBO and Magic Fingers beds.

The ghoul who'd served up the toxic brew returned and took a pencil from behind his pink ear. "Get you something?" he asked.

Chandra scanned the hand-scrawled menu on the chalk-board just behind the waiter/short-order cook. Nothing sounded appealing, least of all the CHEEZY GIRTS, even if they did come with a side of HOMEFIRES. "Just the coffee," she said.

Laughter from the other end of the counter started up again, and some guy in an off-white cowboy hat said, "Well, one thing that Kenyan didn't get away with was taking my guns. I can't even believe how every shooting, no matter what, the liberals start jumping up and down about gun control. How many of those Muslims have driven vans into crowds? How is taking my guns away going to stop anything?"

Chandra shifted in her seat. Her pulse raced. She wanted to leave. Heads nodded up and down. She took another long, slow drink of coffee.

She felt eyes on her and worked up the courage to turn around. Vacant, blue eyes bore into her. She could almost feel her flesh searing at the angry stares. She turned back around, lifted her mug again, and drank. Dainty sips were replaced by urgent gulps. She chugged the remains of her coffee until grainy bits at the bottom collected in her mouth. A large chunk of something bitter lingered on her tongue. She worked it against her front teeth and plucked it out with her forefinger and thumb. It had been some sort of pill, but before she could consider what kind exactly, her head buzzed and her vision blurred. Sounds roared in her ears, but she couldn't make out words. Her eyelids sagged, and she felt herself slump forward. The coffee mug smashed against the floor, and the sickly thud of her forehead against the edge of the counter sent stars and blackness across her field of vision.

Something held her in place. Her forehead throbbed all the way across. Instinct compelled her to reach up and inspect the source of the pain, but her arms were immobile. Rope fibers scratched the flesh of her wrists. It was the first sign that something was wrong.

Her eyelids felt glued together. She struggled a few times to open them before she was successful. Everything seemed foggy. The room was blurry, but she heard the distinct crackle of a fire. The smell of ash and burning cedar filled the air. There was a creaking sound as well, but she couldn't find the source. She blinked a few times to combat the persistent blur, and the room came into focus. She had no idea how long she'd been out or how she'd wound up here, wherever *here* was.

Her arms were tied to the posts of a large, wood-framed bed. The mattress was thin, and it sagged in the center. The room was cluttered with half-empty soda bottles, a kerosene lamp, yellowed newspapers, and various articles of clothing strewn across lime-green carpet.

Some of the blond people from the restaurant were there, seated on an orange, threadbare sofa, staring at her. The short-order cook stood, walked over. As he drew near, she noticed the glint of light off metal. He was holding a hunting knife, the kind they use to gut deer. It was antiseptic clean. All of the blood drained away from her face by the time he reached the side of the bed and looked down at her. He appeared much bigger from this vantage point, and Chandra felt the chill of terror slide from the tip of her tailbone to her knees. The man studied her like an insect pinned to a board. He said nothing, but his face contorted into a bitter sneer, as if he'd caught a whiff from the bottom of a bait bucket.

The fog was slow to lift from her mind, but she knew clearly and logically that they were going to lay her open from collarbone to pelvis. And there was nothing she could do about it.

The man watched her for a few more seconds before he walked away. Her hands struggled against the ropes, but she'd been tied too tightly. Her fingers tingled.

"Heh. Just keep on struggling. You ask Old Bertha over there what we do to people who try to get away."

The creaking started up again, and she lifted her head to find a woman sitting in a rocking chair by the stove. She didn't look like the rest of them. She had thick, dark hair that puffed out in all directions. Her nose was hooked with a large lump in the bridge. It was too large for her face, which had the texture of beef jerky. Her mouth was little more than a slit beneath that massive nose.

The old woman stopped rocking and stared at Chandra with sunken eyes. Her expression was one of resignation. *Was she being held against her will, too?*

She got up and approached the bed, stopping just above Chandra's head. The woman opened her mouth to reveal the raw, infected stump where her tongue had once been. Then she retreated back to the rocking chair.

The cook motioned to the children sitting on the couch to leave the room. When they shuffled off to another part of the house, he approached the bed again and glared at her. "You know why we brought you here?" he asked.

The most Chandra could do was jerk her head back and forth. The fear that snaked its way down her spine now radiated across her entire body. It reverberated like a palsy across her being.

"You're a cockroach. And like all cockroaches, you have to be exterminated."

The word "exterminated" wormed into her brain and festered there. The Nazis used that word. This man and his kin, most likely inbred to keep their line pure, were monsters, forged in the same fire as Nazis. Pity flickered through her mind for a moment. She *should* pity them, but the unparalleled hatred that glowed in the man's silvery blue eyes bore into her soul. She felt poisoned by it. A rage she'd never known possessed her. She struggled against her restraints so hard the ropes dug thick welts into her skin. The flesh twisted and wadded. Blood puddled just beneath the fibers. She wanted to break the bonds and rip him to shreds.

Her struggles seemed to please him. His bucktoothed mouth contorted into a smile. He stepped away from the bed and into the recesses of the house where the children had gone.

There was no way she could break free. The elderly woman rocked by the fire, afraid to intervene or uninterested in

Chandra's plight. The revolting vision of the old woman's severed tongue led Chandra to believe fear is what anchored her to the chair.

The cook emerged again, this time holding a long, black fireplace poker. The sight sent Chandra's stomach into flips. He walked to the stove, shoved open the thick metal door, and put the poker against the red-orange embers. He studied it as it heated, tilting his head from side to side like a confused puppy.

Chandra's muscles strained, all of them together, and when he removed the glowing poker from the flame, she jerked against the ropes so hard, the fibers worked their way into the layers of skin. Her wrists burned.

The man crossed the room in a couple of steps and studied Chandra's body. He decided on a spot—her right cheek—and pressed the glowing tip of the poker against the flesh. A screaming, angry pain ripped through her body, and the ropes dug deeper into the skin. The charcoal smell of her own burning skin made her gag, and a lump of vomit crept its way into her throat. She swallowed it down, panting and heaving. Her body shuddered and convulsed. She couldn't keep her feet still. They twitched of their own volition.

Tears spilled from the corners of her eyes. Her cheek throbbed, and she felt the delicate tissues peel back to a raw, bloody patch. Through tears, she watched the expressionless blur of a head that waved side to side in silent examination. She batted her eyes, and the tears cleared away. The old woman by the fire rocked, but she stared into the stove's flames.

She closed her eyes and blocked out her captor, escaping into herself and willing herself out of this place. She willed herself to be at the table with Nana and Aunt Gloria, and maybe even Antonio if only she could be sure she meant more to him than the occasional hookup. She thought of holidays past, gathered around the table, back when Mama was alive, savoring the succulent turkey, relishing the sage and celery of the dressing, and basking in the warm glow of familial love.

There'd been years when she was away, and it'd been a different kind of familial love then. For a few years, she was stationed in Heidelberg. Family had been her fellow soldiers and some friendly locals who regaled them with legends from the birthplace of Yuletide lore. On leave one December, she'd even made the long trek to Graz, Austria, for Krampusnacht.

It had been like taking a peek into Hell itself. Horned, long-tongued demons danced about, illuminated by fire. The ordeal was fascinating, even if she wasn't particularly frightened by it.

After the festivities, she'd spent the evening in a tiny pub, enjoying a heavy beer and chatting with a slight, bespectacled Austrian man. He spoke fluent German, but his English was hardly conversational, so she was able to practice the German she'd picked up in Heidelberg.

He sipped a wheat-colored beer and smirked about the parade. "A tourist trap, because people are curious. They want to know about our traditions, but there's one even more frightening. No one ever celebrates her. Almost no one even speaks of her."

Chandra had leaned in. "Tell me about her."

He swallowed his beer, and the glow of his cheek faded to stone-white. "When I was a kid, Mother warned us that if we told lies, Frau Perchta would come and punish us." His tone was severe, and the happy-go-lucky demeanor he'd worn throughout the evening dissipated into a sort of depression.

Chandra ribbed him about it. "You sound so serious. Aren't those just stories?"

He looked over his glasses at her and frowned. "To some, they are stories." Here, he took a long drink. "But to me, they're all too real. I've *seen* her."

Chandra pressed her lips together to stop herself from laughing. "You can't be serious," she'd said.

"I was about six or so. It was an honest mistake. I'd broken Mother's favorite vase, one she'd picked up on holiday in Pienza. I told her Gerta, my sister, broke it. She believed me. Gerta got punished for it, and I didn't think much about it until around Christmastime. You see, Perchta gets her power in the weeks after Christmas. One night, maybe a week or so after Christmas, I was asleep, and there was a screeching sound coming from my window. My eyes opened wide, and I went to the window to see what it was. On the other side, I saw a wrinkly woman with a long, hooked nose and sharp fingernails scratching at the glass. Her eyes were enflamed with anger. I knew instantly it was Perchta coming to make things right. I ran right up to my parents' room, screaming. I confessed everything then and there. I told them I'd broken the vase and lied about it, and I begged them not to let the angry old lady get me and take me away." He smiled after this and chuckled a little. "Yes, I can see why you'd think that's a silly story, but I promise it's true."

Her mental escape was interrupted by footsteps approaching the bed again. This time, the blonde hostess from the restaurant stood over her. She held a thick, wooden paddle in her right hand. Her eyes were flat and emotionless as she raised the paddle up and brought it down on Chandra's belly. The pain cracked through her before she could even prepare herself for impact. All of the air puffed from her chest, and she wheezed trying to breathe. She pressed her eyes closed again, hoping her attacker would assume she'd lost consciousness, but another crack came down on her shoulder. This time, there was a snap, but she didn't dare cry out.

She steeled herself against another strike, but it never came. Footsteps retreated. All she could hear was the crackling of the fire and the *thump-thump, thump-thump* of the rocking chair against the floor.

Her eyes popped open, and she turned to the woman by the fire. She tried a couple of times to breathe, but the pain in her ribs kept her inhalations shallow.

"You've. Got. You've got to. Help. Me."

The woman continued to stare into the fire.

"Help."

The woman turned slightly. The fire glow illuminated her hooked nose. The realization struck Chandra out of the blue. She couldn't believe it hadn't occurred to her before, but the Austrian man's story no longer seemed stupid. Perchta was here.

"They're. Lying. To you," Chandra puffed out, the pain wracking her.

The woman's head turned, and for the first time, Chandra saw her eyes. They burned with anger.

"You have to let me out."

She stopped rocking and stood, steadying herself against the chair. She moved like a ghost to the bedside and hovered over Chandra's face. The old woman's wrinkles and jowls were prominent from this bottom-up vantage point. Her hair frizzed everywhere.

Chandra scanned her mind for the right words. "They did that to you. They cut out your tongue, didn't they? They don't want you to tell the truth. They're keeping me here because they hate black people. They silenced you because they hate women like you."

The words dumped out of her mouth, rapid-fire, to find something, anything, that would coerce the old woman to assist. A figure darkened the doorway. The man was back with the hunting knife, the blonde woman following closely on his heels. They were done playing with her.

She nearly screamed out, her pleas turning to gibberish as sobs burst from her heaving chest. The man and his knife were at the bedside. The whites of his eyes completely encircled his irises. Blood dripped now from the ropes as she pulled all of her weight against them. She felt her bottom lift from the saggy mattress. The knife glowed in the firelight as he lifted it.

An explosion made her heart jump. Flames leapt from the stove. Chandra lurched forward, howling in pain at the wounds on her wrists. The knife clanked against the floor. She watched the old woman's profile against the flames roaring from the stove.

The ropes that held Chandra in place loosened, and she felt them fall away. The woman frowned and spread out an arm, indicating the window with a pointed fingernail.

"I don't know if I can move," Chandra said.

The woman closed her eyes, and the stabbing, mind-wracking pain in her ribs eased to a heavy ache. Her breaths came in painful bursts, but it felt as if the worst of the pain flittered away.

Chandra struggled to her feet. The wounds that encircled her wrists throbbed.

The short-order cook and his blonde wife/sister approached again, even as the flames jumped and popped behind them, and Chandra's heart clogged in her throat. The old woman turned to face them like a warrior preparing for battle.

She held up an arm in a protective, motherly gesture as the blond people charged forward. The flames roared over the metal in a burning-hot display of anger. The two blonds stumbled backward. The hostess shrieked and held an arm over her head.

Chandra edged backward until she hit the window with her rear. She turned the metal lock and shoved open the wooden frame until the frigid chill worked its way inside, battling the flames rising up around the stove. There was a flash and another explosion that sent the blond people running into the home in search of safety.

Chandra threw a leg over the windowsill, and hesitated at the dizzying sight of the ground below. The approaching flames made the decision for her, and she dropped a dozen feet until her boots hit the snowbank below. A jagged pain ripped through her ribcage on impact. The lower half of her body became mired in the freezing snow, but she marched forward, into the blue blanket, struggling against the thick powder toward the faint lights beyond the trees.

She turned once and saw a wall of flames engulf the wooden home. Smoke billowed from the windows as the fire licked the roof.

A twinge of guilt overcame her, and she fought the urge to go back and rescue Perchta. The desire to survive won out, and she marched on into the pine forest, shallow breaths fogging in the cold. Each step sent pain ripping down the front of her body. Her legs wobbled and burned. She put her hands on her knees and sucked in a hot, painful breath. Red blobs splatted against the blue-white snow, and she straightened herself. She didn't know how bad it was, but she knew if she didn't keep moving, she'd never make it out of the woods to find help.

Trees hovered close, hanging thick with snow. Her boots crunched against the frigid ground as she waded along, arms windmilling to keep herself upright. Her breath was jagged and sporadic, plagued by the persistent ache in her ribs and her shoulder.

The sky had cleared, and above the sagging branches, stars flickered blue and white against the stark blackness of night. The blanket of night made her feel anything but safe. The nagging sensation that they were coming made her ears perk.

She wobbled ahead faster. It couldn't have been more than a quarter of a mile to the lights.

Night animals, swathed in black, hooted and screeched. A flutter nearly made her scream out. An owl, she reasoned, swooping down to capture a mouse.

The low, dull hum of the highway rose up as she approached the lights, and the sight of the motor lodge and restaurant made her pick up the pace. Her rig might even be there, she thought, as streams of fog puffed from her mouth. She envisioned pulling the rig out of the lot. She might need an overnight in the hospital to get checked out, and then she could haul ass for Atlanta.

The forest grew darker, and a whoosh of icy air ripped through her and froze her down to her skeleton. Thick plumes fanned from her mouth as she watched the trees wave in this strange wind.

Shadows played against the lights, now only a few hundred feet ahead. A branch crashed down just behind her, and she halted, rigid in her fear. Her breath huffed sporadically, liquid rattling in her throat.

Black wings flapped above her, blowing her hair in all directions. She fell to her knees and covered her head with her arms, but the beast was upon her. She watched the hair-covered hooves touch down, and the awful face, twisted in a sort of delighted hatred, wormed its way in front of her as she cowered. Its yellow eyes glowed, and its fangs jutted, ready to rip flesh. It wanted her to witness her own demise. The hot, putrid breath fogged in her face as it bore its fangs. It went first for the charred, blackened flesh that the poker had already cooked. The sharp pain of tissue and muscle rip-ping away from the bone sent her into a glacial terror. The shock of imminent death drove her deeper into the snowbank, and she knew then why you should never stop in the Pine Barrens.

Left in a Manger

Larry Hoy

Left in a manger
Too young to fight back
The little babe meat
   Whimpered and wept

The wolves they drew close
Brought by the sound
A more tasty morsel

Was not to be found

The cattle are lowing
Shuffling away
Trading their life
For the one in the hay

A lick, just a taste
Be sure that it's fresh
Bite deep and rip
The hunger is less

Blood soaks the straw
Gone is the lamb
Just another night
In Deathlehem

NAUGHTY

Steven Van Patten

"Not my best work," Murphy said as he stared at the Christmas tree. Of course, this tree wasn't so much a festive decoration as it was bait.

Murphy stepped out of the beige living room into the near-by light blue dining room and took a seat in a chair in the furthest corner. He didn't want "Santa" to see him until it was too late. As the lights from the substandard tree blinked and pulsed, they cast changing shadows and colors over the plate of cookies and the glass of milk sitting on the dining room table some thirty feet away.

At 11:37 p.m., he checked the gun, releasing and then slapping the nine-millimeter's clip back in before slipping the firearm back into his waistband. Not that he expected a gun to be useful under the circumstances. It wouldn't be the first option, that's for sure.

Around midnight he craved a cup of coffee, but thought better of it. No sense in giving away his position now. Besides, he'd only end up having to piss.

It wasn't until 12:39 a.m. that he heard the first jingle of sleigh bells. Then something large inexplicably began moving in the living room, blocking the light from the Christmas tree from spilling into the dining room. There was a series of *thuds*. Murphy could only assume that Santa was placing the presents.

Santa's footsteps were heavy as he walked away from the tree towards the dining room table and the cookies. He stopped and stared at them for a moment before turning his head toward the staircase that led to the bedroom. Murphy took note of that before he finally interrupted.

"What's the matter, Santa? You don't like oatmeal raisin?"

The jolly old man turned and faced Murphy. "Ho, Ho, Ho! You know the rules, little boy! Now I have to take the TV back!"

"Fuck you and your TV! I want to know why you fucked my wife?"

"Ho, Ho, Ho! I have fucked a lot of people's wives. If you're referring to the lady of this house, well, she was new and tasty! She was awesome! Is she not home? Are you the husband? You're not mad at ol' St. Nick, are you?"

"Cut the shit, asshole! You're not Santa Claus, and you're not some philanthropist that's also a locksmith. You're an incubus."

Santa shot him a wry smirk. "Figured that out all by yourself, huh? Are you some kind of demon expert? Ho, Ho, Ho?"

"Well, I had nearly two years to become one," Murphy answered. "I guess I should have been more concerned when I first moved my family here and the neighbors were all telling me about Shady Hills' personal Santa Claus. They said they didn't know who it was or where he came from, but he'd show up like magic and leave all sorts of expensive gifts, especially for the less fortunate of the town."

"Ho, Ho, Ho, but there are rules!" Santa dragged one of the chairs out from under the dining room table and sat down. For a demon whose secret was out, his mood was rather cavalier. "On Christmas Eve, your whole family should be in bed before midnight, or you get nothing!"

"And since I had moved here with my wife and kids to a six-figure job in the middle of August, none of this was immediately relevant. Our first Christmas came and went, and we didn't see you."

"You and the wife also had a dinner party, if I remember correctly," Santa added. "Your last guest didn't leave until after one a.m. Ho, Ho, Ho!"

"And clearly you had other houses to go to. About six months later, I noticed the string of miscarriages at the hospital, but I didn't put it together because, like I said, you hadn't come here. But I did find it odd that I had to run insurance paperwork for thirteen stillborn babies within the timeframe of a month for such a small population."

"That's right. You were hired to be the new hospital administrator." Santa finally started eating the cookies, seemingly out of boredom.

"*Was*, as in past tense," said Murphy. "I got laid off that June. Wife's a social worker, so she doesn't bring in much. Unemployment insurance was a joke. It didn't take long for us to become financially strapped."

"Well, this is a mighty big house. Ho, Ho, Ho!"

"Pam and I were arguing all the time. 'Why did we move here?' 'Why can't we leave?' Blah, blah, blah. So, when my mother took ill, I took the easy way out that Christmas. I left for Nebraska to go be with her, knowing that now that my family qualified as 'less fortunate' the Christmas gifts would be taken care of by this omniscient neighborhood Santa I had been told about."

"And I did. I even left you a new electric razor because that last piece of shit of yours had dulled out. And believe it when I tell you, I know something about trimming beards! Ho, Ho, Ho!" Santa placed a red-gloved hand over his belly and laughed.

"Yes, you also left me with resentful kids." Murphy's eyes narrowed at the wave. "All those toys and video game systems you gave them somehow diminished me in their eyes. And Pam, of course, was extra cold. I'm not just talking about her demeanor. I'm talking about the first time we had sex after Christmas."

"Was she a little reserved? Unresponsive? Ho, ho, ho!"

"No! I mean her vagina was cold!"

"A potential side-effect. Ho, ho, ho! Doesn't happen to everyone," Santa explained.

"I feel so much better knowing that after you knocked my wife up," Murphy said.

"The babies are always stillborn," Santa said. "And at least I didn't leave you with another mouth to feed. Ho, ho, ho! Unfortunately, Santa never did like condoms!"

"You are not Santa!"

"Can I tell you another secret?"

"Sure."

Santa leaned in. "My powers, and I do have them, have restrictions as far as married women go. I mean, I picked this town because of all the single mothers. Every Christmas Eve, most of them are drunk or high on pills and expecting me to show up with an X-Box or the latest Lego set anyway. But here is the thing, Murphy! I can't seduce a married lady until her husband cheats on her first."

Murphy's eyes and Santa's smile widened simultaneously.

"I can see from the look on your face you didn't know that. I can see that you never thought your ongoing friends-with-benefits relationship with Heather was going to come with a price tag. And while you were back in Nebraska taking care of your mother, you stopped off to see Heather, didn't you? She probably greeted you at the door wearing something sexy. Your tongues were probably inside each other's mouths the second the front door slammed shut. And after you tore off her lingerie and got all up in her, you lay there all hugged up together. She went on and on about how much she missed you. Naturally, you made small talk, and she even asked how your wife and kids were doing, which almost took you out of the mood. But you got hard again. You fucked her again. You both came, and it was so good!"

A terrible quivering had begun in Murphy's stomach. Santa's description of the two hours he'd spent between the airport and his mother's house were spot on.

"Well, while you were with Heather, I was here. Now, what you need to understand is that as an incubus I need to tap a certain amount of sexual energy to sustain myself. In the past, I've tried keeping a few wives. But even with two or three women, I end up killing them. The strain is just too great. To spare myself the remorse of killing these beautiful creatures whose sweet spirit nectar I depend on, I spread the burden across the town. I have found that if I bed about thirteen or fourteen women every Christmas Eve, I'm good for the year. The best part is, none of the women die, and except for the miscarriages, no one's life is disrupted. I'm over a thousand years old, so I've amassed the wealth I need to afford enough video games, iPhones, Air Jordans, and designer jeans for everyone involved. And to keep it fair, if I get to a home and the woman has a faithful husband, but they're broke, I give them stuff anyway. That hasn't happened in a while, though."

Murphy pulled the gun from his waist and pointed it at Santa. "Don't you want to hear the rest?" Santa asked.

"The rest of what?" He glanced down to make sure the safety was off. "You're a demon, some sick fucking demon and I have to send you back to hell."

"You still don't know the full story. While I have the power to seduce, I am not a rapist. Your wife gave herself to me willingly. They all come willingly. In fact, she came downstairs as I was putting down the presents. She was wearing a nightshirt and panties. I told her she was being a bad girl by leaving her bedroom before I had left. She asked if I was going to spank her. She was half-joking, but I took her up on it. I surprised her with my speed and strength as I closed the distance between us and put her over my bended knee and gave her tight little ass three good whacks."

Santa glanced at the gun, then back at Murphy's face. Murphy could see he was enjoying this.

"Then I let her go, but it was done. She had become excited. I could smell it building up in her. Her heart raced as I came close again, close enough to rub her arm and whisper in her ear. I told her that I am but a weary traveler, but I bring tidings of great joy. Had you been a faithful husband, my words would have meant nothing. More than likely, she would have turned around and gone back to her bedroom. But my words went right through her. In her ear and straight to the tip of her clitoris."

Santa banged his fist on the dining room table as if he were cheering himself on, causing Murphy to jump and the plate of cookies to rattle. "She led me right here and yanked her panties off. I took her doggie style, right here on this table."

Murphy heard the gun go off, but he was only dimly aware he'd pulled the trigger. Santa blinked hard as his body jolted back. A circular bloodstain formed over his midsection.

"You shouldn't have done that," Santa said after a moment. He was in pain, but his eyes defied any sense of real worry.

"Why not, fucker?" Murphy asked.

"Because some people are very protective of me."

"Like who?"

"Like Pam, your wife."

The sound of jangling house keys was immediately followed by the front door swinging open. Pam was wearing a long, black wool coat and bright red scarf. "Was that a gunshot? What the hell is going on in this house?"

"Short version, I shot Santa here while he was dropping off presents."

Pam's eyes widened as she walked up to them; she made brief eye contact with her husband before she turned and fell on one knee next to Santa and looked him over. "How dare you!"

"How dare I? You fucked a demon! If that's not grounds for divorce—"

"Really? You're going to go there, 'Sleepless in Nebraska'?" Pam fell to Santa's side and took his hand. "Don't worry, honey, I'm going to take care of you."

"You're going to take care of him?" a livid Murphy repeated. "Where are our kids?"

"The kids are still at my mother's, what do you think? I wasn't going to put them through two unnecessary drives in one night!"

Santa's eyes opened. "Pam?" He sounded weak, much weaker than he had earlier.

Staring at the gunshot wound, Pam put a hand on Santa's shoulder. "Santa, I'm so sorry I wasn't here. This idiot husband of mine tricked my own mother into telling me that she was sick. The lying sack of shit actually told her my immortal soul is in danger. But I'm here now, sweetie."

"Your immortal soul is in danger, you dumb whore!" Murphy shouted. "I have a good mind to shoot him again!"

"You better not!"

Santa took Pam's hand. "Hey, Sweetheart. Ho, ho, ho. I'm glad you're here. There wasn't enough space under the tree for one of your gifts. I wanted to hand it to you personally. Just reach under my belt."

"Forget that now, Santa! You're hurt, I need to get you upstairs!"

"Get him upstairs? Have you lost your mind?"

"Before you do, reach under my belt."

Pam did as she was told, ignored the blood and slipped her right hand under the large black belt buckle, expecting to find something hard and ready. She wasn't disappointed.

"You bitch! Even now, you're going to give him a handjob? With me standing right here?"

"Not exactly," she answered as she pulled her hand out of Santa's trousers and produced a snub-nosed .38 caliber handgun. In one fluid motion, she aimed and fired.

The space where Murphy's left shoulder connected to the rest of his body erupted with a hot and piercing pain as he felt himself being pushed backward. His gun and his head hit the floor roughly three seconds apart from one another. The gun bounced and slid out of reach as he found himself having to fight to stay conscious. The last words he heard before he blacked out were: "Pam, you have to help me heal.

I still have deliveries."

"I know, honey. I know."

"We have to save Christmas! Ho, ho, ho!"

Minutes later, Murphy came to. His shoulder was still on fire, and the upper third of his shirt was matted in blood. He forced himself to sit up only to see that both Santa and Pam were gone. That's when he noticed the rhythmic thumping that seemed to be coming from upstairs. Initially, he couldn't imagine what was causing the noise, but it became obvious once he stood up and saw a trail of clothes strewn across the house. A large pair of shiny black boots next to Pam's much smaller red snow boots on the kitchen floor. Santa's red, white, and blood-stained jacket next to her black one on the living room couch. A large black belt and red and white pants next to a pair of women's Levi's on the stairs that led to the bedrooms.

At the foot of the stairs, he could hear them.

"Ho! Ho! Ho!"

"Yes!"

"Ho! HO! HO!"

"That's it! Right there! Take it!"

"You're doing it, Pam! The wound is nearly closed! HO! HO! HO!"

"That's good, baby! Now, go harder!"

"HO! HO! HO!"

"Give it to meeee…"

Murphy turned back around and retrieved the gun. "I hope you two assholes are having a good time because now you're both fucking dead! And there's not a court in the country that would convict me!"

He finally saw the underwear pile—a white lace bra and matching panties next to white boxer briefs and a white XXXL t-shirt—when he got to the top of the stairs. He cocked the hammer of his gun and charged the bedroom door and slammed into it full force. The door swung open, and splinters flew as the doorframe gave way.

"AHHHHH!"

He screamed as he emptied fifteen rounds into what turned out to be an empty bed. Each of the four pillows had erupted into a cloud of feathers in the onslaught.

"You've been a very bad boy, Murphy!"

The voice had come from behind him. He turned and saw a naked, well-endowed, and gleaming Santa towering over him. Pam, also naked, was slung over his right shoulder, her bare ass next to his head. It was as if sex with Pam had made Santa taller and stronger. He thought to hit Santa with the empty gun, only to have a very meaty hand suddenly grip his throat hard enough for him to gag.

"No more Christmas for you!"

It was the second time this evening that Murphy found himself fighting, and failing, to stay conscious. Only this time, as he felt the vertebrae in his neck giving way, it dawned on him that he wouldn't be coming back this time.

Santa watched until all the light left Murphy's eyes, then dropped him on the floor. Then he stepped over Murphy's body and gently placed Pam on the damaged bed and covered her with a single sheet. She wasn't dead, but she was close. The sexual energy she had expended to help him had all but drained her. He silently promised to make sure her next Christmas would be fantastic, if she lived.

Stepping over Murphy's corpse again, Santa walked through the house, found his clothes, and got dressed. Five minutes later, he'd be gone. The night was young by his standards, and there was still much to do.

S*EQUEL

DG Critchley

had shut off the radio, which was nothing but Christmas music anyway, and was just about to start my research when the phone rang. Normally when I'm about to start working, I'll let it go the answering machine, but I was expecting a call from my new literary agent. One of the great advantages of currently having the best-selling horror novel in America is that the stink of money makes the publisher pay attention to the cash cow. And Harry may have been new to being my representative but he was an old-school literary agent and a champion at fawning over his two-legged revenue streams.

I sighed to myself and grabbed the phone. "Merry Christmas, Harry."

Harry had a set routine, and caller ID had not altered his routine. "It's me, Harry. How's America's favorite gore-meister?"

"I don't know, Harry. I'll ask Stephen King next time I see him." Harry asked the same question every time and I answered it the same way every time. I suspect Harry used the verbal foreplay to justify his percentage.

I looked out the window past rows of baby Christmas trees. A hawk was soaring over the Manuxet River in the distance. It was late December, but the weather had been unseasonably mild. The ground was still soft and the river clear of ice. Not very Christmas-like, but it beat shoveling snow. I decided to forego the niceties before Harry's chatter completely killed my creative mood.

"Harry, *Blood Keeper* is a bestseller and I love that fact. But it's only one book and if my soon-to-be ex-wife Melissa has her way, I don't know if I'll see another royalty check before the bank decides I can't pay the mortgage on this farm." Buying an old dairy farm and converting it to a Christmas tree farm was my idea. In another 2–3 years, it would be a revenue source in case the book thing faltered. Ironically, I myself had not put up a Christmas tree this year.

I heard Harry light a wooden match on his thumb and start a cigar. That was a good sign. "That's why I'm calling. You've lived in Massachusetts for five years, correct?"

"Yes," I said, beginning to feel the vein in my forehead start to throb. I looked out the window again and decided it wasn't a hawk, but an eagle. "We've been over this, I've lived in Pentucket for five years, but I married Melissa in California. Dean, my former agent, felt that getting married in a community property state gave Melissa a claim for half the royalties in spite of the prenup agreement."

He exhaled into the phone. I suspected nobody borrowed Harry's phone without a hazmat suit. "Well, I bounced it off the legal department and they say Dean was whistling Dixie. Massachusetts divorce law applies. They're not divorce law specialists, but they say you're fine at first glance. Under Mass law, you should get about two-thirds of the assets as the higher wage earner. And that's not factoring in that Melissa ran off with Dean—she committed adultery and took off. A judge is going to take that into consideration."

I smiled. Harry wasn't telling me anything my divorce attorney hadn't told me. I was just making sure everyone knew how deeply troubled I was by her cleaning out the joint checking account and taking off with my agent.

"Yes, my divorce lawyer can't locate them to serve the divorce papers, so I'm suing for divorce by abandonment and hoping for a default settlement. I still think there's something fishy—Dean was a lot of things, but greed was his most endearing trait. I can't imagine he'd walk away from his percentage of *Blood Keeper*."

I could imagine Harry squinting at his notes. If it had percentages or dollar signs, Harry could remember every detail. Everything else was a little hit or miss. "We'll take his percentage out of the checks and put it in a holding account. When he reappears, it'll be sitting there waiting for him. When he asks for it, we'll have the boys in legal take it to a judge and have him declared in breach of contract. If he doesn't show up in a couple of years, you have him declared legally dead. Either way, you get his 15% back."

"Harry, you've given me the best Christmas present. Now I feel like I can get back to actually writing something instead of this business crap. And although I'm sure he'll show up when the money runs out, I love the idea of having Dean declared dead."

Harry was not a fan of horror or my odd sense of humor. "Listen, as much as I hate to interrupt your really creepy musings, the VP wants to know how your next book is doing and when can he have a rough concept to start the marketing people thinking?"

I paused. "Well, I haven't got the final details in place quite yet, but the story will be about a serial killer with an overdeveloped sense of irony. He tortures his victims, but he kills them by removing a body part that he finds appropriately humorous. So, when he kills an alcoholic, he cuts out the liver, when he kills a model, he skins her face off alive."

The silence on the other end was because Harry really didn't like anything about horror but the commission.

I patiently tried to explain. "It's an experiment in seeing how far black humor can go before it de-evolves back into true horror."

Harry was now out of his comfort zone and we both knew it. "That sounds like something the marketing department would come up with."

"So give it to them as a head start. Tell them it's an early Christmas present. I should have a finished draft in a few days," I said, looking at the clock.

"Well get back to work." It was getting close to Harry's lunchtime and the bartender worried if he was late.

"That's the plan. Thanks, Harry, and Merry Christmas." I hung up the phone. Time, happy hour, and Harry's 15% waited for no man.

I strolled over to the gurney where the backstabbing excuse for my former literary agent lay bound and gagged. The little beads of sweat were beginning to mess up his expensive coif, and the fear in his eyes was great enough to overwhelm the Botox treatments. Dean was beginning to suspect that I was not pleased with being cuckolded and I assume that the gag was the only thing preventing the weasel from begging for his life.

"Dean, old buddy, I'd thank you in the foreword for the inspiration you're about to provide, but I technically have not seen you since you ran off with Melissa, so that would be awkward to explain. So, please excuse the snub—it's nothing personal."

I looked down at him. "Frankly, I'm having trouble with this part. You see, the concept requires something ironic to be removed surgically, and since we both know you don't have a heart, that kills my first choice, so to speak."

Dean didn't seem to notice the clever pun, but then again, he did seem somewhat distracted by the shiny row of surgical instruments on the tray near his head.

"Dean, old pal, I'm stymied. My second choice would be to castrate you since your dick is what got you into this mess. But that's only ironic to me. It doesn't scream "agent" like it should to my adoring readers. I mean, Melissa was easy— she broke my heart." I stepped aside to give Dean a clear view of the jar holding the exorcised part of my dear, late wife.

Dean's eyes widened far beyond what I'm sure his plastic surgeon would recommend and a muffled shriek managed to work itself out through the gag. That was useful—I jotted down a note to include that part as Dean began to thrash beneath his restraints. Of course, it would do him no good; the restraints were designed to hold a far stronger, albeit equally involuntary, participant in my anesthesia-free "literary research."

I'm not sure if the sweat rolling down his ashen face was getting into his eyes or if he was weeping. It would be a moot point momentarily. He would be weeping, and shrieking, and begging for a quick death that would not be coming.

I looked out the window, savoring the muffled noises. I was beginning to think it wasn't a hawk or an eagle, but rather a buzzard. That meant I needed to bury Melissa deeper before the ground froze. I'd fix that in a few days when I finished with Dean.

"Dean old buddy, please consider this your official termination notice. You have however inspired me. As my literary agent, you're entitled to 15% of *Blood Keeper*. But, since you violated my trust, I'm going to reclaim that commission."

Fear clouded comprehension in his eyes, and unless I missed my guess, the king of power lunches was in the process of soiling himself.

"Dean, here's a fascinating little factoid. The body mass of a man of average weight and height such as yourself is composed of, among other things, 12% fat, 45% muscle, and more importantly, 15% skeleton."

Dean suddenly realized how I planned to get my 15%, and the muffled mewling sounds were truly impressive. I just hoped I could translate the glorious noises into appropriate prose.

I picked up a bone saw.

Rudolf, the Gold-Nosed Butcher

Stuart R. West

"Tell me again, Zayde. Tell me the story of Rudolf." Awake and sugar-wired, David tugged the blanket up to his chin. He settled into bed to await the tale, one of which he never tired.

His grandpa, on the other hand, looked sleepy. He rubbed his bearded chin as his eyes narrowed. The robe over his arm drooped, exposing a six-digit number, one which followed

David's thoughts like a shadow. "David, how many times have I told you this tale?"

"I dunno. A zillion? Please, Zayde?"

"Very well." His grandpa cleared his throat, the way he always did before he told a story. Honestly, David wondered why Grandpa had ever told him the tale in the first place. While David was no baby, the story was scary. Probably why Grandpa'd warned him not to tell his parents about it. "It'll be our little secret," he'd told David with a wink. But since David's parents were stuck at the Denver airport, the ice storm locking down half the country, what they didn't know wouldn't hurt them.

The menorah's candlelight glowed in Zayde's eyes, active and watery looking. "A long time ago, in an awful, awful place where our people were sent to die, there—"

"Why?"

"Excuse me?" Grandpa sat up, folded his hands over his cane. His beard draped over the cane's silver lion's head, giving it an old mane.

"Why were our people sent to the camps to die?" Maybe it was a silly question, one better suited for little kids. One David had never asked before but had never stopped wondering about since Grandpa started telling the story.

"David, that's—that's not a simple thing to answer. People have debated it since it happened. But I suppose it's because of hate. Hatred of…" Grandpa closed his eyes. His lids twitched as if his eyeballs were knocking to get out. "The Nazis hated us because we were different. They didn't understand us, were afraid of us. Prejudice. Do you know what that means, David?"

"Sure." *Not really.* But David wasn't going to ask.

Grandpa chuckled, dry and scratchy as sandpaper. "Of course you do, of course you do." He folded back into the chair, his bony knees cracking. "When I was just a boy, even younger than you—" He pointed the tip of the cane toward David. "—I was a prisoner in one of these hellish camps. I'd long lost my family and was alone. But the Nazis... They kept me around. They made me their running boy. I believe I amused them. All but one of them...the *worst.*" Grandpa lowered his voice, but his bushy eyebrows climbed high. "His proper first name was Rudolf. I never knew his last name, didn't care to... But around the camp, Rudolf was known as the Gold Butcher."

David shuddered, clenching the blanket tighter and making sure as little of his skin was exposed. Just because he didn't believe—not really—in the legend of the Gold Butcher didn't mean his imagination didn't bully him.

"The Gold Butcher was a terrible sight. Gussied up in his tight, grey uniform, he'd parade around the campgrounds with his razor-sharp chin held high like some kind of damned show horse. All six-foot-four of him. And you never wanted to look him in the eye, David. If he caught your gaze, it's said he swallowed your soul whole. Added it to the hundreds of Jews that he'd already slaughtered. He enjoyed his torturing and killing, too, more so than the beloved gold he hoarded. He was the worst of the many monsters at the camp. The stories I could tell you... Well... You could see the evil in his eyes. You could *feel* it. Colder than the ice outside." Grandpa tapped the window with his cane, the panes of which were glazed over like fancy cupcakes.

"But the worst thing about how Rudolf looked, David, you know what that was?"

David's bedspread traveled up to his nose, the blanket taut as a stretched rubber band. When he nodded, the bedsprings squeaked. "His gold nose."

"That's right, David. His gold nose. You remember how he came upon his gold nose?"

This time David couldn't find his voice. Or it had abandoned him. He nodded, forcing a dry swallow.

"One of the prisoners, one of the Butcher's victims. As a last act of defiance, he bit off the Nazi's nose and spat it back at him." Grandpa's eyes closed and he shuddered. "I hate to think what the Butcher did to that man."

The silence hung over them like the worst humidity. Finally, David mustered the courage to speak. "Did you see that happen, Grandpa? I mean, when the Butcher got his nose chewed off?"

"No. No, I didn't. But I tell you, little one, it's the truth, hand to God." He raised his hand. "After that day, the Butcher wore a gold-plated nosepiece attached to his face by what looked like four spider legs. It's said he fashioned the nosepiece from gold fillings he extracted from his victims' teeth. Used long, burning-hot pliers." Grandpa jabbed a hand out in jerky swordplay. "Snip, snip, snip!" He ended with a thunderclap of hands. His cane dropped.

David jumped. His tongue played with his one gold filling, made sure it held firmly in place.

"Anyway, history tells you how the story ended. The Nazis fell. We few survivors were liberated, but there wasn't much to celebrate. Not after all the death and nightmares of the camps." Grandpa turned his head and stared out the window, lost for a moment.

"But… What happened to the Gold Butcher?" David knew the answer; heck, he'd committed the tale to memory, not to mention his recurring nightmares. Just because he knew the outcome, though, didn't mean he had to like it. It seemed kinda dumb, really, hoping for Grandpa's story to change, for a new, happier ending. But sometimes it's okay—even for bigger kids—to hope for a happily-ever-after.

"Well… There's the problem, isn't it, David? They never

found the Butcher. To this day, there're still people hunting for him. But *we* know, don't we?" Again, Grandpa leaned forward. Darkness stole his eyes. Candle-lit shadows danced behind him, forming all sorts of ghouls and monsters. "Every Hanukkah, the Gold Butcher's ghost is resurrected. For eight days and nights—" Grandpa pointed toward the menorah. The candles burned much too quickly, nearly snubbed out now. "—the Butcher travels the world in his golden sleigh, pulled by the skeletons of the damned, his tortured victims. And he looks for young Jews to add to his collection of souls. He enters their homes, starts with their gold teeth—" He made a twisting gesture, a key unlocking a door. "—then throws their bodies into the fireplace. Then he opens his uniform, peels back the flesh—" Grandpa opened an imaginary door in his sweater. "—unfolds the ribs, one at a time—" Like peeling an invisible banana, Grandpa tweaked away his ribs, then threw his hands wide. "—then pulls in the poor child's soul."

Outside, the wind howled, worse than a wolf caught in a trap. Snow flew in a cloud, twirled, a miniature tornado. Not quite done yet, the wind wheezed, reminding David of how his bubbe—his grandma—sounded before she'd died of pneumonia. Fingers of ice stretched from a tree limb and scratched at the window.

David didn't care how it looked. He yanked the bedspread over his head. "Why, Grandpa? Why does the Butcher want our souls?"

Grandpa hesitated, something he didn't often do. Usually, he had comments ready for everything. "I suppose it's because of hatred again, David. Just like in the camps. Prejudice."

"But… It's not real, right, Grandpa? You're just making stories up, right? Like the other kids' stories about Santa Claus?"

Grandpa's cane dropped. The rocking chair creaked when

he rose, but not as much as Grandpa himself. Quicker than David had seen him move, Grandpa hurried toward the bed and sat next to David. He cradled an arm around David; his hug was warm, but he smelled as weird as always.

"Oh... Of course I'm just making stories up. Never mind this crazy old man. I'm just set in my ways, telling ghost stories for the holidays. Remembering ones from my child-hood and passing them on."

"So... It never happened? None of it?"

Beneath David, Grandpa's arm stiffened. He stroked his beard, confused looking. "That's right, David. None of it hap-pened." Although David didn't buy it, not for a minute, espe-cially not with the way Zayde's voice made a quiet, little tick. The way it grew weak. Another adult lie. "The Butcher's just a made-up story. I'm sorry I frightened you. I didn't mean to. Now, I think I've kept you up past your bedtime. Hopefully, your parents will be home tomorrow, weather and God per-mitting." But he'd said it more like a question and stared out at the storm.

David glanced at the menorah. Only the tallest candle, the *shamash*, remained lit. Darkness crept into the room as surely as the Gold Butcher himself. "Grandpa?"

"Hm?"

"Can we relight the menorah?"

Grandpa wouldn't let him relight the menorah. To him, tradition meant everything, while David didn't understand half of the old traditions. But that night, David understood the threat of the Gold Butcher. Sure, deep down, he knew it couldn't be true, but that didn't matter. He believed in the Butcher enough to resurrect his Yoda night light, the one he hadn't used since he was a little boy.

It seemed like forever since Grandpa had gone to bed. Of course, David knew how time played tricks, especially at night, even forming dreams of not sleeping. But tonight was different. He knew he'd been awake the entire night, felt every second ticking to the beat of his heart.

Silently, he'd recited the three Hanukkah blessings, the *brachot*, several times. Then he did it again. He tossed and turned, rumpling up his sheets like the snow-covered landscape outside his window.

He stayed alert to the raging storm outside, listening and watching. Low-hanging branches dragged their ice-tipped fingers across the windows, *tap-tap-tapping* for David's attention. The Gold Butcher wanting to come in.

He meant to outlast the night. Wait for morning. Stay alert, on guard. What else could he do? He wouldn't just willingly let the Butcher swallow his soul.

In the night light's sour yellow glow, he stared at the menorah and considered sneaking downstairs to get replacement candles. He felt safer with them lit. But it was the eighth night, the final night of Hanukkah, the last night of the Gold Butcher's yearly appearance. Another couple of hours and he'd be safe for another year. He *could* make it. Surely it wasn't too long until daylight.

Right?

Sick of arguing with himself, he decided to get the candles. He kicked back the covers and got out of bed. In his closet, he unburied his slippers—the silly, childish, bear-faced ones he'd put away last year—and stuffed his feet into them. Like a good friend, they hugged his toes tight, a little too tight.

Outside his bedroom, on the landing, he paused, listening. The wind wailed, crying now. He knew snow fell silently, but he heard it anyway. Heard it twist and twirl and lash out angrily with frost-biting strength, like sand tossed up against the house in full buckets.

And, of course, he heard Zayde. His snores, the so-bad-David's-parents-complained-about-them snores. Tonight, though, he welcomed them. A little bit of comfort in this worst of nights.

His feet *shh-shh-shushed* across the floor, little secret whispers. At the top of the stairwell, he looked out through the foyer's two-floor window, a window so big and scary that it invited in all of the night's creatures. With the snow still falling, it seemed odd the landscape looked so brilliantly lit, so eerie in Winter's blue light.

His hand on the rail, David flew down the stairs. At the bottom, a cold wind sliced beneath the door and stabbed at his ankles. Gusts blew against the door, forming voices: *"Let me in... Let me in..."*

David raced for the kitchen. With a shaky hand, he flicked on the light. The sudden blast of illumination burned his eyes, temporarily blinding him. He made his way to the junk drawer and opened it, careful not to explore too quickly so he wouldn't cut his fingers on scissors or a razor blade. He found the box of candles, snagged the lighter next to it.

One hand clutching his survival gear to the chest, the other on the light switch, he froze.

Outside, in the night, in the distance, he heard something. A horrible sound.

Clack, click, clack, clickety-click-click...

It sounded like ice breaking slowly across a pond, or maybe an entire deck of cards attached to a bicycle's wheels, or dried husks of trees falling like dominos in a forest or...

But he knew exactly what it was.

Clack, clickety, clack, clickety-click-clack...

The sound of bones, skeletons, rattling against one another. The Gold Butcher's legion of the damned delivering their master to David's house.

Clack, click, clack!

The ruckus rose, so loud it shook the walls. Hanging pans swayed like pendulums. David leaned into the kitchen door's arch and clamped his hands over his ears. His chest throbbed as the skeletal army brought the Butcher closer. Closer, ever closer...

Click, clack...clackety...clack.

Their march stopped, the golden sleigh landed. David flipped off the kitchen light, cocking his head like a dog that had heard something would. Silence. A suffocating blanket of snow created a weighty silence.

Navigating his way around the dark kitchen, he found the cutting block of knives and withdrew the largest one. His heart banged inside his chest as he thought of being pulled inside the Butcher's ribcage. He sucked in a deep breath, sought out hidden bravery. Felt his childish teddy bear slippers hugging his feet and lost hope.

His breath still captured, he listened. A large branch cracked beneath the weight of ice. At least he hoped it was a tree branch.

As his breath slowly slipped out, something tromped outside the front door. Onto the stoop. Another tromp. Boots, no doubt about it. Heavy, Nazi boots muffled by the snow. The Butcher's boots, he knew it, just knew it.

Oh my God, he's gonna eat my soul!

The knob on the front door rattled. Then clicked. The door swung open with a mouse's squeak, so tiny.

A gust of wind blew through the house, the freezing, dead breath of the Butcher. The knife shook in David's hands, growing heavier by the second. He didn't want to die in the dark, in the kitchen. By himself. His parents would never know what happened to him. He needed Zayde, he'd know what to do.

He just had to get past the Butcher and up the stairs.

He realized he could go the other way. The long way. Into the den, around the stairs, through the family room, and then up.

On tiptoes, David moved into the hallway. The waxed floor nearly yanked one slippered foot from beneath him. He staggered against the wall. Uncle Chet's photo slid off its hook. David pinned it to the wall with his shoulder to keep it from crashing to the floor. Carefully, he reached up, took the picture in hand, and set it down on a side-table.

Down the hall, the Gold-Nosed Butcher stood in front of the open door, silent as death. David gasped. Snow dust whirled behind the dark figure. Winter's creepy blue glow outlined the intruder's body: the peaked cap; the form-fitting, waist-length tunic; the trousers flaring up before being tucked into jackboots. He stood at quiet military attention. Unmoving. Looking at David. Or at least David thought he was looking at him. He couldn't see his eyes, his face, and was thankful for small favors.

David withheld a scream, turned. Tore into the den. His slippers slapped against his heels. His heart filled with pain, beat with panic. His knife gripped firmly in both hands, he let it lead him. Ready to stab it into the heart of the beast, even though he knew the beast had no heart.

Into the family room, David leaped. Something snapped at his back. Knife up, he whirled. Heat flushed him. Flames cracked from the open fireplace. By forgetting to put out the burning fire, Grandpa had made the beast's job easier.

Behind him, David heard two quick steps and a boot slap down. He turned to face his death. There stood the beast, taller than any adult David had ever encountered. An awful odor rolled off its rigid body, smelling like rotten fruit or vegetables on a hot summer day.

David gagged. Stepped back, closer to the fireplace. And screamed. *"Grandpa!"*

The Beast remained silent. And as it took two slow, jack-booted steps forward, David saw why. A grin stretched the Beast's mouth wide. Inside lay blackness; no teeth, no tongue, nothing but a dark so deep, David knew that many souls had drowned within. Above the gaping hole, the Beast's gold nosepiece reflected the fireplace's flames, bright and alive. Four taut, black strands held the false nose in place. But the eyes were the worst, worse than Grandpa had described.

The eyes glowed cold, pale. A blind man's eyes. They looked at David, yet saw nothing. Tiny, tortured faces swirled in the whites, swam into focus, then faded away as if they never existed.

With another scream, a nonsense cry birthed from his chest, David plunged the knife into the Butcher's heart. Or where its heart should have been. David withdrew the knife with ease and staggered back.

The monster's military jacket fell open. Its grin grew, impossibly so, too large for any human. Bones cracked. Flesh peeled away from the Butcher's face, his chest, drifting to the carpet like yellow ash. And still, it smiled.

As in Grandpa's tale, the Butcher played his exposed ribcage like a xylophone. Lovingly, he plucked one bone, then the next, opening all of them to expose a dark void.

"Farzeenish!"

Behind the beast, Grandpa's cane rose. He brought it down hard on top of the Butcher's peaked cap, then did it again. The cap slid sideways and fell. The last of the Butcher's facial flesh flaked away. Grandpa attacked again. A crack formed at the top of the skull. Like a breached dam, yellow liquid spurted from the hole.

The Butcher howled, tottered, uneasy on its feet. It turned to face Grandpa, raised its arms to attack.

Grandpa flipped his cane around, the silver lion-headed handle a much better weapon.

"Die, damn demon!" Grandpa swung like a muscled carny, drawing on surprising strength. "David, help me push it toward the fireplace!"

David gave the creature wide berth, arced around to join Grandpa, who drove the beast forward, his cane a cattle prod.

The cane struck the Butcher's jaw. The creature's skull whipped to the side, and the gold nosepiece flew off, bouncing across the floor. At a feeble run, Grandpa threw his shoulder into the beast. Winded, Grandpa lurched back, panting, bent over as if sick.

A coughing fit overtook Grandpa. He gripped his arm and toppled onto the coffee table. Magazines flew, remotes clacked. An ashtray spun off the table's edge. The table teetered before choosing a direction and spilling Grandpa onto the floor.

"*Zayde,*" David cried. But he couldn't worry about Grandpa, not now. Although weakened, the beast wasn't destroyed yet.

David plunged the knife upward. It glanced off the Butcher's jawbone, slid sideways, and nearly took David down with it. Using his momentum, David stumbled around in a tight circle. Upon return, he shoved the knife deep into the Butcher's dark chest. It hit something, something David couldn't see. But it felt deep and thick and wet and...

Oh God, I hope I'm not stabbing innocent souls.

Upon the knife's withdrawal, the beast bent over. Bones snapped and contracted inside the uniform. A vacuum of unknown origin sucked air through the chimney, drew the flames higher. As if yanked on invisible wires, the Butcher flew back into the fire. Its gloved claws, its jackboots scrabbled at the brick sides while the rest of the body roasted.

David kicked at the beast's fingers still clinging to the brick. The hands and boots released. The compacted creature burned, charred. The uniform smoldered, curled inward. Dark ash flew up the chimney.

On the hearth above, David grabbed a can of lighter fluid. He unleashed all of the can's contents onto what remained of the beast.

Whomph!

A flood of fire unrolled from the fireplace. David jumped back, the heat near unbearable. With an arm raised for protection, he inched toward the raging fire and slapped the safety doors shut with the fire poker.

David watched as a rainbow of liquid and bone and ugly things better not thought of melted. An awful smell filled the room. A scream, as high-pitched as the wind David had heard earlier, erupted from the thing. And David swore, swore on his future children's graves and hoped that day would never come, he saw two pale eyeballs glaring at him. Fighting the fire. Holding onto the last small part of its horrible unlife.

The beast as good as destroyed, David rushed to his grandpa and dropped to his knees.

On the floor, Grandpa tugged at his shirt. His mouth opened and closed like a grounded fish. One leg kicked, then the next, a dead man's jig. Blood-red veins swam into his eyes, matching the color of his face, and stared beyond David. In tears, David grabbed his zayde's cold, lifeless hand.

Thrack! Crack!

David whirled around at the sound. The fireplace doors had opened, one still slightly swinging. A jackboot stepped out from the dark hole, followed by a glove-covered hand. David wiped the tears from his eyes, unsure of his vision, his sanity. The top of the Butcher's cap appeared in the fireplace, slowly,

slowly lifting.

With a scream propelling him, David raced for the front door. He had to get out, had to escape, had to...

The door opened. From the yard to the stoop, a wall of skeletons blocked his escape. Greeted him with hungry skeletal grins. Bones entwined, skulls connected in a never-ending, rattling train of bones. The Butcher's army of tortured souls.

David slammed the door. Afraid to turn around. He didn't need to. He felt the presence behind him, cold and dead. A shadow fell over him.

David turned, shaking. Warm urine ran down his leg.

The Butcher, once again wearing his gold nose, grinned. It opened its jacket, its chest, its ribs. And sucked the screaming child in...

CREEVY'S TREES

Kerry E.B. Black

An underlying stench of decay tickled his senses as Adam set the pine tree's trunk in the base. "I must be imagining things," he thought, as he added water to hydrate the Christmas tree. His children, Bree and Chancey, hopped about with excitement as he set lights atop the prickling branches. "Ouch!" He plunged his thumb into his mouth to keep blood from speckling the carpet.

"Daddy's sucking his thumb!" Bree squealed.

Chancey set tiny fists on his hips. "Hey, I'm not allowed to do that. Why're you?"

Adam glared and resumed stringing the lights. Bree dropped a box, yielding the unmistakable sound of glass breaking. "Sorry, Daddy. It slipped."

He rubbed his temple. "Where's your mother? She should be here for this fun family experience."

Bree stood taller. "She's shopping with Aunt Crystal. She said since she's done everything else around here, like cooking and cleaning and hanging all the other decorations and wrapping the presents, we should put up the tree."

"Shopping my ass," Adam muttered around another pricked finger. *Probably at the bar, sipping peppermint schnapps.* He cleared a growing obstruction in his throat. His voice sounded strained as he said, "Garland, please." He stepped back. The red, white, and silver plastic garland made the pine look like a bizarre candy cane. "Does it look even?"

Bree clasped her hands beside her cheek. "It looks perfect."

He tousled the child's hair. "Glad you think so. Let's get the ornaments on before the game starts."

Chancey's finger ventured into his nostril. "Should we sing carols?"

"Dude, finger out of the nose. Sure, you can sing as you hang the ornaments." Adam threw away Bree's dropped box with its fragmented antique glass. He found a sparkling splinter in his wrist. "Dang, decorating is dangerous."

The tree quivered as the kids hung ornaments as high as their reach allowed. Adam hung the pieces above their heads to even the display.

"Oh, Daddy, it's the beautifulest tree in the whole world! Where did you find it?"

Adam ducked his chin, wiping the back of his neck with a calloused hand. "Old lady Creevy's yard." *Crazy bird kept enough trees on her acreage to stock a forest. She could do without this one.*

Chancey thrust out his chest like a miniature detective, rocking on the balls of his feet. "I thought Mrs. Creevy said we couldn't buy any of her trees. She said they were important to her."

Bree tutted. "No, Chancey. She said they were sacred. Like at church, how the cross and stuff are sacred. It's nice that Mrs. Creevy changed her mind and let you buy one, Daddy."

Adam grunted. *Bought one? Yeah, that's it.* "Where's the star?"

"Right here!" Bree rushed to retrieve the box. Chancey raced her. The children collided, bloodying both noses.

He yelled over the kids' crying, "Great, you're going to look fabulous in pictures with your swollen noses. You best not have black eyes in the morning or your mom's going to kill me."

They elbowed each other as they rushed to the bathroom to staunch the blood flow.

An odd crackling like an old person's laugh drew his attention. Tree sap dripped from a spot on the trunk where a limb broke during transportation. He'd been in such a hurry to tie the thing to the top of his car and get away before the Creevy bat realized he had cut the tree that in his haste, he snapped some limbs.

Christmas lights turned the amber sap crimson, then green, translucent and fascinating as it formed an enlarging bulb. Another cackle sent chills through his spine. *Bet my wife's playing a trick.* "Not funny." he said, looking about. The merriment escalated, echoing through the room.

Bree trembled in the hallway, eyes wide over the bloodied hand-towel she pressed to her nose. "Daddy, what's that?"

Chills raced through his spine. *Not my imagination, then.*

She hears it, too. "Don't know." He waved her away. "You and your brother go to your rooms. Close the doors tight. I'll come get you soon."

She clung to the rag, tears dripping into a splatter-pattern that resembled a Santa hat. Her voice quavered. "Okay, Daddy."

The room reverberated with ear-shattering glee. Decay wafted through the room. Adam gagged. From the enlarging pool of sap, a being formed. Pointed ears, an angular nose, and thrusting chin made a hideous caricature of "a right jolly old elf." Its face split into a smirk, displaying needle-sharp teeth.

Adam gawked. "What the...? Get out!"

It steepled its fingers, obscenely long claws clicking like breaking ice. "Leave, Sonny? You brought me here." It over-turned the candelabra. Flames kindled in the fake evergreen garland, smoldering.

Adam reached to quench the fire. Sharp, hot pain followed by a thud. His arm fell to the ground. He screamed and squeezed the stump. Sticky blood geysered from the wound. "What the fuck?"

The parody of a gnomish St. Nick licked its claws.

"Get out of my house!" Adam lunged at the thing, head lowered like an enraged bull.

It side-stepped, ragged red sleeve buffeting Adam as he careened past, stumbling to the ground. Adam flipped over, feeble from blood-loss. His vision swam.

Its clawed toes scratched the hardwood, horrible grin mock-ing. Fire charred the wallpaper, and the smoke detector screeched. "Your family's tree needs a star."

His wife's voice quivered, "Adam, what the hell's going on?"

The satanic Santa tipped its witchy chin. "Ah, a perfect tree topper!"

"No!" Adam lurched from the floor to tackle the thing as its nails flashed toward her head. Three bodies hit the floor. The room blurred, a blizzard of blood, and then blackness.

Adam struggled awake, strapped to a squeaking stretcher. An EMT's deep voice said, "Domestic. Police'll arrest after he heals. Kids look beat up. Social worker has 'em."

Black charring. A strangled scream caught in Adams' throat. His decapitated wife's wide-eyed horror stared from atop the tree, dripping gore like tinsel on the branches below.

CHRISTMAS MOON

David Bernard

Three a.m. in Fort Lauderdale is one of the few times the city seems quiet, at least if you avoid the strip bars and the airport. And as much as I normally enjoy both the solitude and the strip joints, tonight I had no use for any of it. December means only one thing to me—the Christmas Moon Maniac. For the last ten years, a serial killer had struck during the December full moon, and this was the first night of that full moon. I started my career back in the 70s covering the

Miami crime beat, so I know a thing about psychos and serial killers, and I don't mean just the elected type. The Christmas Moon Maniac was different. Every year for ten years running, he struck like clockwork, always during the full moon. Sometimes one victim, usually two, and sometimes more, all ripped to pieces. The bodies were of all ages, races, and gender. The only thing they had in common was the need to identify the remains through dental records and DNA. What I could never understand was how this lunatic could limit himself to once a year. The mutilations indicated a rage that he should not have been able to bottle up for a year at a time.

I work the graveyard shift for the *Florida Sun Coast Daily Tribune* because I hate the new editor. Harris is one of these hotshot MBAs with no actual journalism experience who's more concerned with the bottom-line profit margin than getting the story right. The way he slashes text out of a perfectly good story, I suspect he's the red pencil equivalent of Jack the Ripper. Not that Harris would know who Jack the Ripper was or that a red pencil was a tool used for editing back in the good old days when editors worried about content. So, even with a solid 17-years' worth of seniority at the *Trib*, I work the overnight shift to keep my sanity and avoid punching Harris repeatedly in the throat. Each afternoon I wake up and hope the idiot didn't again butcher my stories to make room for another condo foreclosure sale notice. Again and again, that hope is in vain.

To be honest, with the state of journalism today, I don't mind the overnight shift too much. Investigative reporting is a dying art in a world where anyone with a cell phone and a little good timing can take a front-page photograph and what little fact-checking gets done involves Wikipedia. Working days now means you get to write human interest stories (none of which are really that interesting) and attend press conferences (irrelevant political doublespeak). At least the night shift gives you felonies, fatalities, and "stupid drunk" stories; any story about a stoned frat boy driving a stolen golf cart off a bridge is more interesting than a retired school teacher who developed a new hybrid of zinnias.

With December's full moon arriving, the Broward County District Attorney was getting nervous. With Christmas two weeks away, the merchants were screaming murder because people were driving out of the county to finish their shopping, putting up with Palm Beach County prices rather than be caught out at night. Last year, the Christmas Moon Maniac had struck in Bahia Mar, and the yachting crowd was not happy about their entitled brethren getting sliced and diced. More importantly, getting blood stains out of teak wood decking is apparently very expensive. If the idle rich jet set was unhappy with the DA, it meant the funding for his expected run for the governor's office was at risk. So while I uneasily searched for a killer in the industrial areas near Port Everglades with a shiny Smith & Wesson Model 686 double action revolver in my pocket, most of the city police, the county sheriff, and the local state trooper barrack patrolled the upscale neighborhoods.

The DA's office, in all their infinite wisdom, had determined that the murders originated near I-595 around the airport and Port Everglades on the first night and had gradually spread westward into the more urban areas. This, our clever district attorney explained, meant that the psycho started his annual reign of terror in the lightly traveled industrial areas and then worked his way downtown. I had figured that out with a road map and color-coded push pins eight years ago. But I had also noticed that the attacks on the first night of the full moon always occurred closer to the industrial area between the airport and Port Everglades.

The first night had been cold by Florida standards. By

3:00 a.m., the mercury had dipped into the mid-50s. I hadn't seen anyone on foot in hours, and car traffic was lighter than usual. Between the non-Floridian cold and everyone knowing full well what a full moon in December meant, the city was holding its breath. I was cold and getting footsore as the moon began to set. The sun was due to rise in about 45 minutes when I decided to give up and check the police blotter. I was sure the Christmas Moon Maniac had attacked someone somewhere, but it looked like I guessed wrong as to where. And if it was another blue-haired dowager in a gated community, the DA's gubernatorial aspirations were toast. On the upside, if it was another tourist like four years ago, the Governor would have the National Guard down here in a heartbeat. It didn't stop the killing, but there's nothing like a few machine gun-toting, part-time soldiers to make the snowbirds feel safe.

Suddenly the hair on the back of my neck stood up. I didn't see anything on the empty street, but I knew something was wrong. I ducked into the doorway of the office of a warehouse complex. With a locked door behind me and a couple of cheesy fake pillars on either side, whoever was following me had to come at me in a straight line, face to face. I already had the revolver cocked and waiting. I noticed the night had gotten quiet—no crickets, no tree frogs—only the occasional sound of a car on I-595 in the distance. The effect was almost supernatural.

Suddenly, whatever happened passed and the sounds of the night returned. I slowly released the hammer and remembered to breathe again. I didn't know what had just happened, but I had a bad feeling. That's when the scream started. It was a scream of pure terror followed by a gurgling noise that fortunately didn't last long. I pulled the gun out of my pocket again and, against every survival instinct in my body, ran toward the noise. By the time I covered three blocks, I could see blue lights flashing. Someone had called the cops, and they had responded with uncharacteristic speed for this neighborhood. I arrived on the scene right after the deputies. While they were busy throwing up their coffee and doughnuts, I got a good look. It was the Christmas Moon Maniac's work, and the mutilation was as horrific as ever.

I recognized the tattoo of a topless nun on a forearm, one of the larger remaining intact body parts. Only one man had that tacky of a tattoo—Tomás Mason, pawnshop owner, reputed drug dealer, suspected pimp, and alleged dealer in kiddie porn. It wasn't a great loss to humanity to see his steaming intestines wrapped around a fire hydrant, but considering "Mad Dog" Mason was over six and a half feet of heavily armed, ill-tempered, walking psychosis, the Christmas Moon Maniac just earned himself some serious street cred.

One of the cops, in between dry heaves, motioned me off. I didn't argue; I'd seen enough. Between Mad Dog's rap sheet and a history of the Christmas Moon killings, I had my story composed before I reached the *Trib* offices. I filed my story and went home. Then I did what I did every year, I pulled my files on the killings and looked for something I missed while I cleaned my gun.

The next afternoon I went through the paper. Sure enough, that idiot Harris had again slashed my story to the point of incomprehensibility. Anyone who still wonders why the print media is dying just needs to look at his ham-fisted attempts at editing. It did nothing for my mood when I realized my last good pair of shoes was caked with Mad Dog's blood. Trying very hard not to think about it, I put them on and tried to scrape the blood off as I walked down to the police station. The cops, of course, knew absolutely nothing. I managed to sneak in to see the coroner, Dr. Detaranto, but even my favorite forensic chatterbox was doing a sphinx act. I wasn't sure if he was afraid of the Christmas Moon Maniac or the District Attorney, but I was getting nowhere, just faster than usual.

I grabbed a quick meal at the pizza joint near the police station. Even though the place was crowded, it was as quiet as a tomb. Whoever turned Mad Dog Mason into chopped meat had seriously spooked Fort Lauderdale's boys in blue because no one was talking. I did notice a lot of the boys were toting weaponry that was definitely not standard police issue.

I gave up and stepped outside. The sun was beginning to set. Another fifteen minutes or so, the moon would be rising and the second night of the Christmas Moon would begin. I guessed right as to where to look last night, but the second night was always a crapshoot; second night attacks had happened all over Broward County from Pembroke Pines to Lauderhill.

I decided to go back to the previous night's carnage. Mad Dog was not the type to go down without a fight, so it was safe to assume he had been jumped from behind. If I was lucky, I could find the killer's hiding place. If I was really lucky, the psycho dropped his driver's license for me to find. If you're going to be unrealistically optimistic, why not aim high?

The corner was amazingly clean; everything had been scrubbed down, and I could detect a hint of bleach still in the air. The DA was definitely not taking chances—the only way you'd know a man had been ripped to shreds at this spot was the fact that the corner was cleaner than the rest of the sidewalk. Even the fire hydrant sparkled like new.

I looked for any alleys or blind spots where someone could jump Mad Dog, but the area was well lit with no obvious hiding spots, so either the Christmas Moon Maniac could jump off a two-story warehouse without breaking both ankles, or he could cross a city block so quickly that Mad

Dog had no time to react.

The street light above me suddenly clicked on, and I damned near had a coronary. I'd lost track of the time. It was already dark, and the moon was just clearing the open space where the candy-striped smokestacks of the old power plant at the port used to sit on the horizon. A plane came in for a landing at the airport, and as the engine noise faded, I realized it was deadly quiet again, just like it was right before Mad Dog was ripped to shreds. A random thought popped into my head about how I had lived in here long enough to start referring to landmarks that were gone. I might have even relaxed a bit at my own insight.

Then I heard the howl. I tried to convince myself that some-one's dog was feeling lonely, but I wasn't buying a word of it. I tucked my hand into my coat and cradled the gun. It did not reassure me. I decided it was time to move somewhere less open, less deserted, and less likely to afford me the oppor-tunity to see my own intestines.

I started back toward the police station at a brisk pace. The brisk pace became a determined jog as another howl ech-oed through the empty night, closer this time. If I was the paranoid type, I'd swear I was being stalked. The Christmas Moon Maniac never struck in the same place twice, so there was no reason I should be as terrified as I was rapidly be-coming.

I tripped over the curb and almost lost a shoe. Then it hit me—my shoes. They were the shoes I wore last night and still had Mad Dog's blood caked on them. I suddenly had the crazy idea that whatever was doing the howling must smell the blood of its last victim and was wondering how it sur-vived. Of course, that would make the killer some sort of animal, which was impossible. Even a gator didn't do the kind of damage the Christmas Moon Maniac inflicted, and alligators didn't howl like a wolf.

I was about to take off my shoes and see if I could break the four-minute mile barefoot when the howling sounded in front of me; I was being outflanked. I looked for somewhere to hide, but there was nothing in either direction but the endless corrugated tin wall of a boat storage warehouse. Suddenly, under a streetlight ahead of me, I saw a man hunched over like a gorilla. Correction—a man hunched over, wearing a fur coat. As it came slowly toward me, I could see it was covered in coarse fur with an elongated snout bristling with jagged teeth where his face should be. It paused a moment and began casually shuffling toward me again. The first thought through my mind was that whatever it was, it was playing with its food, which in this case would be me. My second thought, as I pulled the gun out of my pocket, was that it looked nothing like Lon Chaney. Lon Chaney? Fangs, fur, claws, full moon. Werewolf?

I didn't have time to rationalize how I made that leap in logic because the creature was coming closer. I took the initiative and emptied the gun into it. My Smith & Wesson uses .357 Magnum ammo. Normally this will do enough damage to a human body to reduce a target's internal organs to liquefied meat. I had decent aim, and I nailed the werewolf at least three times in the dead center of the chest. Instead of collapsing into a bloody heap of dead, it stepped backward with the impact, and then stood there. With horror, I watched the bullet holes pucker up and close. Looking decidedly angrier, it snarled and leaped at me.

I tried to dodge, but it raked me with its claws as it passed by. I could feel blood already soaking my shirt. I threw the gun at it and turned to run. It slammed into me from behind back before I took a step. I hit the ground hard, and the momentum carried the monster over me and head first into the lamp post. It seemed to be stunned from slamming into the pole, but with the new gashes on my neck and shoulder, I knew I was losing blood too quickly to outrun it. I struggled up onto my knees and looked for anything I could use as a weapon—a stick, a rock, a bazooka.

I reached for my cell phone to dial 9-1-1 and brushed my pen. Then it dawned on me. My pen was silver plated, a gift from my editor back when I made the mistake of leaving Miami for Fort Lauderdale. If it was a werewolf, wasn't silver was supposed to repel it? Or was that a vampire? I hadn't seen a horror movie since the 60s. Even if it wasn't silver that hurt a werewolf, I could poke a nasty hole in him. That would annoy him for a good two to three seconds, but at least I'd go down fighting. I gripped the pen like a knife and watched the werewolf shrug off slamming face first into the metal pole. It was definitely not in the mood to play with its food anymore. It leaped at me again as I brought the pen up and tried to brace myself. A solid wall of furry muscle slammed into me, claws and teeth ripping into me as it knocked me flat on my back. I hit the sidewalk again, even harder. Between slamming my head on the concrete and the wind knocked out of me, I just gave up and waited for the final blow, trying to remember how to pray. When the deathblow didn't come, I opened my eyes. Lying next to me was the creature, face first on the sidewalk, with the pool of blood collecting around him. It appeared I was less dead than he was. However, just in case, I decided to make a run for it. I tried to stand up and couldn't. I looked down and saw a rib poking out of my shirt and a ragged hole in my pants where my knee cap used to be. I decided a nap sounded very good.

By the time I came to, the cops had shown up. The beast was now a very large, very naked, and very dead guy, but I was in no position discuss the matter. They flipped the body over, and there was my pen sticking out of his heart. I was getting light-headed, and I was pretty sure it was blood loss, not elation over being in slightly better shape than the naked, dead werewolf guy. I tried to stand up again, but I never made it. I just sort of floundered helplessly in the growing puddle of blood that was mostly mine. I decided it was time for another nap.

That was the last thing I remember until I woke up hand-cuffed to a bed in the ICU at Holy Cross with four broken ribs, a collapsed lung, a concussion, a missing kneecap, and enough empty blood transfusions bags to make the Red Cross wince. There was also a homicide detective waiting most impatiently to have a little chat about dead guys, serial killers, and his entry in the police department pool about how many stitches they needed to close me back up.

By the time Lieutenant Muñoz was done grilling me, I was thinking getting chewed on by a werewolf wasn't the worst part of my night after all. I filed my story from the hospital bed with a borrowed laptop. I assumed that a werewolf terrorizing Fort Lauderdale was front page headlines.

The next day, I discovered my potential Pulitzer was now a front page story of how the DA had single-handedly stopped an international serial killer. The nice thing about being in an ICU is that I could listen to the beeping speed up on the blood pressure monitor as I read the story. The dead guy was a Herr Wilhelm Franz Mueller, an in-house auditor for a German airline. He traveled from airport to airport, reviewing the records of the local operations, and like precise German clockwork, he arrived to review the books of *Luft Deutsch* operations at Fort Lauderdale airport each December and had done so for the last decade. The DA conveniently "forgot" to mention that Mueller's autopsy showed Mad Dog Mason's DNA between his teeth and my skin under his nails. I decided not to ask what they found in his stomach.

Luft Deutsch provided Herr Mueller's work schedule to the State Department to expedite the investigation's quiet completion. Mueller's schedule coincided with carnage and killings in cities across the world. No one had made the connection because of the different countries involved.

I healed much faster than anyone expected. The DA offered me a simple deal: if the werewolf story went away quietly, so would any potential charges against me for killing a German citizen. *Luft Deutsch* offered a sizable "consulting fee" for my "inconvenience" that included a non-disclosure clause. No one would believe my story, so I agreed to anything and everything. I took my consulting fee and agreed to schedule a knee replacement after some of the stitches came out. I was quietly discharged from the hospital. I never did get my pen back.

I didn't do much for the next few weeks but try to sleep and read the *Trib*. Reading the paper was as painful as usual, but sleep was difficult because of nightmares of the werewolf running through downtown Fort Lauderdale. He'd look at his reflection in a storefront, and it wasn't a werewolf, it was my decaying corpse. The pain pills helped me sleep for the first week, and then I seemed to develop a tolerance for them. Other than my missing knee constantly aching, I wasn't in pain, and the pills didn't help me sleep either; I just gave up on them. I gave up on reading the *Trib*, too. The typos and the hack jobs that Harris seemed to think constituted "editing" were driving me nuts. I actually snarled at a dangling participle.

I continued to heal much faster than expected. The stitches were itching, so I removed them myself with a pair of manicure scissors. And I felt better than I had in years. I woke up one morning and discovered my missing knee was as good as new. My reflexes were back, my hearing had improved, and I'd swear my bald spot was filling in. I had a sneaky idea why, and when the only scar that didn't fade away was in the shape of a pentagram over my heart, it was a clincher. Surprisingly, it didn't bother me as much as I expected.

My dear editor Harris wants to have a meeting "as soon as I'm feeling better." He has no idea how good I actually feel. I only use the crutches so that people won't ask how I can walk without a knee. No one wants to discuss "my ordeal," and I prefer it that way. Rumor has it in the newsroom that the werewolf story has made me a liability to the paper, so I expect the meeting will be a discussion of my immediate "medical retirement" due to injuries in the battle with Herr Mueller. Heaven forbid that the truth gets in the way of the advertising revenue stream. I've scheduled the meeting to start about fifteen minutes before the full moon next week. Harris may be giving me the boot, but I got a little going away surprise for Harris. Let's see how he likes being on the receiving end of a little indiscriminate slashing for a change.

GOBLIN FRUIT

Harold Hull

ondon, 1890

Snow landed atop roofs and chimneys, temporarily hiding the filth that lay underneath. Boys and girls with soot-covered faces ran through the streets. They made their through the slums, not daring to branch out into Kensington or Chelsea or any of the other places where the wealthy lived. And just as the poor children stayed in their districts, so did Wesley

Turner.

He walked through Westminster wearing his best: a gray vest, charcoal coat, and black top hat. A monocle perched within the confines of his socket. He limped along, supported by a silver-plated cane, with his free arm intertwined with that of his wife, Mary.

Mary, a plain-looking woman, glanced up at her husband and smiled, doting on him as she always did. She kept her head wrapped in a bonnet and carried an empty basket.

It was December, and they were heading to the marketplace.

As they walked along the cobblestone streets, they passed stands filled with every conceivable good one might desire during the Christmas season. A mustached, rotund merchant stood beside a collection of toys: nutcrackers, dolls, and delicately carved wooden animals. He offered an array of red, green, and gold crackers for the children, teasing the young boys about the wonderful surprises held within. There were food stands, with geese and chickens strung up like ornaments, and freshly baked pies made of mincemeat, the aroma wafting through the market. A group of carolers stood singing "Hark! the Herald Angels Sing," their voices carrying over the constant chatter of merchants and prospective buyers.

Wesley stopped in front of a stand selling fine jewelry and picked up a silver necklace. An engraved, oval locket hung from the chain. "Come here, dear," said Wesley. "Turn around." He loosened the clasp and laid it out over the top of Mary's chest before binding it again.

She faced him. "Do you like it?" she asked.

"It's wonderful." He caught the merchant's attention and gestured toward the necklace. "What do you want for it?"

The merchant gave him the price and Wesley paid it.

They strolled on through the market, not stopping again

until they reached a stand Wesley found most delightful. It was a fruit stand, wedged between two shops, a darkened alley trailing off behind. The man selling the fruit had a rough look about him, and Wesley presumed he must've been gutter scum from Whitechapel. He wore a poor-boy hat and brown trousers, with a torn overcoat to keep warm. His hair was tangled, and it was unclear whether the man had bathed recently. But the fruit he sold made up for his ragged appearance.

On either side of the stand were two barrels filled with red apples, lemons, and oranges. Crates were stacked in front and held raspberries, mulberries, cranberries, blackberries, bilberries, gooseberries, barberries, and any other kind of berry imaginable. Wesley had never seen so many different types of fruit in one place. There were baskets of cherries and melons on top of the stand, along with apricots and pomegranates, dates and strawberries, pears and figs. His mouth watered.

"G'day, friend," the fruit seller said. "Name's Ainsley. Anything I can interest you in?"

"Everything looks wonderful," said Mary.

"Aye, I grew it all on my own farm. Fruit you've probably never seen before."

"Some I haven't seen in years," Wesley said. "How did you grow the citrus, if you don't mind me asking? We don't have the climate. Are you a Spaniard?"

"Do I look like a Spaniard, friend?" asked Ainsley. "I grow it the same as everything else, and I've got my ways. Old ways. Mysterious ways."

"However you do it, it's quite remarkable. We'll fill our basket, if you don't mind."

"Certainly."

Wesley picked through the crates, scooping up cranberries and gooseberries and dropping them into the basket. Ainsley stood behind the stand watching, his lips moving in a silent tally of the cost. Wesley thought the poor man odd and might've scoffed at the idea of purchasing anything from such a low-born, but the fruit before him stood out like magic in a darkened place. There was fruit he hadn't tasted in a long time; some he'd never tasted at all.

When their basket grew heavy, Mary set it on one of the few empty spots left on the stand, while Wesley topped it off with pomegranates.

"Have you ever had them before?" asked Ainsley.

"No," Wesley said, "but they look delicious."

"They are, but they're not like the others. You cut them straight in half and pick out the seeds. It's the seeds you want to eat. They pop in your mouth and out comes the juice."

"And how much will this all be?"

Ainsley stuck a finger up. "Hold on. There's something I want to show you." He bent down, scrummaged through a box underneath the stand, and stood back up holding a shimmering, pink fruit, oval in shape and as smooth as a blade. "This, friend, is called a Goyba fruit. Very rare. It's similar to a pomegranate in the way you eat it. Slice it carefully and peel it back, then take the seeds out. I like to take one seed at a time, put it on my tongue, and swallow it whole. If you bite down on them, it'll taste bitter, so don't do that. But if you put them on your tongue, it's like breathing in an angel." He grinned, then placed the Goyba fruit at the top of Wesley's basket. "It's complimentary, seeing as though you've bought so much today and I'm mighty appreciative of that."

"Thank you," said Wesley, slightly taken aback by the man's kindness. "I'll make sure to try it tonight."

The sound of children snickering emanated out of the blackened alleyway behind Ainsley. It was too dark to make out much, but Wesley could've sworn he'd seen shapes rummaging around. For a moment, he thought he'd seen two tiny red dots.

Eyes. But that was a preposterous notion, and he dismissed it outright. He paid for the fruit, bid Ainsley farewell, and headed home.

* * *

The wind whipped the side of Wexcraft Manor. A fireplace kept the study warm; the wood crackled as embers floated up the chimney. Wesley sat in an armchair beside the window, the shutters tapping incessantly against the glass. He held a book with his left hand, and with his right, he lifted a glass off the table beside him and drank. Smooth, aged scotch ran down his throat. He placed the drink and the book aside and stood. Mary had filled a bowl with apples and pears. The Goyba fruit sat on top. He took it and cut it with a finely sharpened knife, making an incision around the circumference, then splitting it in half.

It was like opening a bag of pearls. Dozens of seeds lay nestled within the fruit. They were just as Ainsley had described: pink, oval, and shimmering. Wesley plucked one out and let it fall onto the middle of his tongue. He sucked and tasted the juices running out. It was sweet and reminded him a bit of honey, but with a tinge of plum mixed in. When the nectar had finished running down his throat, he swallowed the seed, careful not to bite into it, as Ainsley had warned. He picked another seed and ate it, savoring every drop of juice that seeped into his mouth.

The wind and snow continued beating against the side of the house, but he paid no mind to it. Inside the manor, he was warm and safe and relaxed. He had plenty of good books, and now, he had delicious fruit. He returned to his armchair and continued devouring the Goyba fruit until every last seed was in his belly.

Only then was he full.

* * *

When morning came, Wesley found himself feeling un-well. He staggered through the house, trying to find Mary. His body was burning up. Even his insides felt as though they were on fire. Sweat streamed down his forehead and cheeks. He toppled against the hallway wall, nearly knock-ing down a portrait, but regained his balance with the assis-tance of several servants.

"You should sit down, sir," said his maid, Catherine. "I'll find Missus Turner for you."

He was helped into the ballroom and put upon a chair beside a window. The sun had risen halfway over the horizon, its beams lighting up Wesley's reddened face. He unlocked the latch and opened the window. Cool air hit his skin, but it did nothing to lessen the sweat dripping off his nose and brows.

Behind him, a half dozen servants were busy decorating the room. On Christmas, his children and grandchildren would visit, and everyone would be stuffed into the ballroom to open gifts and sing carols. Garland and wreaths were strung up around the room. Tapered white candles were situated in can-dlesticks over the fireplace. The Christmas tree was set up near a double window overlooking the street below. Lights wrapped around it. Red bows and children's toys—dolls, nut-crackers, wooden boats, and instruments—were situated within pockets of the tree.

Wesley had looked forward to helping decorate, or at least watching and sipping brandy, but he couldn't concentrate on anything other than the pain in his stomach.

He'd been so distracted with his own misery he hadn't

noticed Mary entering the room. "You look dreadful," she said, hovering over him.

"I feel dreadful," said Wesley. "I don't know what's wrong with me."

She felt his forehead. "You're running a temperature. I'm going to send for a doctor. Catherine will help you back to your room."

With the help of several servants, he pushed himself out of the chair and forced his body upright. It took a moment before he became steady enough to walk, then slowly he took a step forward.

His belly felt heavy. Everything did.

He took another step. His legs buckled under his own weight, and he toppled to the floor.

People were gathering around him. He saw Mary's panic-stricken face, heard her shouting his name, and tried to reach out to her. She took his hand and fell beside him, her fingers running through his hair. Grave faces surrounded him, but a few of the servants stayed back, barely within Wesley's range of vision. He could've sworn he saw them grinning.

Then, his world went dark.

❄ ❄ ❄

Over the next three weeks, his life became a series of vignettes: in and out, day and night, awake and unconscious. He knew when Mary was there because she was the only one who ever touched his hand or face. He could hear the doctor's voice, but it was always at a distance. The servants would move him around, change his sheets, and empty his bedpan, but they never bothered to talk or comfort him in any way. Mary was the only one who truly cared.

She whispered into his ear, told him everything would

be all right, that the doctor believed he'd eaten something poisonous, but that it would eventually work its way out of his body.

Although he couldn't prove it, Wesley knew it had been the Goyba fruit that had caused his ailment. "He sold me poisonous fruit," he told Mary.

"Yes, dear, he did. An inspector went to find the man, but no one's seen him. He vanished."

At the end of the third week, Wesley's fever broke. Strength returned to his body, although the stomach pain remained. The doctor examined him and declared his recovery a Christmas miracle. Wesley wasn't sure about that, but was glad he'd be able to spend Christmas day with his family.

It wasn't until he attempted to get out of bed that he realized his stomach had grown.

Standing with the support of Mary and two servants, he glared down at his increased gut and wondered what kind of poison could cause swelling like this.

What kind of fruit could cause a man so much harm?

* * *

Wesley endured an unceasing agony throughout the Christmas festivities. When finally the gift giving was over, he excused himself and retired to his bedroom. Catherine helped him into bed. It took only a few minutes before he fell into a slumber, and it was a dreamless, deep sleep that latched onto him.

But when he awoke, he did so screaming.

Writhing in the bed, sheets twisting around his limbs, he rolled over and fell off the edge, landing hard onto the floor. There was something wrong with his stomach. Something very wrong. He could feel movement. Tiny hands and feet clawing around.

"You should return to your bed," he heard Catherine say.

He turned and saw her, along with several other servants, standing against the wall.

"I need...a doctor," he said.

"It's too late for that now."

Slowly, he rose to his feet and maintained his balance. He had some strength in his legs. All the pain was concentrated in his midsection. "Mary," he said, moving toward her bed. Then, he stopped.

Something laid on top of her. It was three feet in height and had the anatomy of a human, although Wesley suspected it was no human at all. The creature burrowed into her stomach, digging an even deeper nest than it had already created.

"Lord in heaven," said Wesley, sobbing. "Help me, Lord. Help me." He staggered backward out of the room and into the hallway. His head spun. The hallway seemed to shrink and heave. He swayed from wall to wall, knocking down portraits as he fumbled along. *I'm dreaming,* he thought. *I must be dreaming. Or in a delirium. This can't be real. This can't be happening to me.* But then he saw them at the end of the hallway. The outlines of tiny creatures shuffling in the shadows. He needed to get away from them before they buried their nails into his belly like they'd done to Mary.

He stumbled into the ballroom, collapsing onto the floor.

Instinct told him to get up and run, but his body had shut down. He was finished trying to escape. Devils were worming around inside his belly, and he couldn't run from that. He turned over onto his back and stared up at the ceiling.

His servants entered the room and formed a circle around him.

"You looked down upon us," said Catherine. "And so did Missus. Turner. You can't look down on us anymore."

"Please. I'm sorry. Whatever you want—"

"You're giving us what we want. The man told us he'd give us riches as long as we helped him with his babies."

Then, Wesley heard a familiar voice say: "And riches you'll be given." The circle parted, and Ainsley stepped to the forefront. He shook his head and said, "Sorry to see you in such a state, friend, but sometimes sacrifices are needed in order to keep my children happy."

Wesley croaked a single word. "Help."

"Can't," said Ainsley. "It's nearly time. It doesn't take as long for goblins to be born as it does for humans."

The creatures came into the light then, revealing gaunt bodies with reptilian flesh the color of ferns. Within their sunken eye sockets were red specks. The goblins wove lithely around the servants until they surrounded Wesley.

"Try to relax," said Ainsley. "Draw your final breaths knowing you're a part of something greater, a tradition older than man." He bent down and stripped Wesley of his shirt.

His stomach had doubled in size since the morning. He lifted his neck and watched dozens of little hands pushing out, making imprints upon his belly. Nails were cutting into his innards. They were scratching and biting, desperate to free themselves. A dot of blood formed near Wesley's navel. Then he noticed the fingernail jutting up out of him. Streams of red wound down his sides like flowing water trailing down a hillside. He wailed, tears filling his eyes. Another fingernail came up out of his stomach, then another.

All at once his belly opened, and a multitude of goblins was born out of him, tearing away from their artificial womb. The bloodied children took their first breaths and were welcomed into the world with open arms.

ABOUT THE AUTHORS

David Bernard is a native New Englander who now lives (albeit under protest) in South Florida, a paradoxical place where, when temperatures drops below 60°, locals break out parkas to wear over their plaid shorts and sandals. His previous works include short stories in anthologies such as *Snowbound with Zombies* (Post Mortem Press), *Legacy of the Reanimator* (Chaosium), and *Twice Upon an Apocalypse* (*Crystal Lake Publishing*).

Kerry E.B. Black lives in the land where George A. Romero's Dead dawned. Some of this first-reader for Postcard Poems and Prose's works has crept into anthologies and online journals. Please follow the author on Facebook: www.face-book.com/authorKerryE.B.Black , Twitter: @BlackKerryblick, and at https://kerrylizblack.wordpress.com/.

Rose Blackthorn is a writer, dog-mom, and photographer who lives in the high-mountain desert, but longs for the sea. Her short fiction and poetry have appeared online and in print with a varied list of anthologies and magazines, including two prior Deathlehem anthologies. More info can be found at: http://roseblackthorn.wordpress.com/; http://www.facebook.com/RoseBlackthorn.Author; http://amazon.com/author/roseblackthorn; and https://twitter.com/rose_blackthorn

William D. Carl is the author of five novels, including *Bestial, The School that Screamed, Out of the Woods*, and the first book in the Gone Noir Saga, *Three Days Gone*. He has had over thirty short stories published in anthologies and magazines like *Jamais Vu, Out of the Gutter, The Many Faces of Van Helsing, In Laymon's Terms, Now I Lay Me Down to Sleep*, and *The Gruesome Tensome*. He writes a bi-weekly column for cinemaknifefight.com called *Bill's Bizarre Bijou*, which highlights the weirdest movies you've never seen. He lives in Pawtucket, Rhode Island with his partner of twenty-six years and a large, slobbery dog.

DG Critchley lives in northern New Jersey, mostly for the hot Texas weiners, but will deny it if pressed on the issue. Predominantly a mystery writer, Critchley's stories most recently appeared in the Thanksgiving mystery anthology *The Killer Wore Cranberry #5* and *Murder Among Friends*, a charity collection of mysteries for the John Greenleaf Whittier Birthplace museum.

Mark L. Eshbaugh is an author, artist, and musician. He has written a number of non-fiction books about photographic subjects, and contributed to several textbooks about art. To date his creative writing has appeared in anthologies, graphic novels, on film, and in song. He lives in Massachusetts with his wife and son.

G.H. Finn is the pen name of someone who keeps his real identity secret in order to escape the eternal wrath of the ever vengeful, eldritch Elder Gods. And to avoid paying library fines.

Having written non-fiction for many years, Finn began writing short stories in 2015 and has had over 60 short stories accepted for publication as of 2017. He especially enjoys mixing genres (sometimes in a blender, after beating them insensible with a cursed rolling pin) including mystery, horror, steampunk, sword-and-sorcery, dark comedy, fantasy, detective, dieselpunk, weird, supernatural, sword-and-planet, speculative, folkloric, Cthulhu mythos, sci-fi, spy-fi, satire and urban fantasy.

G. H. Finn's links: Website: http://ghfinn.orkneymagic.com/; Twitter: @GanferHaarFinn; Facebook: https://www.facebook.com/g.h.finn/; Amazon Author's Page: UK http://www.amazon.co.uk/G-H-Finn/e/ B0147L6E66/; US http://www.amazon.com/G-H-Finn/e/B0147L6E66/

Dan Foley grew up in Northern New Jersey. He has lived on the east coast, the west coast and points in between, including two nuclear submarines. He has lived in Manchester, CT. since 1985. His genres of choice are horror and paranormal suspense.

He is the author of the novels *Death's Companion, Reunion, Abandoned,* and *Wolf's Tale,* the novellas, *Intruder and Gypsy, and* a collection of short stories *The Whispers of Crows.* All are available through Amazon and B&N. He has also published in various anthologies and magazines in the U.S. Canada, England and Australia. Find him at www.deathscompanion.com, or on Facebook at www.facebook.com/dan.foley.31

R.A. Goli is an Australian writer of horror, fantasy, speculative and erotic horror short stories. In addition to writing, her interests include reading, gaming, the occasional walk, and annoying her dog, two cats, and husband.

Her short stories have been published by Broadswords and Blasters, Fantasia Divinity Magazine, Deadman's Tome and Horrified Press among others. Her fantasy novella, *The Eighth Dwarf* is due for release Spring 2018. Check out her website https://ragolifiction.wordpress.com/ or stalk her on Facebook https://www.facebook.com/ragolifiction.

Larry Hoy: Biker – Writer – Legend
When not at work, Larry can be found on the back of his motorcycle. Trips have taken him through three countries and maybe a third of the states. Over those years he has collected an endless supply of stories. Now, on days when he isn't thundering down backroads, he has been spotted putting

some of his stories down on paper. This is one of those stories.

Other high water marks in his life include his wife and daughters. Together they have shared many adventures and somehow come out safe on the other side. The family also trains in Kempo-Karate, where they earned enough belts so they can all hold up their pants.

If you are fortunate enough to see him out and about, please wave him down and tell him how much you loved the story. He gets off on stuff like that.

To find out more you can contact him at: https://larryhoyjr. wordpress.com/

Harold Hull lives in Maine with his family. He is a graduate of The University of Maine and works for a local non-profit. He is currently working on a YA horror novel.

Christine Lajewski was born and raised in Flint, Michigan and moved to Massachusetts in 1976. She currently resides in Norton, Massachusetts. She is a writer, retired alternative high school teacher, a teacher/naturalist at Massachusetts Audubon and a haunt actor. Her first novel, *JHATOR*, which explores death and grief from a Buddhist perspective, was published in 2014. *Bonebelly*, a horror novel that involves a creature's individual hell and a haunted attraction, is due out by the end of 2017.

Leslie J Linder lives and works in Downeast Maine. Her non-fiction has appeared in Neo-pagan magazines including *SageWoman*, *Circle Sanctuary*, and *Witches & Pagans*. Leslie's poetry has appeared in journals and zines including *Wicked Banshee*, *Forage Poetry*, and *Rat's Ass Review*. In fiction, Leslie enjoys exploring vegan-related themes in genres like Horror and Science Fiction. Her debut horror novel entitled, *Revenant: Blood Justice*, is out from Black Rose Writing. She also has a short story, "Catharine Hill," out in the *Northern Frights*, an anthology edited by David Price and published by Grinning Skull Press.

Nick Manzolillo's writing has appeared in over forty publications including *Wicked Haunted: An Anthology of the New England Horror Writers*, *Grievous Angel*, *Thuglit*, *Red Room Magazine*, and the *Tales To Terrify* podcast. He has an MFA in Creative and Professional Writing from Western Connecticut State University. By day he works as a content specialist for TopBuzz, a news app. He lives in Manhattan and spends the little free time he has growing a beard.

Kurt Newton's dark fiction has appeared in numerous publications including *Weird Tales*, *Dark Discoveries*, *Weirdbook*, *Shock Totem*, *Black Infinity*, and

Hinnom Magazine. He lives in Connecticut.

Raised on a healthy diet of creature double features and classic SF television, **Gregory L. Norris** is a full-time professional writer, with work appearing in numerous short story anthologies, national magazines, novels, the occasional TV episode, and, so far, one produced feature film (Brutal Colors, which debuted on Amazon Prime January 2016). A former feature writer and columnist at Sci Fi, the official magazine of the Sci Fi Channel (before all those ridiculous Ys invaded), he once worked as a screenwriter on two episodes of Paramount's modern classic, Star Trek: Voyager. Two of his paranormal novels (written under my rom-de-plume, Jo Atkinson) were published by Home Shopping Network as part of their "Escape With Romance" line — the first time HSN has offered novels to their global customer base. He judged the 2012 Lambda Awards in the SF/F/H category. Three times now, his stories have notched Honorable Mentions in Ellen Datlow's *Best of* books. In May 2016, he traveled to Hollywood to accept HM in the Roswell Awards in Short SF Writing.His story "Drowning" appears in the Italian anthology *The Beauty of Death 2*, alongside tales by none other than Peter Straub and Clive Barker. Follow his literary adventures at www.gregorylnorris.blogspot.com.

Joseph Rubas is the author of over 200 short stories and several novels. His work has appeared in *The Horror Zine*, *Thuglit*, *All Due Respect*, *Culture Cult*, *The Storyteller*, *Nameless Digest*, and others. He currently resides in Albany, New York.

Sheri Sebastian-Gabriel's fiction has appeared in *Devolution Z* and a number of anthologies. She lives in New Jersey with her two sons, her daughter, and a Hellhound named Nya.

Karen Thrower is a native Oklahoman, wife, and mother to a rambunctious four-year old. She holds a Bachelor's degree in Deaf Education from The University of Tulsa. She is also a member of Oklahoma Science Fiction Writers and serves as the Vice-President and Facebook 'Wizard'. She has been featured in issue #5 of "Gathering Storm Magazine" and will be seen in the January 2018 edition of "Broadswords and Blasters."

Steven Van Patten is a celebrated writer and Brooklyn native. When he's not creating scary stories, he can often be found stage managing television shows. His TV work includes various MTV, VH-1 and FUSE shows over the last twenty years as well as Comedy Central vehicles, *The President Show* and *The Nightly Show w/ Larry Wilmore*. He also fills-in occasionally at ABC's *The View*.

He has penned four novels; The *Brookwater's Curse* trilogy is about an 1860s Georgia plantation slave who becomes a vampire, and *Killer Genius: She Kills Because She Cares*, features a hyper intelligent black woman who becomes a serial killer with a unique socio-political agenda. His short horror fiction is popping up everywhere, including *Hell's Kitties*, a horror anthology edited by April Grey. He's also developing a children's book series based on the childhood of the human son of vampire Christian Brookwater, the main character in the *Brookwater's Curse* series. Steven, or SVP can be found on Facebook and under @svpthinks on Twitter and Instagram. He also serves as one of three hosts of the Beef, Wine and Shenanigans podcast, an internet radio show that comically explores the African-American perspective of horror, science-fiction and superhero genres.

Bev Vincent is a contributing editor with *Cemetery Dance* magazine and the author of several books; most recently, *The Dark Tower Companion*. His work has been nominated for the Edgar, the Stoker, and the ITW Thriller. A recipient of the Al Blanchard Award, he is also the author of over 80 short stories and numerous essays, interviews and book reviews. Learn more at bevvincent.com or follow him on Twitter @BevVincent.

Stuart R. West is a lifelong resident of Kansas, which he considers both a curse and a blessing. It's a curse because… Well, it's Kansas. But it's great because… Well, it's Kansas. Lots of cool, strange and creepy things happen in the Midwest, and Stuart takes advantage of them in his books. Call it "Kansas Noir." Stuart writes thrillers, horror and mysteries usually tinged with humor, both for adult and young adult audiences.

Stuart spent 25 years in the corporate sector and now writes full time. He's married to a professor of pharmacy (who greatly appreciates the fact he cooks dinner for her every night) and has a 25-year-old daughter who's dabbling in the nefarious world of banking.

To be one of the cool kids on the block, subscribe to the Stuart R. West-Worlds newsletter for upcoming book info, free stuff, and absolutely no recipes: http://eepurl.com/c34zpv.

If you're still reading this, you may as well head on over to Stuart's blog at: http://stuartrwest.blogspot.com/

Sheri White lives in Maryland with her family. She's a mom to three girls, ages 28, 22, and 19, and has instilled a love of all things scary in them as well. Her two-year-old granddaughter will be next. Her husband Chris is very understanding, and a little unsettled at times.

In addition to reading and writing horror, she's also the editor of *Morpheus Tales* magazine. Sheri's fiction has been published in many small press magazines and anthologies.

 **Grinning Skull Press** Presents

The Place where it all started

O Little Town of Deathlehem

Twas the fright before Christmas,
And all through the town,
Not a soul stirred,
No one dared make a sound…

Welcome to Deathlehem, where…
…Krampus, not Santa, brings the holiday cheer…
…the lights on the tree, so festive and bright, skitter and crawl and possess
a lethal bite…
…malicious little elves, not a jolly one, know if you've been naughty—or
nice…
and
…family gatherings often turn deadly.
So enter…if you dare.

A collection of 23 holiday horrors benefiting the Elizabeth Glaser Pediatric
AIDS Foundation.

Return to Deathlehem

Slay bells ring,
Kids are screaming,
In the lane, snow is blood stained.
There's nowhere to hide,
Krampus has arrived,
There'll be feasting in a winter slaughter land…

Welcome back to Deathlehem,
…where the office Secret Santa proves more dangerous than a game of
Russian roulette…
…where trips to Grandma's house are fraught with danger…
…where a traditional Nutcracker poses a threat to a pair of would-be
thieves…
…where ghosts of Christmases past haunt and take vengeance against the
living…
…and many more!

Twenty-three more tales of holiday horror benefiting the Elizabeth Glaser
Pediatric AIDS Foundation

Deathlehem Revisited

You make this a Christmas to dismember,
Killing feelings in the middle of December,
Strangers meet, one unwillingly surrenders,
Oh, what a Christmas to dismember…

Welcome back to Deathlehem…again!…
where a mutated Christmas has a taste for human flesh…
…where a trio of trespassers are terrorized at an abandoned holiday-
themed tourist attraction…
…where elves thrive on the torment delivered to others…
…where holiday shopping drives people to commit extreme acts of
violence…
…and many more!

Twenty-three more tales of holiday horror to benefit The Elizabeth Glaser
Pediatric AIDS FoundationPediatric AIDS Foundation